MURDER FOR CHRISTMAS

An absolutely gripping cozy murder mystery full of twists

JEAN G. GOODHIND

A Honey Driver Murder Mystery Book 8

Originally published as
The Ghost of Christmas Past

JOFFE BOOKS

Revised edition 2022
Joffe Books, London
www.joffebooks.com

First published by Accent Press Ltd. in Great Britain and the USA as *The Ghost of Christmas Past* in 2014

This paperback edition was first published in Great Britain in 2022

Cover art by Dee Dee Book Covers

ISBN: 978-1-80405-523-6

PROLOGUE

Maine, USA

Carols were playing on the prison's loudspeaker system and two guards were positioning a blow-up Santa Claus behind an iron grille.

Professor Jake Truebody coughed to get their attention. Reluctantly, one of the guards sauntered over.

'What's up, doc?' He slapped his lips Bugs Bunny style.

'My file's gone missing.'

'Sorry about that, Professor. Was it important?'

On a scale of one to ten the prison guard's concern didn't rate too highly. A weapon rated eight to ten. Contraband in the form of drugs, cell phones, or hooch, rated six or seven. A visiting professor's paperwork rated as highly as a pair of six-year-old sports shoes or a worn-out jockstrap. A big fat zero.

The professor tried to curb his impatience. 'It was to me. It contained a letter for mailing and some course work in factual history. The prisoners were looking forward to that.'

The prison officer's expression went a little skewed as concern vied with amusement. The amusement won.

Grinning he said, 'Nothing too bloodthirsty I hope, Prof. You know how keen the governor is to protect our inmates from too much blood and gore. Tom and Jerry are obviously on the banned list, and he's debating the sexual undertones between Snow White and the Seven Dwarfs.'

The guard exchanged a sly wink with his partner. They both grinned.

Jake Truebody blinked nervously before twigging that the guard was only joking. Humour at the large penitentiary where the professor took a history class was part of the scene. Everyone made jokes; the prisoners, the guards, the visiting lecturers, the medical staff, and even the governor. It helped them all cope with the endless grind of dealing with the same offenders, the same hopelessness year in and year out.

Once the joke came to him Jake Truebody only managed a small, tight smile. Prison surroundings were depressing at the best of times and off-the-cuff humour did nothing to relieve it as far as he was concerned. A man of deep social conscience, he took what he did here very seriously. To his mind teaching history two hours a week to a bunch of lifers was his way of giving something back to the community. The prison guards were here all the time; a little light relief helped them cope. The professor didn't make jokes. Neither could he always work out when somebody was being serious or when they were not.

The prison guard's comment was taken more seriously than it should have been.

'I've been careful regarding subject matter. No gore, just interesting details relating to interesting time periods. Just lately I've been covering outstanding women in history,' explained the professor with his usual enthusiasm for the subject he loved.

'Covering them?'

'Figuratively speaking,' returned the professor, a scarlet flush spreading from gizzard to hairline.

The guard, who relished innuendo but regarded history as hogwash, raised a pair of bushy eyebrows in mock concern. 'Not too sexy I hope, Professor. The governor is very . . .'

'Yes! Yes. I know,' replied the professor hastily. 'The governor doesn't like a syllabus with too much sex in it either. I don't go there. There were some personal papers in with my course notes. I've been penning a brief biography of my life. It's thrown up some surprises that are worth investigating, so I would like the papers back. You will keep an eye out for them?'

'You bet I will.'

Once the professor's back was turned, the guard let one corner of his mouth lift in a sardonic smile. Why would a prisoner bother to steal a visiting professor's paperwork?

'Not like it's non-negotiable bonds or a cell phone,' he reiterated to one of his colleagues later when they were on other duties. 'Is Santa sorted yet?'

His partner assured him that Santa was firmly incarcerated behind the mock prison bars. 'He won't get out of there. Better get on with the job, I suppose.'

Tinsel and glass baubles were set aside to make room for paperwork. Two prisoners were being released right now, just a few weeks before Christmas. One had managed, by some legal botch, to gain early release. He was the second that day. The first one had been released two hours earlier. It didn't do to release in batches; they could form a team. Birds of a feather flock together, but criminals flocking together was not a good idea; so stated the governor, who fancied himself as something of a wise man when it came to criminal behaviour.

'Merry Christmas,' they shouted after the second released prisoner of that day.

The prisoner turned round and gave them the finger.

The guards laughed.

They both prided themselves on knowing their charges well — very well.

'Just history. What goof would want notes on history or the professor's life? A little skag or a bottle of hooch — now you're talking.'

They laughed at the professor's naivety as they turned away from the last chore of their shift, confident in their perceived knowledge of all human behaviour.

* * *

The sleet that had threatened all day came at the front of a deep depression blowing in from the Atlantic coast. It smelled of sea salt, fresh and biting cold. Night had closed in early. Burdened with what remained of his papers, both private and work related, Professor Truebody ran for his car, piled the papers on the front seat, and gunned the engine.

Sensible people were heading home, glad there were only two weeks to go before Christmas. The extremely sensible were already there, sheltered from the storm and the early darkness. The night was bleak, the roads like a river, so he took it slow while musing about his future trip to Europe.

He smiled. 'Jake,' he said to himself, 'you're a lucky devil.'

Picked out in his car headlights, he spotted a lone figure standing at the bus stop just two hundred yards from the prison gates. The man was tall and carried a bundle beneath his arm. The face looking straight into the headlights was familiar and he recognised him as a former prisoner and a keen attendee at his history class.

He hummed 'God Rest Ye Merry Gentlemen' and felt good. Really good.

Bringing the car to a stop he asked the ex-con if he wanted a lift.

'I think I know where you're going. I'll take you there. Save getting drenched at the bus stop,' he said, generosity oozing out of every pore.

A sudden gust grabbed the door and papers whirled around the car as the man got in.

'There' was the halfway house that most prisoners ended up in while on parole. He figured this guy would be no different despite the air of betterment he had about him.

'Hell of a night,' he added.

The newly released prisoner only nodded, his eyes wide and his prison pallor bathed by the headlights of infrequent vehicles passing in the opposite direction.

The professor felt equal measures of pity and jubilation as he observed the way the man was drinking in the multicoloured Christmas lights, plastic snowmen, and lit up reindeer lashed by wind and rain — not a snowflake in sight.

Jake's enthusiasm for history and concern for lesser mortals got the better of him.

'Look. I noticed you attended the majority of my history classes and also that you were very interested in genealogy.'

'You bet,' the man replied. 'Nice to know where you come from, who your pappy was; stuff like that.'

'It certainly is,' said the professor. He paused, his mind drifting to the research he'd carried out into his own family.

'You know where you come from, Professor?'

'Yes. It meant a lot of research, but it was worth it. Now if you'd like to continue on the outside, perhaps with a view to further study and a degree . . . ?'

The man, whose name, he recalled, was Wes Patterson, looked at him. 'I may do.'

'Well. If you're not doing anything else . . .'

The storm came in with a fury, sweeping water across the road along with branches torn from trees. The sleet was turning heavier, flakes of snow hammering against the windscreen.

The car skidded.

'My,' the professor said breathlessly. 'That was close.' His heart thudded in his chest and beads of sweat had broken out on his forehead.

Ahead of them was a roadblock and police halting traffic, detouring the few cars out to take a right turn rather than go straight on. The halfway house for prisoners was straight on. Truebody took the detour prescribed.

'Grim weather for the time of year. Should be snow by Christmas proper,' he said once he'd straightened the car and breathed easy again.

Wes Patterson agreed. 'This storm's real bad. Likely to get even worse, so I hear.'

He sounded almost enthralled at the prospect. It occurred to the professor that the recent guest of the federal authorities was loosening up a little. It was no big surprise that prisoners incarcerated for long periods were a little withdrawn when they were first let out. Adjusting was daunting. Suddenly they had to think for themselves and mix in with decent folk again.

'I don't think we're going to get you to the halfway house tonight,' said the professor. 'I reckon the best thing we can do is to make for my place. You can stay there the night. I'll phone the halfway house either tonight or in the morning and explain there was a problem — not that they can't see the problem for themselves,' he added dryly.

The bulky body of the man sitting beside him seemed to sigh with relief. 'Whatever you say, Professor. I'm sure we'll be comfortable at your place.'

'Perhaps we can discuss your continued study of history,' Jake said cheerfully, noting that the man had said 'we'll be comfortable'.

'I'm sure we can,' said Wes. 'And your interest is much appreciated. I think early American History would suit me best. I'm particularly interested in the early settlers and their relationship with the Native Americans they encountered.'

The professor nodded. The man was finding his feet, regaining his confidence. 'A good choice. A very good choice indeed.'

Jake felt himself swell with satisfaction. Back in the prison they'd called Wes Patterson 'The Legend'. Others assumed it was to do with his crime and the way he'd handled his legal case, finding a technical loophole that the professional defence lawyer had failed to see.

Jake preferred to take the view that it had something to do with his interest in history.

'You'll do well, Wes.'

'I will?'

'I guarantee you'll never offend again.'

'Is that so?'

The man didn't sound as if he believed him.

For his part, Wes Patterson knew he'd latched onto the right subject. His friend Sheldon had told him that. Sheldon was well informed on history though touched in the head. Anyone who thought himself the reincarnation of a long-dead Native American had to be that didn't they? Not that he was always a Native American. Sometimes he was other things; historical characters Wes had never heard of. Sometimes he was a vampire or a ghost. Sheldon was into the supernatural as well as history and they were great buddies. That was the best bit.

The weather and the night weren't getting any better. Branches, leaves, and rolling trash cans were being blown around like wedding confetti. Not a soul was in sight, not a dog, not a cat, not even a bird.

Professor Truebody peered through the windscreen of his Japanese coupé, fully prepared for problems but confident of dealing with whatever came his way. On the street where he lived all the lights were out.

The professor stated the obvious as he turned into his drive. 'Looks like the power's down.'

Pausing for a split second, his hand on the car door, the professor peered at the dark outline of his house. The sudden gleam of a flashlight passed over one of the windows and was gone.

'Anything wrong, Prof?'

Jake narrowed his eyes. There was no light now. Just darkness.

'I thought I saw a light inside. Must have been my imagination.'

Papers firmly tucked beneath one arm, his bulky briefcase bumping against one leg, Professor Jake Truebody headed for his front door, opened it, and stepped into the darkness. Wes Patterson followed him, not quite able to believe his luck.

CHAPTER ONE

On the other side of the Atlantic, in the city of Bath, Christmas lights had been switched on and the weather was cold. Overnight frost lay like icing on the mansard roofs of the eighteenth-century buildings. The frost from the night before remained *in situ* all day before another frost thickened what was already there. Snow was threatening to fall.

Honey Driver was out shopping and minding her own business, though not for long.

'That's him!' somebody shouted. 'That's him that's been sticking red noses on the reindeer. I saw one in his bag.'

Gasps of surprise were expressed on steaming breath.

'Grab him,' shouted someone else.

Honey Driver spun round. As Crime Liaison Officer on behalf of Bath Hotels Association, vandalism wasn't usually part of her remit, but she was in the right place at the right time.

A young man was standing next to one of the fibreglass reindeers that had appeared *in situ* once the first of December hit.

'Stay where you are,' she shouted, and immediately had second thoughts. He was bigger than her. She needed backup. Better still, a weapon. With a flourish she pulled the

French stick she'd just bought from its wrapper, brandishing it like a baseball bat over her head. She could still smell the newness of it, fresh bread straight from the oven.

The young man with the half-opened holdall took one look at her and scarpered.

'Hey! Come back here!' Honey gave chase. Luckily, she was wearing flat boots. Heels would never have worked.

All over the city, day after day, people had come across the same act of vandalism; red noses stuck on the fibre glass reindeers displayed around the city. Worse still they were stuck on with super glue and they just wouldn't come off. The burgeoning of red noses had made headlines in the *Bath Chronicle* and the *Western Daily Press*. The reindeers were a fund-raising thing, each about four feet tall, decorated by celebrities and artists and placed all over the city at park entrances, on parapets, and at either end of the Royal Crescent.

The front-page article suggested that someone knew who was doing the dastardly deed and, what's more, was protecting their identity.

I'll make the front page too, Honey thought as she gave chase through an arcade of shops linking one main thoroughfare to another, the sight of her trusty bread baton raised high over her head causing shoppers to scatter.

He ran down towards the city's elegant spa, newly renovated with a rooftop hot tub and a view over the city. He made a side move to where there had been an alley — now blocked off.

Honey cannonballed into him.

Winded, his knees crumpled and he collapsed against a wall.

'Don't hit me!'

His arms were folded over his head, his eyes on the French stick.

The bread stayed upright for no more than a few seconds before bending in the middle and flopping sideways.

The young man looked surprised. His jaw dropped onto his chest.

'Gotcha!' Honey glowed with triumph. 'Waste not, want not,' she murmured as she folded the bread in half and tucked it inside her coat.

The young man looked petrified. 'What do you want?'

He had big brown eyes and long lashes and reminded her of a spaniel. She had a soft spot for spaniels but refrained from patting him on the head.

'You! I want you.'

'You're mad!'

Honey was breathless, but also excited. She could see the headlines now: 'BATH HOTELIER NABS PHANTOM RED NOSE VANDAL.'

First, she needed his confession. Someone had sworn they'd seen the red nose in the cloth holdall he was carrying. And he had been standing next to one of the reindeer, one arm leaning nonchalantly on it prior — no doubt — to doing the dirty deed. The bag containing the evidence nestled at his feet.

'Show it to me,' she demanded, placing her arm across his chest, pinning him to the wall.

He stared at her. 'Not bloody likely. I've heard of women like you.'

'Oh, yeah?'

'Yeah. Old birds that chase after young men and lust after their bodies. You're a pervert!'

The penny dropped. This dork thought she wanted a peek at his privates.

'You wish! And cut the "old bird" bit. I caught up with you, didn't I? Now! Let's get down to business. You've got a red nose in your bag. It was seen by a member of the public.'

'Oh no, I ain't!'

'I suppose you're going to tell me next that you're not the vandal who's been sticking red noses onto decorative reindeer, reindeer I might add who are destined to be sold off to raise money for charity.'

'No. I'm not. I'm a plumber.'

'Prove it.'

Eyeing her warily, he bent down, unzipped his bag and brought out a ballcock, the little round thing that controls the water level in a lavatory cistern. It was a red ballcock.

The bag also contained tools, brass connectors, and tape, all of them things a plumber would use. There were no red noses.

Honey chewed at her bottom lip. Well, this was embarrassing! That was definitely a ballcock, not a red nose. She felt obliged to make amends.

'Er . . .' She started hesitantly. 'Look. I've got a leaky loo in the ladies cloakroom at my hotel. Do you think you could pop round? I'll pay you top dollar.' She decided it was the least she could do.

The young plumber swiftly zipped up his bag. What he said next was heartfelt and to the point. It was also pure Anglo-Saxon, and the second word was 'off'!

CHAPTER TWO

Honey related all this to Mary Jane while the latter was applying a subtle shade of auburn dye to Honey's hair. Or, at least, Mary Jane had informed her it was auburn, though whether it was subtle or not hadn't yet been confirmed.

It was Mary Jane's opinion that the noses did something for the reindeer.

'They should have had red noses in the first place. It's the right time of year for reindeer to sport red noses.'

'I wonder where he's getting them from. He must have quite a stash.'

'Never mind where he's getting them from. In my opinion they're going to the right place.'

Honey began trilling 'Rudolph the Red-Nosed Reindeer'. She was feeling happy and festive — until Mary Jane took the towel from her head.

'Aghhh!'

One glance in the mirror was all it took to write off having a very Merry Christmas. Her hair had turned the colour of a bunch of neon carrots.

She covered her eyes with her hands and made a wish. 'Please make it go away.'

'Aw, come on,' urged Mary Jane in her broad Californian twang. 'We all have a bad hair day now and then.'

Honey shook her head and refused to come out from cover. 'This is not merely a bad hair day. It's the wrong colour. It's cataclysmic.'

'Cataclysmic?' Mary Jane pulled her spectacles halfway down her nose, picked up the box containing the home colouring kit, and checked the details. When she frowned her eyes almost drowned in wrinkles.

'No. That's not what they call it. It says burnished copper on the box. Yep!' She nodded. 'Burnished copper.'

'Carrot,' Honey exclaimed, her voice filled with horror. 'It's burnished *carrot*.'

Not having taken on board that Honey had heard her the first time Mary Jane took another look at the fancy name.

'Well, it says burnished copper on here.' She shook her head in a forlorn manner and made a clicking noise with her tongue. 'I followed the instructions to the letter. All I can say is that there must be something in the water altering the shade.'

The statement was typically Mary Jane. The fault was not hers. It was never hers. She was one of those brazen folk who approached everything in a 'can do' frame of mind even when it was perfectly obvious she could not do! Hair colouring was right up there on the list.

Honey was beside herself. 'Well, this is definitely not burnished copper, glowing copper, or any kind of auburn shade. Just look at it!'

Mary Jane looked at Honey's hair, flinched, and averted her gaze, fixing it on a bare rose bush outside the window.

'I can't be seen over Christmas like this,' Honey despaired. 'Wake me up around mid-January.' Blaming herself for trusting Mary Jane's supposed hair-colouring skills, she hid her head under a cushion and groaned.

Mary Jane's air of supreme confidence was undiminished.

'Oh come on, Honey. Not looking at it won't make it go away. I find a little meditation helps when things aren't going exactly as planned. I beef it up with some in depth conversation with Sir Cedric. He gives good advice.'

To an outsider who didn't know her and hadn't a clue who Sir Cedric was, Mary Jane sounded philosophical, as though the long-dead knight worked on behalf of the Citizens Advice Bureau, dispensing words of wisdom over a cafe latte and a club sandwich. The truth was that Sir Cedric was dead, and had been for over two hundred years.

'Maybe ask him if he knows the phone number of a good hair colourist.'

The likelihood of Sir Cedric being able to help in this instance was extremely remote, mainly because he'd never used a phone in his life, or a hair colourist for that matter. Sir Cedric had worn a wig, tight britches, and white stockings; hair washing — or any kind of washing for that matter — had tended to be on an infrequent basis.

Mary Jane shared a room with Sir Cedric, though of course you wouldn't notice his presence. Only Mary Jane could see him walk through the wall or out of the wardrobe. No one could prove or disprove that, but then, the tall, lanky, and *very* eccentric Californian was a professor of the paranormal so considered herself an expert. Everyone accepted her eccentricities and never questioned Sir Cedric's existence.

Mary Jane gathered her things together, got up from the chair, and stretched her thin frame. 'I really should be going. But don't you fret about your hair, Honey. Look at it this way; you won't need a costume for a fancy dress party with hair like that.'

'Sure. I can go as a clown. I won't need to wear a wig.'

'Aw, now, come on up from out of your boots.' She rubbed Honey's shoulders, shaking her slightly as if to dispel the despair from her body. 'Come on. You handle *crime*. You can handle this.'

Honey was not reassured. 'My hair *is* a crime. Just look at it!'

She felt like adding *and it's all down to you* but checked herself. In all fairness, she was as much to blame. She'd chosen the home-dye kit after all.

'It'll get put down to seasonal madness — like wearing fake reindeer antlers and long white beards. We all do that. Besides, you won't be going out much,' said Mary Jane dismissively. 'No crime-fighting and stuff.'

Honey conceded that she was right about the wearing of fake reindeer antlers. Mary Jane herself was wearing them, the bright red clashing with her lounge pyjamas of pistachio green and shocking pink.

Sighing deep into her boots — or at least her reindeer-shaped slippers — Honey hoped she was right. Nobody would judge her a serious crime-buster with hair this colour. She wanted to be taken as a serious antidote to serious crime — not that she'd felt that way at first.

The position of Bath Hotels Association Crime Liaison Officer had been foisted on her in the first place.

On the day in question, Casper St John Gervais, Chairman of Bath Hotels Association, had insisted that she'd agreed to do the job the night before, during a presentation given by an Australian wine producer. Honey had consumed most of a bottle of Shiraz, which had put her in a state of mind to agree to almost anything.

The very next day she'd accepted the position, following a surge of excitement at auction when she'd bagged a pair of bloomers said to have belonged to Queen Victoria. It had struck her that the Queen of England and Empress of India had worn very large knickers for a such a small woman. The price had been pretty huge too, but Honey had been pleased. The day had gone well — until Casper phoned and reminded her of what she'd done. The job of Crime Liaison Officer had landed on her. And Casper had been clever. He'd bribed her to take it on.

'I'll make sure that your rooms are filled in the shoulder months.'

How could she refuse?

'Just for a while,' she'd told herself. Business was always slow in January and February. She'd have been a fool not to accept the offer.

Contrary to what she'd expected, she found that she liked the job. She'd also ended up liking the irascible police officer, Detective Chief Inspector Steve Doherty, he of the unshaven good looks and wall-to-wall street cred. They'd rubbed each other up the wrong way at first. Now they just rubbed each other — especially in private.

'Does it really look that bad?' The colour wasn't nearly so dazzling when she narrowed her eyes.

If she was hoping for reassurance it wasn't forthcoming. Mary Jane headed for the door.

'I'll go talk it over with Sir Cedric. It's bound to make things better.'

'For whom?'

No reply. Mary Jane had bounced out of the door as though she were meeting some old friend for afternoon tea.

Honey was left filled with despair. She held her head in her hands and felt a little like Cinderella, in no fit state to go to the ball. Luckily for Cinderella, her fairy godmother had come to her rescue but there was no sign of one hanging around Honey Driver's pad. The only one she knew of was playing in the pantomime at the Theatre Royal. Still, it wouldn't hurt to make a wish would it? She closed her eyes.

Please make it go away. Turn the clock back. Make everything as it was before.

Having carrot-coloured hair was not the first disaster of the Christmas season. Another one hit her in the face like a sausage-filled frying pan.

For some stupid reason that no one could quite recall (though accusing fingers were pointed in her direction), the Green River Hotel had missed the copy deadline for a very important marketing brochure. This particular brochure was the one produced by the English Tourist Board and distributed to just about everywhere, including, so it was rumoured, places as diverse as Timbuktu, Timor and Tokyo.

Her daughter, Lindsey, had pointed out that their bookings for the coming year were not as prolific as they should be and the finger was pointed firmly in her direction. Honey had forgotten the deadline.

Expletives were followed by excuses. 'I've been busy.'

'We've all been busy.'

She was cool with this. 'We'll get over it. You'll see. Everything will be fine. It's just a little hiccup.'

'More haste, less speed,' Lindsey had replied.

Honey found a hat to wear. No way was she running through reception looking like an escapee from a circus. Lindsey looked up as Honey dashed past. There had to be a hairdresser with space to take her.

'I need to go out. I won't be long,' she shouted over her shoulder.

Lindsey guessed what she was up to. 'You won't get in anywhere. I won't say I told you so, but I did tell you so. Just like that advertising you said you wouldn't forget — but you did.'

Cripes!

Swamped with guilt, she paused to button up her dark green coat and wind a bright red knitted scarf around her lower face. This wasn't about hair. This was about missing the advertising deadline.

You wouldn't listen. You're stubborn. You always were.

Honey presumed the damning voice in her head was the down-to-earth side of her nature, the one with feet firmly planted on the ground and an unerring accuracy of judgement. Her other self, the one in everyday use, possessed a 'fly by the seat of your pants' attitude and a flippant approach to judgement. Tossing a coin seemed as good as anything.

That was probably what had happened with the brochure; she'd tossed a coin, rather than bothering to study the trade generated by last year's brochure.

With more conviction than judgement, she told herself that everything would sort itself out. In the meantime, she lost herself in the crowds, occasionally darting into a hair-dressing salon, in the vain hope that they could fit her in. They all threw her pitying looks.

'Sorry.'

There were twelve days to go until Christmas, and all through the busy streets and ancient alleyways of Bath people were spending as though their pockets were bottomless, their bank accounts bursting with cash.

Fearlessly they eddied in and out of small shops, big stores, and the shop selling hot pies and pasties, the delicious aroma of the latter drawing them in — along with the need to keep up the energy levels.

The atmosphere was seasonally electric; Christmas greetings passed between total strangers and two groups of carol singers in Abbey Churchyard competed with renderings of 'Silent Night' and 'God Rest Ye Merry Gentlemen'. The latter won the battle of the eardrums, but only because they were accompanied by a tuba player.

Strings of decorative lights danced overhead brightly sparkling against the leaden sky. The eyes of shopkeepers were sparkling too. The tills in the crowded shops were jingling. Jingle bells and a one-horse open sleigh just couldn't compete with the sound of a busy cash register.

The Christmas Market was in full swing, dozens of little individual stalls selling everything from homemade chocolates to clothes made from recycled material.

Honey lingered by the stall selling scented candles, breathing in the smells of tangerine, pine needles, and roasted chestnuts.

Everything was lovely and people were noticeably friendlier at this time of year. Everyone was doing a brisk trade, including hotels and restaurants. Office parties were their lifeblood at this time of year and the Green River Hotel was no exception to this seasonal fervour. The last slot for an office blowout had been scooped up by the end of August.

Casting all concerns about next year to one side, Honey entered the shopping fray, very much enjoying being part of the seasonal throng.

She was still feeling good, despite her hair, when she set down her array of Christmas wrapping paper, presents and last-minute decorations against the reception desk back at her hotel.

Lindsey put down the phone.

'The Grigsby and Jones group for the office party has been cancelled.'

Honey's smile froze then shattered.

'No!' The booking referred to was a conglomeration of different companies, making up a total of around seventy people; the Grigsby and Jones group had had twelve guests attending. Parties were meant to look crowded. Twelve empty seats would leave a big gap.

'Well, at least this close to the event we do get the keep the full amount paid, they aren't entitled to a refund . . .' Lindsey caught the look on her mother's face. 'They did settle the full amount, right?'

Honey bit her lip.

'Half.'

'Mother!'

'I trusted them.'

'This. *Is*. A. Business!'

'I did phone them a few times.'

'Obviously not enough!'

Honey accepted that she thoroughly deserved this dressing down. She knew her own weaknesses, her tendency to dance around things.

Never mind. She would bounce back.

'So what's their reason for cancelling?' she asked.

'One of the partners has run off with a client's money and the other partner's wife. The remaining partner and staff are in no mood to celebrate. The firm's had to fold. I think the employees are going to a local pub to drown their sorrows.'

A cancellation at such a late date had Honey fuming. It would be double-o-great to pick up a late booking, but the chances were pretty slim.

She swore.

Lindsey shook her head, shot her mother a pitying look, then left her to it.

Honey slid into the swivel chair behind the reception desk. She patted her head. The hat would have to stay in place. There was no way she was going to show her head of hair today. Hair, advertising, and now a cancellation. Life just wasn't fair — well not to her anyway. A big cloud of mucky gunk was hovering above her head. She wished it would go away.

Her fairy godmother must have been listening. Suddenly the phone rang.

'I saw you're doing Christmas parties. I know it's short notice, but can you accommodate ten for the meal three days hence, plus rooms? I'm giving my staff a last-minute one-off Christmas Special, a big thank you for their efforts throughout the year.'

Honey punched the air and silently thanked her fairy godmother.

'Yes. Yes. I've got that. Christmas party for ten. Plus rooms. Mallory and Scrimshaw. Right. I'm afraid I'll have to charge you for the full amount this late in the day. This will cover the meals and rooms. Bar bills and drinks at the table will be charged extra.'

'That's exactly what I expected.' He gave her the exact date he wanted. 'I also want to book all ten for Christmas Day lunch — if possible. Can you squeeze us in?'

Honey felt as though she was floating close to the ceiling. 'I most certainly can.,' Even if I've got to hire trestle tables and put them in reception, she thought to herself. Things were brightening up. 'Right. Now if you'd like to give me your credit or debit card details . . .'

It wasn't professional to sound so bubbly when taking a booking, but she couldn't help it. It was a miracle! This was what Christmas was all about . . . although sitting bottoms on empty seats was small fry compared to having wise men from the east bring you a chunk of gold and pungent perfumes.

The company booking the event sounded slightly Dickensian: Mallory and Scrimshaw. The debit card number, security code, and everything else checked out. The name of the individual wasn't needed on a phone booking so she didn't bother to make a note of it. Grab the booking and run. There was a more pressing problem she had to deal with.

CHAPTER THREE

'What do you think? Do you think people will stare?'

Lindsey regarded her mother's hair.

'You can be as honest as you like,' said Honey.

Lindsey cleared her throat. 'It's a very . . . positive colour. That's all I can say.'

Honey grimaced. The message was loud and clear. 'Sure. As in, neon sign in trashiest part of town.'

'I can try contacting a few salons, but I can't see us having much luck.' Lindsey was nothing if not supportive.

Although grateful for her offer, Honey knew the score. 'I tried. It's the wrong time of year. Office parties and all that. Everyone wanting to look their best. I've tried every salon in the civilised world.' Well, it wasn't quite the entire world, but Bath was a big slice of it as far as she was concerned.

'I could get you another colour — something to calm it down?'

'No.' She shuddered. 'Nobody but a professional is ever touching my hair again. I've resigned myself to spending the Christmas period with my hair hidden. I figure there must be something more festive than a knitted hat, though. I could wear one of those sparkly carrier bags on my head and tie the red rope handles under my chin. That might do the trick.'

Seeing as there was nothing else she could do, Lindsey announced she was off to the gym. How she found time or enthusiasm, Honey couldn't fathom, except that her daughter planned her day methodically. She was never flustered, always in control — sometimes Honey wondered whether there'd been a slip up at the hospital and her real daughter, the one like her, was driving some sane family steadily batty.

Things could be better. What better way to make herself feel better than to indulge in a little comfort eating. She located a bag of chocolate marzipan, then filled up a vibrating footbath with warm water and a rich moisturising gel, set it before the sofa, and surrounded herself with fat cushions.

The vibrating footbath had been a birthday present by her darling daughter. Lindsey was nothing if not practical. Hotel people suffered for their trade — or at least their feet did.

Eating chocolates while soaking her feet was sheer decadence; what else could she do to make herself feel better? Her gaze alighted on the ornate mirror. She frowned. There were too many mirrors about the place, but that could be fixed. Draping them with holly, mistletoe, and spangled reindeer with big red noses would minimise their impact.

She sighed. 'Well! Can't sit here daydreaming.'

As she reached for the first envelope from the pile she'd brought over from the hotel, her free hand strayed to the bag of marzipan chocolates. There were only six of Thorntons' best dark chocolates in the bag. This would be the third that she'd eaten. She eyed it speculatively. Hell, it didn't look so wicked as all that. She popped it into her mouth.

'No point in saving any,' she muttered. 'I'll need the energy over Christmas.'

She turned her attention to the bundle of mail.

She opened one Christmas card after another with pretty scenes of fat-breasted robins, glittery stars or snow-bound coach and horses outside old-fashioned inns. Something about the latter — Victorian Christmases focusing as they did, on family, cold weather and warm fires — hit the right chord. She thought of Dickens, plum puddings, and visions of sugar plums dancing on heads — or people slightly off their heads by virtue of how much brandy and rum had been mixed into the plum puddings. She reminded herself to check with Smudger, the hotel's chef, how generous he'd been with the alcohol. She didn't want a repeat of last year when a party of vicars had rolled out of the bar after Christmas lunch, barely coherent for evening prayers. And all they'd had was one sherry each . . . and very large portions of plum pudding smothered with brandy cream.

The very last envelope caused her to pause and take stock. The address was handwritten and in the most beautiful script; calligraphy at its best.

She fingered it tentatively. It wasn't stiff enough to be a card. A letter? Now who did she know who didn't use email?

Seemingly of their own volition, her fingers began to tap dance around the gummed down opening. Why the hell was she feeling so nervous about this? She answered her own question.

'Bad vibes,' she muttered.

She began ticking off the reasons the letter was making her feel so disconcerted.

Number one, the address on the envelope wasn't typewritten. That was the first alarm bell. The second was the beautifully rounded copperplate script. She knew nobody of her intimate acquaintance who could do that.

And it was addressed to Mrs *Hannah* Driver. That meant it wasn't from a close friend. She couldn't recall how long it had been since people had ceased calling her Hannah and started calling her Honey — except for her mother. Gloria Cross had picked the name Hannah and figured it was there to stay and to be used, even though she was the only one using it.

All these things conspired to make Honey's nerves tingle and her toes curl up. Handwritten letters were as out of date as sedan chairs and penny farthing bicycles but it was the postmark that really dug deep into her soul. The return address was a town in Maine not far from Rhode Island.

Rhode Island! The place name gored a hole in her heart and sent a prickly feeling down her spine. With those two little words her deceased husband Carl rose from the dead — though hopefully only in letter form. The thought of him traipsing into the Green River Hotel demanding a bed and her presence in it was nothing short of a nightmare. He'd drowned. He was fish food. As forgotten as yesterday's stale bread.

But was he? It was Christmas and all good ghost stories were told at Christmas. A plot line from some TV mystery series flashed into her mind where the wife had awoken up covered in blood. The scene had taken place on a boat far out at sea. Of her husband there was no sign and the unfortunate wife was accused of murder. She had done time but when she got out she followed the few clues she'd mustered and tracked him down. Turned out he was alive and with a young wife and baby in tow. Well, at least Carl hadn't done that to her. He'd just drowned in the middle of the Atlantic. His body had never been found.

Another awful scenario popped into her head from a clichéd American soap opera. 'Hi, Honey. Here I am. I'm not dead. It was all a mistake. It was really my twin brother that died.'

She shivered as she blinked the image away.

Mindful that the envelope was turning soggy thanks to the steam from the footbath, she placed it to one side.

Once it was out of danger of becoming a mushy mess, she towelled off her softened toes and rubbed her heels with Vaseline — which though cheap really did the trick — then added a few dollops of Moulton Brown foot replenishment. The Vaseline did the deep-down work; the more expensive product smelled lovely and added gloss to a winter-worsened instep.

She then began to read the letter.

Dear Mrs Driver,

You may not remember me as it is some years since your husband and I . . .

The letter went on to confirm the time of arrival of a Professor Jake Truebody. He'd booked a room for the Christmas holiday, as already confirmed by email.

Honey turned cold.

Lindsey chose that moment to come barging into the coach house they shared at the back of the hotel. The coach house no longer bore any resemblance to a place reserved for a coach and pair. The bedrooms were downstairs, the living room and kitchen upstairs to gain the benefit of the views and the light — the latter more so than the former. Chimney pots and mansard roofs were hardly the stuff good views were made of.

Lindsey looked at her. 'What's up with your cheeks?'

Honey blustered. 'It's the steam. They always go pink like that.'

'They're not pink. They're pale. As though you've seen a ghost.'

'It's the hair colour. It makes me look paler.'

'Ah! It would do.'

'If I can't get a salon appointment, I think I'll wear a cloche hat over Christmas. I'm sure my mother can find me a flapper dress — or something.'

'Not so easy now she's no longer in the second-hand fashion trade.'

Honey agreed. Her mother had been a partner in a shop dealing in high-class cast offs. She'd recently informed them that she'd branched out into something else. A dating site for the over-sixties which Honey thought was a great idea. Matchmaking for seniors might mean she would leave Honey alone.

Honey cleared her throat. 'Lindsey, there's a man coming to stay over Christmas.'

'Well, there's a big surprise. In my experience, people do tend to stay in hotels over Christmas. What's special about this one?'

'Nothing. He's . . . American.'

Lindsey looked amused. 'We can't hold that against him.'

Honey cleared her throat for a second time. 'His name's Professor Jake Truebody.'

'I know.'

'You do?'

'I checked the list of guests this morning.'

Lindsey sounded her usual efficient self. Nothing fazed her. Now for the crunch.

'He says he's an old friend of your father.'

It was just a tightening of her daughter's smile that gave it away; Lindsey was affected, though hardly knocked sideways.

She nodded her chin slowly. 'I see. Is he coming to see you?'

'It would seem so, though it might be sheer coincidence — a bit of sightseeing and following up my name. I don't know the man. At least, I don't think I do. I don't recall the name.'

'What's his reason for coming then?'

Honey shrugged. 'I don't know. He strikes me as strange and a bit of a show-off.'

'A show-off?' Lindsey frowned as she took the letter. Her eyebrows arched when she noted the beautiful handwriting. 'Wow! Someone's taken a lot of trouble. What's he like?'

Honey spread her hands, palms upwards. 'I've already told you, I don't recognise the name.'

'I take it you didn't know all of Dad's friends.'

'No,' said Honey with a grimace. 'He was pretty secretive about some of the female ones too.'

'This is a *guy*.'

'With a name like Jake, he would be.'

'Truebody. It's a fairly unusual name.'

Honey shook her head. 'As I said, never heard of him.'

When her phone started to trill like a strangulated budgie, she knew it was Doherty. She hoped he was going to suggest having a drink with him at the Zodiac Club — their favourite watering hole, the place where hoteliers and pub landlords congregated around the midnight hour, unburdening their problems and generally getting pissed.

He did indeed suggest meeting her there, and she agreed.

'I'm also calling to let you know that I persuaded Mark Bennett, the plumber you chased, not to press charges.'

'Ah! Thank you.'

He grinned. 'I told him it was an age thing.'

CHAPTER FOUR

Two days after the letter arrived and Mallory and Scrimshaw had filled the gap left by the firm of lawyers, Honey Driver went shopping. In her pocket was a folded-up shopping list. At her side was Doherty.

'I didn't think you liked shopping,' she said to him.

'I don't,' he shrugged. 'But it gives me a chance to see the sights.'

While rounding the corner into Milsom Street, they paused briefly to look at a multicoloured reindeer. According to the sign etched into its base, it was titled *Rainbow Reindeer.*

'Otherwise known as the red-nosed reindeer,' remarked Honey. They both clocked the red plastic nose someone had added to what was supposed to be an artistic exhibition. 'Still no idea who's doing it?'

'No. They've been caught on a few security cameras, but they're wearing a hoodie and the pictures aren't too clear.'

'Snowing when it isn't snowing?'

'Yep. That's about how clear they are.'

A white mist had descended on the city and icy air nipped at noses but the Christmas decorations were bright and shone on bravely regardless. Only in the narrowest of side alleys where the lighting was minimal did the mist hold full sway. Buildings that were old when Jack the Ripper was a lad loomed darkly, their outlines muted into mere phantoms of what they really were.

Honey knew Doherty was bound to ask her the million-dollar question and it was making her nervous.

'So, have you told her yet?'

Attempting to divert Steve Doherty's attention to the big task of present buying had not worked. He'd given her a ring to wear. His intentions were obvious — and honourable. The ring hadn't yet seen the light of day. Everything was on hold.

'Steve, I'm a bit busy at present, Christmas arrangements and all that . . .' An excuse.

'Are we engaged or not?'

'Of course we are . . . but does it have to be public knowledge just yet?'

'I'll tell her myself.'

'No! You don't need to. OK, call me cowardly, but I have to choose the right moment.'

She pretended to find a shop window showing a briefcase supposedly suspended in mid-air and surrounded by holly and mistletoe particularly interesting. Actually it was far from it. A briefcase rated a D minus on the exciting present scale. D for dull.

'I wouldn't use it,' said Doherty. 'So don't buy me one.'

'I wasn't going to. How about socks?'

'As long as they don't have snowmen on the side and jingle when I walk.'

She gasped. 'But, Steve, that's exactly what I had in mind!'

Talking nonsense was ducking the issue, but at this moment in time she was into ducking. She hated feeling like a silly teenager. A silly teenager deserved to feel guilty about declaring her intention to tie the knot. Here she was on the wrong side of forty-five — far from being a silly teenager but feeling as though she was. This had to stop.

Doherty made her feel guilty. Lindsey made her feel guilty. The number one coward card kicked in. When all else fails, make a viable excuse.

'This isn't the right time to ask me about this. I'm expecting a crowd in the dining room, the last office party, thank goodness. Also I'm not looking my best. Mary Jane did my hair . . .'

'Mary Jane isn't qualified to do hair.'

'I know that. You know that too. You've seen the colour.'

'So why did you let her?'

'I was in a hurry. It's turned out all wrong and wasn't really my colour in the first place.'

'It's *definitely* not your colour. It belongs to Coco the Clown.'

Earlier, Doherty had almost choked when he'd seen the colour and asked if she happened to own a wig.

'I'd be far more confident about announcing our engagement if my hair looked normal.'

'I'm not saying that your hair isn't likely to sap your confidence, but let's be honest, you're making excuses.'

He was quite right of course. Doherty had given her a ring — which she hadn't worn yet. He'd asked her to marry him. No time schedule for that, but she had pointed out that she needed to run it past Lindsey first, and that was the problem. She just couldn't get up the courage to tell her daughter — well, not yet anyway.

Over the years, mother and daughter had discussed such an eventuality in a very grown-up manner. But that had been when the whole idea was imagined, not real. Getting real was a real problem. A real, REAL problem.

'Tell you what, I'll tell her on Christmas Day. You'll be there, won't you?'

'Honey, you have no backbone.'

'Yep, but I've plenty up front.'

'I've noticed.'

No prizes for guessing what he wanted for Christmas.

'OK. Let's do the deed on Christmas Day. I'll hold you to it.'

* * *

Honey's nose was pink by the time she got back to the Green River Hotel, and her concern about bookings for next year was hurting like a hole in her head. There were other things to worry about, and they were all whirling around at the same time, crashing into each other and getting muddled.

Telling Lindsey that Doherty had asked to marry her had to be put to one side for now. She told herself that she'd get round to it in her own good time. Some might view her as cowardly. They'd probably be right.

Bath was busy. The Green River Hotel was busy.

From the beginning of December the office parties had been in full swing. On top of that everyone was out eating and drinking and clogging up the shops.

On the whole the atmosphere at the Green River was full of festive friendliness and everyone was happy to help out.

From kitchen staff to chambermaids to reception cover, everyone was entering into the spirit of things, even though they were working over the holiday period. A lucrative cash incentive — double time and a day off in lieu — helped to ease the pain. Plus a slap-up dinner on the big day itself.

At times like these it was a case of all hands on deck, the dishes, the waitressing, and the pulling of pints in the bar. That included the boss. She'd even bought in an extra supply of rubber washing-up gloves. It paid to be prepared.

'Roll on New Year,' she muttered to herself, then threw herself into the fray, though not until she'd found something better than a knitted hat to cover her head. She found a black velvet cloche hat, part of a 1920s fancy dress outfit, that hid most, if not all, of the offending hair colour.

First stop, the engine room. The kitchen.

In every hotel, every restaurant, it's accepted as fact that the kitchen is the hub, a sacrosanct territory where the head chef reigns supreme.

Smudger Smith was just such a chef, totally in charge of his little kingdom. A true professional with a temperament best described as tetchy, he took great pride in the standard of his cuisine. Criticism of said cuisine was best done at fifty paces and while wearing running shoes. Smudger was sensitive about his cooking.

That didn't mean he didn't play hard too — only the week before he had been found snuggled up to a turkey in the cold store. When roused from his slumber he'd muttered something about stuffing a girl from Iceland.

Honey poked her head around the door. 'Everything OK here?'

Smudger kicked the oven door shut and glared at her as though she'd accused him of murder.

'Are you insinuating that I'm incapable of coping?'

'Of course not.'

She knew she should leave, but the aromatic mix of rich plum pudding, mulled wine jelly, and almond paste kept her rooted to the spot.

'Turkey ready for the oven?' It was purely an excuse to linger.

The glare surfaced again on Smudger's pink face. 'Why? Are you doubting my ability? Do you want to do the job yourself?'

Her voice went high pitched. 'Of course not,' she squeaked.

Taking over the running of a catering kitchen was the last thing she wanted to do. Forget the glamour trotted out by TV chefs. Catering kitchens were hell on wheels!

She took a backward step. He took one forward.

'I was just checking you were OK,' she said weakly.

'Of course I'm OK! Now perhaps you'll leave me to get on with my job.' His face was pink from heat and agitation.

She judged that right now was the time for grovelling. 'Sorry. I know you're under pressure. Yet another pair of turkey legs, yes?'

He blinked as if he was considering throwing something. She did a quick reconnoitre of the stainless-steel tabletops. No meat cleaver in sight. A definite plus.

After a curt nod, he turned his back and positively flew into action. Pans rattled and kitchen staff ducked.

The mention of turkey legs had certainly pressed the panic buttons. A month of office parties had resulted in a freezer packed with them. This was because most diners preferred the white breast meat. They had enough deep-frozen turkey legs to last them until April. At first the staff had been pleased to take a leg or two for personal consumption, but after all the office parties they'd had, the limit had been reached. Now everyone was refusing point blank to take the surplus home, while pointing out that there were only so many turkey curries they could make — or eat.

'OK. I'll leave you to it. I'm off to get in shape for later.'

'You're already in great shape,' shouted a voice from the washing-up area. A tinsel-trimmed halo bobbed above the stainless-steel shelving.

Rodney 'Clint' Eastwood was scrubbing pans, piling plates into the dishwasher, putting one batch away before reloading another.

Clint, who sported a whole gallery of tattoos over his body, had added a little seasonal trimming. An angelic halo, formed from wire and covered in tinsel and coloured balls, sat on his head. Baubles usually found on a Christmas tree hung from his ears. He looked like an overgrown house elf from Hogwarts.

'Thanks,' she shouted leaving the kitchen to its tasks and expelling a gasp of relief as she let the door whoosh shut behind her.

* * *

At reception, musing on Mary Jane and her ghost stories, Lindsey wasn't immediately aware of someone plonking a suitcase down and leaning over the counter.

'Hi. I'm Jake Truebody. You must be Lindsey Driver.'

Startled, Lindsey looked up.

'Sorry. Did I startle you?'

Blue eyes twinkled behind owlish spectacles. He offered his hand. 'You're wondering how I know your name.'

'I took your booking?' She smiled courteously.

He beamed broadly. 'Oh, I've never spoken to you. I booked online then wrote a letter. I like writing. There's nothing on God's earth like the written word facilitated with a proper pen and bottled ink.'

'Ah, yes. I saw your letter.' She hesitated, not sure quite how to interpret the way he was looking at her. 'You said you knew my father.' It was all she could think of to say.

He took off the black hat he was wearing and smoothed back his hair. It was long and curled over his coat collar.

'We set up a business together. 'Course, you wouldn't know that. You were young when he died. I don't suppose you really knew him that well.'

'No. Not really.'

Feeling oddly awkward, Lindsey turned away. Usually brimming with confidence, he'd bowled her over. He'd known her father. She'd met few people who'd known her father, only mainly relatives in the US. Every so often she got a card or a present from someone she didn't remember.

She found the email confirming his booking. 'If you could sign the register entering your passport number and address in the box provided.'

He took the pen and did as requested.

'And if I could check your passport details against the particulars you've written . . .'

He handed her his passport. The address was in Maine and he looked more or less like his photo: long face, horn-rimmed spectacles, a black felt fedora and greying hair curling over his collar. Passport photos were never very exact.

'The mug shot was taken some time ago,' he said laughingly.

Lindsey smiled. 'They're never very flattering, are they!'

He agreed that they were not.

The passport number also checked out. Everything seemed to be in order.

'Room Sixteen,' she said, handing him the key.

Just for a moment — the very slightest of moments — he held on to her fingertips and gazed into her eyes.

'You really do look like your father, Lindsey.'

The comment made her pause. 'Do I really?'

'Absolutely.'

He thanked her and headed for the stairs.

She watched him go before entering the name, passport number and address on the system. There it was: Professor Jake Truebody and an address in Maine. Everything checked out — with the exception of his handwriting. It was neat enough, though not as elaborate as the letter her mother had shown her.

His arrival unnerved her. Maine was where her father had lived and this man claimed to have known him. But what was he doing here?

She rechecked the handwriting on the registration form. The capital letters were elaborate, though certainly not calligraphic standard, though writing of that calibre must take time.

She wondered if she'd inherited her mother's suspicious mind. Amateur sleuths had to be endowed with suspicious minds. Perhaps it ran in their family, and why not? A Sherlock Holmes-type gene could easily lurk in their blood.

But he'd mentioned her father. That alone was enough to make her curious to hear more.

Later she'd wonder at the impetuousness of her next action, but for now she was driven. She dialled the professor's room.

'Professor, I've been thinking about you knowing my father. I'd like to hear more about your friendship — if that's not too much trouble.'

She sensed a withholding of breath and figured he was seeking a get-out clause. No problem. She could do that.

'If it's not too much trouble,' she said again. 'Please feel free to say if it is.'

'No. No trouble at all.'

She sensed it wasn't quite true, but she'd asked and he'd accepted.

'In return perhaps I can take you on a tour of the city? Just let me know the kind of places you like to see.'

'That's very kind of you,' Jake Truebody said. 'History is my subject. That's why I'm here and quite frankly I would be mighty grateful to be taken around by Carl Driver's daughter. But if it's any trouble . . .'

'No trouble at all.'

'Then I accept. What's there to protest about when a pretty girl like you is offering to hold my hand?'

'Bullshit,' muttered Lindsey as she put down the phone. Jake Truebody was here for a reason, though what that reason might be was anyone's guess. Hopefully it was nothing to do with upsetting her mother's life.

CHAPTER FIVE

Eight days before Christmas. Party night had arrived.

Professor Jake Truebody stood aside to let the first of the Mallory and Scrimshaw Christmas party guests through the door into reception.

Honey had so far avoided any contact with the man who claimed to be an old friend of Carl's. She really didn't want to go there and besides, she was just too busy.

A self-assured young man with floppy hair leaned over the reception desk.

'Mallory and Scrimshaw. Are we the first?'

Honey confirmed that they were and beamed her brightest smile. The booking for ten persons, office party, rooms, and a forward booking for dinner on Christmas Day had turned up. Not that she'd doubted they would; payment having been made up front. Employees never looked a gift horse in the mouth. In her experience, if the boss was paying, they were up for it.

'Welcome to the Green River Hotel. Now if you'd just like to sign in, we can get you settled in your rooms. The party starts at eight, so you've got plenty of time to get ready. Complimentary glasses of champagne will be served in the bar from 7.15 p.m.'

The plastered on smile threatened to crack her face in half. The countdown had begun; they only catered to residents and Christmas dinner diners over the holiday, easier to cope with than firm's parties and people checking in and out. Christmas office parties were great for those attending, but for the staff twenty or so parties on the trot were pretty wearing. This was the last.

The sight of the Mallory and Scrimshaw crowd helped put her in the festive mood. Each and every one of them — with the probable exception of a woman with blue/black hair and a chalk white complexion — were as pink-faced as chocolate-box cherubs. The weather outside was nippy for December. Cold snaps like this weren't usual until January. This year was proving the exception; snow had fallen and ice had been spotted on the Avon floating like crisp white pancakes. Rumour had it that the stone polar bear standing on the roof at Bear Flat — a particular area of the A37 — had been seen to shiver.

'I can't believe this,' said one wide-eyed blonde, her eyes taking in the crystal chandeliers, the Louis XIV style furnishings and the pale blue walls.

Assuming she was referring to her taste in décor, Honey puffed up with pride. 'I designed it myself.'

'Oh.' The girl looked puzzled. 'That's nice.'

Honey was disappointed, though consoled herself that judging by the girl's outfit, her taste was more high street than high class.

One of the young men in the party slapped the reception desk and grinned. 'Sam here is a bit overcome — as are we all come to that. This is a big first for us on account of the boss has never dug deep into his pockets for a Christmas "do" before. Come to think of it, he's never been in the habit of digging into his pockets at any time of year. You've heard of Scrooge? Not forgetting the ghost of his old business partner, Marley.'

'Ah. Not forgetting him,' said Honey, though fully aware that she had. 'And when can we expect Mr Scrimshaw to arrive?' she asked brightly.

'He'll be along soon.'

'And Mr Mallory?'

'He's dead.'

Aware that his companions were hanging onto his every word, the over-confident young man almost doubled in size as he further elucidated.

'But Ebenezer Scrooge is a fact and is alive and well — only one nub of coal on the fire,' he added, his voice a parody of Scrooge himself, shoulders hunched and hands like claws.

The small crowd laughed at his antics then nodded in unison and made jokey asides or more assiduous comments that included the words skinflint, tight as a duck's arse, and miserly. Honey just smiled and listened. There was no way she was going to make comment this way or that. Mr Clarence Scrimshaw had booked a five-course Christmas meal and all the rooms so that those of his staff who wished to make merry with alcohol could stay overnight. They were also booked in for dinner on Christmas Day. There was nothing tight-fisted about that.

'Don't know what's come over the old skinflint,' said the confident young man who signed himself in as David Longborough.

'A change of heart?' suggested Honey.

The blonde girl sniffed. 'Didn't know he had one.'

There followed chuckles and clucks of approval. The boy, David, patted the blonde girl's hand.

'Come on, Sam. You didn't do so badly by the old goat.'

Honey slyly observed them, raising her eyes just a teeny bit. Watching guests while carrying out a mundane task is a prerequisite for any dyed-in-the-wool hotelier. She noticed a pink flush spread over the girl's face and reached the obvious conclusion; old Scrooge might have had a soft spot for at least one of his employees.

'There's plenty of hot water, and coffee- and tea-making facilities are provided in your rooms,' she added as she pushed the registration book and a pen beneath each frost-nipped nose. 'Enjoy your party and have a fun time. After all, it is the season of goodwill to all men,' Honey said brightly.

David Longborough chuckled. 'You're right there, darling. We're all going to make the most of it. It might never happen again.'

'Yes,' said a woman with black hair and heavy make-up. 'There has to be a reason for him acting out of character, though for the life of me I can't work out what it is.'

CHAPTER SIX

Mr Clarence Scrimshaw was far too small for his desk. Heavily ornate and made from a rich red mahogany, the desk had been handed down from his grandfather, Percival Charles Scrimshaw.

His grandfather had established the business back in 1905 with one hundred pounds that, as family history would have it, came with his marriage to one Daphne Beatrice Moore, the daughter of a bishop. A further one hundred pounds had come when he'd acquired his partner, Eamon Mallory senior, father of Eamon Mallory junior.

For the most part the company published books of local interest, nostalgic non-fiction titles such as *Bath Chairs and the Nineteenth Century Invalid*, *A History of Green Park Railway Station*, and *Lewd Residents of the Regency Period*.

The last title had been their most successful so far and old Clarence had been keen to get the author to write a follow up — something saucy in the title of course. Bath was a Regency city and you could always count on anyone associated with the fourth Hanoverian king to be a bit racy.

Unfortunately, Arthur Lovell, the author of this insight into the Regency, was unattainable unless a medium was employed to make contact with the hereafter. Arthur had met a sticky end out on the Avon Estuary trying to rescue a cat. The cat had survived, neatly skipping up over Arthur's body as he slowly sank into the Avon mud.

The offices of Mallory and Scrimshaw were situated down a narrow alley which in turn led to a shaded courtyard encased tomblike by other old properties. Cobblers Court had changed little over the centuries except for a better drainage system and plastic guttering. Inside could be described as period, but perhaps more correctly, basic and dated.

Despite the introduction of computers, inside toilets and all things necessary to publish books in the twenty-first century, the premises of Mallory and Scrimshaw still possessed the gloomy atmosphere of an earlier time. Outside an old gas lamp, long converted to electricity, hung at a crooked angle from the wall. Inside the floorboards creaked underfoot and the walls were bumpy.

Not that any of that counted for anything any longer to the aging, miserable old man Mr Clarence Scrimshaw had been.

Although usually dwarfed by his desk when sitting behind it, that was not the case now. His body was presently spreadeagled on the desktop, the handle of a letter opener sticking out of one ear, blood oozing onto a conveniently placed piece of blotting paper.

A gloved hand had put that blotting paper there, and a vengeful, devious, mind had inwardly chuckled with glee at the fact that the old boy used some archaic items, most of which should have been ditched long ago. A fountain pen? Blotting paper? Really?

The job was done. It was time to go.

The floorboards and old staircase creaked underfoot on the way out. Nothing had changed in the world except that Clarence Scrimshaw was no longer in it.

A chill mist had descended on Cobblers Court, blunting the effect of the hanging lantern and the few remaining lights in the building opposite. Office cleaners were finishing up their work on the first floor. On the floor above that the lights were still bright and people were moving around. A banner draped across the windows on the inside proclaimed that a hair stylist had taken up residence.

The cloaked form exited Mallory and Scrimshaw, swept into the alley way and disappeared into the Dickensian mist.

* * *

Manning Reception at the Green River Hotel, Anna, the hotel's Polish receptionist, put a call through to room seventeen without noting the caller's name. It was normal practice to write this down just in case the recipient wished to call them back and had mislaid or forgotten their number. But Anna was in no mood to be that pedantic. She was heavily pregnant and beginning to get threatening twinges. But she wouldn't give in. There was no way she was going to miss the festivities.

Up in his room Paul Emmerson, the company bookkeeper for Mallory and Scrimshaw, was wearing a track in the carpet. His wife was sitting on the bed, watching him, her dark eyes shooting daggers. The call had been for him.

'That was *her,* wasn't it?'

He nodded without looking up, his eyes fixed on the course of his footsteps.

She made a huffing sound. 'Well let him deal with it. He drew up the contract, not you.'

'She's persistent, I'll give her that. She rang me because she couldn't get hold of him at the office.'

'He must have left by now. He should be here, in the hotel.'

Paul Emmerson stopped pacing.

Susan Emmerson winced at the look he gave her. Contempt was written all over his face.

'You don't really think he's going to turn up here, do you? He hates parties.'

'But he'd still come seeing as he paid for it, surely?'

He shook his head, eyeing his wife pityingly. 'You don't really think he paid for all this?'

A puzzled frown accentuated the fine lines that his wife's forty-five years had gifted her forehead. 'Surely, he must have done. And if he didn't pay for it, then who did?'

He shrugged. 'Who cares? As they say, there's no point in looking a gift horse in the mouth. And the old sod owes me. He bloody well owes me.'

* * *

In room nineteen, immediately next door to the one occupied by Mr and Mrs Emmerson, David Longborough was doing his best to choke his workmate with his tongue.

Samantha Brown broke the connection at the exact moment when his hand crept into the side of her strapless dress, a dark green creation that barely kept her greatest assets in check.

'Don't you want me, babe?' He looked hurt, adopting a little boy lost expression that she'd fallen for before.

She pushed him back. 'This isn't about sex and you know it bloody well isn't.'

'Naughty, naughty.' He tapped her lips with his finger. 'Old Clarence wouldn't want to hear you using bad words, sweet Sam.'

'It's your fault. If you hadn't talked me into this . . .' Her smooth brow puckered and her glossed lips pouted. 'If somebody finds out . . .'

'Nobody will find out, and by the time they do, we'll be in London. We'll have no problem getting a publishing job up there. They'll take anybody as long as they'll work for next to nothing.'

Sam's brow remained puckered. 'I thought what we did might get us more than that. We might end up in *prison*.'

Longborough caressed her shoulders reassuringly. The last thing he wanted was for her to come on all serious. For her to come on all sexual was what he was after. He'd put in plenty of time on seducing her and, hey, it was Christmas.

'Now come on. It's party time. We said we were going to enjoy this. Right?'

Her frown lessened. Her smile was hesitant but at least it was happening, and Longborough badly wanted it to happen.

He felt a fresh surge of physical desire. She'd been teasing him all year, all the time thinking that she was in charge, she was the one making the running. She was wrong. Now he had her — or would do very shortly.

They started to resume the position they'd been in, but Samantha held him off.

'Just one thing,' she said before he kissed her again. 'Your tongue tastes of garlic. I'd rather you kept it to yourself.'

* * *

It was four thirty and in room twenty, Mrs Freda Finchley was taking advantage of the hotel's deep bath and plentiful supply of hot water. On the whole, she was quite satisfied with the room and the facilities. She hoped the dinner would be good too and, knowing Clarence, it would be. He was most insistent on getting value for money. Not a penny was spent unless it was stretched to the limit.

The moment she'd received her room key, she'd left the rest of them, glad to be alone; glad to prepare herself for when Clarence Scrimshaw arrived.

This whole arrangement had come as a big surprise. She'd never known Clarence to spend money on employees before. Perhaps if she hadn't been on holiday with her sister in Bournemouth for the past two weeks, she might have known more. Sometimes he opened up and told her his plans. The majority were work related, but just occasionally he would tell her something of his youth and of the early times when Eamon Mallory was still alive.

'So what are the arrangements for Christmas?' she'd asked him on her return.

His eyes had sparkled behind his wire-rimmed spectacles and a mean smile had flickered on his lips.

'Nothing out of the ordinary,' he'd said to her. 'It's just another day. Another year.'

'I think you're going to surprise us this year,' she'd said, smiling at him in the way she'd seen Sam Brown smile at him. 'You deserve a jolly Christmas, Mr Scrimshaw. All the hard work you put in all year.'

His thin lips had smiled. 'I know what I deserve, Mrs Finchley, and I reward myself accordingly.'

'And how do you plan on doing that?'

He tapped his lips with his index finger. 'It's a secret, Mrs Finchley. A closely guarded secret.'

So he wanted it kept a secret. Everyone seemed to be in on the secret, though nobody mentioned it except in soft whispers. To her all the subterfuge had been a little disappointing. She so loved being taken into Mr Scrimshaw's confidence, but she preferred to be there alone. On this occasion everyone knew but did not talk about it — except for the girls talking about what they were wearing, and the guys shooting the breeze about very boozy Christmases they'd had in the past.

As the water tumbled into the bath, she set out the scented toiletries she'd brought with her. First she tipped half a bottle of moisturising bubble bath into the water. The bottle said only a capful, but the stakes were high. Her eyes glistened at the prospect of finally winning the man she'd set her heart on.

As the bubbles piled up, she arranged the bottle of expensive body lotion next to the shampoo, hair conditioner, and deodorant.

She eyed her arrangement with some disquiet, instantly feeling that something was missing, something very important.

'Perfume!' she exclaimed, her heart pounding with excitement. Freda Finchley indulging in perfumed luxury. Whatever next?

Just to confirm what she'd thought she had done, she checked the dressing table in the bedroom. Sure enough, she had placed the perfume there, ready to dab on profusely once she had finished her bath.

Before immersing herself in the steaming bubbles, she stripped off in front of a full-length mirror.

This way and that she turned, finally deciding that she didn't have a bad figure for her age. Clarence would not be disappointed. Now all she had to do was to get him to her room. She was sure that once compromised he would be putty in her hands. No man such as he would want his reputation ruined, would he?

The bubbles broke and reformed around her as she lowered herself into the bath with a deep sigh.

By now he would have found the Christmas card she'd placed on his desk. Once he read that he would be in no doubt what she wanted from him and what would happen if he didn't concur.

Nice word that, concur; a very legal way of saying agree. And he would have to agree. He would have no choice, and once he smelled her perfume . . .

CHAPTER SEVEN

Lindsey was manning Reception when the Emmersons went out. 'We have to visit my mother. She's been taken into hospital,' Paul Emmerson explained. 'Hopefully we won't be long. We've had these little emergencies many times before.'

After popping their key into the receiving slot cut in the reception desk, they were gone.

A draught blew in as the door swished shut, scattering the brochures laid neatly out on an eighteenth-century side table.

Eyeing them disdainfully did nothing to make the leaflets fly back up again. Lindsey went to pick them up.

As she did so, she glanced out through the window behind the side table. Mr and Mrs Emmerson were still outside the hotel. They appeared to be arguing. Whatever the outcome of the argument, neither seemed well pleased. Turning their backs on each other, they stormed off, Mrs Emmerson going in one direction and her husband in the other.

She'd just come away from the window when Mrs Finchley descended the stairs. Her face was pink and she left a cloud of expensive scent in her wake.

'I have to go out,' she said in a flustered manner. 'I need air. There's my key.'

She almost collided with Mary Jane who immediately took the opportunity to introduce herself.

'Hi there. I'm Mary Jane. I don't know whether you've read the notice board in reception, but if you're here over Christmas, I'm giving ghost story readings after dinner on Christmas Day. It was going to be on Boxing Day, but all the excitement and magic will be gone by then, don't you think? Can I count on your support?'

The woman looked at her in a dazed fashion, as though she'd suddenly been shocked into a reality she hadn't known existed.

'Ghost stories?'

'Yes. Christmas ones. They're mostly written by local authors, such as Patricia Pontefract, and American ones. It'll be fun and I'm being sponsored by a local publisher mainly because a whole collection of stories was written by one of his authors . . .'

Mrs Finchley froze.

'A local publisher? And you've got Patricia Pontefract?'

Mary Jane nodded profusely. 'That's right. So how about it?'

The woman nodded. 'If I can, I will. Most definitely.'

Lindsey saw that Mrs Finchley was desperate to get out of the door. Mary Jane had tripped her up — though not for long.

'Unrequited love,' Mary Jane declared as she placed her bag on the reception counter and was handed her key. 'There's a man in that woman's life who doesn't know she exists.'

'How do you know that? Has she had a palm reading with you?' asked Lindsey.

Mary Jane was into table tapping, astrology and other weirdness. Palm reading was a recently added extra.

'No.' She shook her head and recouped her bulbous bag, a shocking pink item with green tassels hanging from the corners. 'No woman would use that much expensive perfume unless she had a man in her sights. And, boy oh boy, was that perfume expensive!'

Samantha Brown suddenly came bolting down the stairs in tears.

Seeing the state of her, Lindsey came out from behind the reception desk.

'Is something wrong?' she asked. 'Can I help at all?'

Samantha shook her head and pushed a paper tissue hard against her nostrils, an action which made her vaguely resemble Miss Piggy.

'Sam!'

The shout came from David Longborough, his long legs taking two stairs at a time, his chestnut hair flopping over his forehead.

Lindsey gave him the once over, her expression finally fixing in set-concrete disdain. She'd met his sort before. There was a hint of Eton about him, the casual confidence that only someone privately educated possessed. However, she sensed there were two sides to this young man. She wagered he was blessed with the quick wittedness of a Cockney boy. Strange that he was in publishing when politics or City trading might have suited him better.

Sam Brown shook off the hand that tried to restrain her. 'Leave me alone, David. I'm going shopping.'

She darted out. He stood looking after her, his expression too dark to indicate disappointment. He was angry.

It was not the policy of the Green River Hotel to get involved with residents' personal lives, and Lindsey had no intention of doing so now. She stepped smartly back behind the reception desk and felt better for doing so.

However, Mary Jane was a natural-born nosy parker. She couldn't help herself. Like the archangel guarding the Garden of Eden, she stood like a statue between Longborough and the door.

'Have we met before?' she asked him.

It was not what Lindsey had expected her to say. Judging by the look on Longborough's face, it wasn't what he'd expected either. The question seemed to pull him up short.

'What?'

'Your face seems vaguely familiar,' said Mary Jane, her eyes half closed, thumb and forefinger pinching her chin as though trying hard to recall where she'd seen him.

'I don't recall ever meeting you, Mrs . . . ?'

'Mary Jane Porter. I'm from the United States. California to be exact.'

'I would never have guessed,' he said, his sarcasm muted but discernible.

'Yes, yes . . . I feel I've seen you somewhere before. Are you from around here?'

'What?' It was obvious he wanted to get past her, but each step to the right was countered with a step from her and each step to the left, likewise.

'My father's family came from London. Tottenham in fact.'

'He would do.'

'My mother's family came from around here.'

'Did they now?'

Mary Jane's expression was very intense and her blockading of the door unassailable.

'Look. Can I get past? I want to catch up with my girlfriend. She needs me.'

'She looked pretty upset. Can't say I believe she needs that — to be upset, that is.'

'Quite frankly, it's none of your bloody business.'

'So what was the name of your mother's family?'

There was no sliding past without Mary Jane's say so. Being tall and gangly came in handy. She filled a lot of space.

Longborough glared at her, his hands perched like claws on his wafer-thin pelvis.

'Look. If it's of any concern of yours, my mother was a Reynolds and her family lived around here for ages. OK? Are you satisfied now?'

Mary Jane's eyes opened wide and she seemed genuinely taken aback. 'Really? Well there's a thing!'

His expression froze. It was, thought Lindsey, as though their resident psychic and tarot card reader had hinted at family secrets. Whatever it was, Longborough slid past her at breakneck speed and out of the door.

'I'll be back,' he shouted over his shoulder.

Mary Jane rested one elbow on the reception desk, her hand fiddling with the fluffy pink hat she was wearing, eyes narrowed, and brow creased in thought.

'So where did you meet him?' Lindsey asked her.

Mary Jane straightened and slapped the desk with one long, bony hand. 'I didn't ever meet him. I have seen an oil painting of one of his mother's ancestors. He looks just like her. I also know that one of his mother's ancestors was responsible for a good man's death. I'm sure they're one and the same. He'd been accused of murder and was sentenced to hang. The truth was that he'd been in his lover's arms at the time in question, but he never betrayed that fact. Apparently she was his best friend's wife. After his execution she used to visit his grave wearing a long black veil. She continued to do it all her life — and thereafter.'

Lindsey just nodded.

CHAPTER EIGHT

The party went with a swing; there were over of seventy people in the dining room, milling around between there and the bar.

A number of part-time staff had been called in, but holes in service emerged which necessitated Honey waitressing where necessary, and Lindsey helping out behind the bar.

In between doing this, Honey offered free drinks to those individuals from each firm participating who had booked the event. No one refused. The only person she didn't corner with a free drink was Clarence Scrimshaw of Mallory and Scrimshaw, publishers. He was nowhere to be found.

'One free drink saved,' she muttered and poured one for herself to compensate.

The dancing went on until midnight; the drinking a little longer, the last barflies being despatched to their beds somewhere around three in the morning.

Honey and Lindsey dragged themselves to their own home, both dog tired.

'Am I tripping over my feet or the bags beneath my eyes?' muttered Honey.

'Both,' Lindsey murmured back before sloping off to bed.

The next day was the big clean up, and there was a lot of cleaning up to do.

Mother and daughter talked as they worked. The current subject was Jake Truebody, the man who wrote elegantly and insisted he'd been a friend of Honey's dead husband.

'I don't remember him. I don't know him, and I'm not going to go out of my way to make friends with him.'

Honey said all this as she backed out from beneath a dining table where a cold roast potato had sat squashed and alone.

Her comment was in response to Lindsey mentioning his arrival; how he'd appeared suddenly like a ghost with his black hat, horn-rimmed spectacles, and the obvious looks of a university professor.

So far their conversations about him had been brief, both of them uncomfortable with his presence. Honey disliked mentioning him because of the ex-husband connection. Lindsey was mulling over how she felt about the man. In a way she was drawn to him because he'd known her father. On the other hand something about him made her wary. So far she'd avoided revealing her concerns, not until she had analysed them properly and worked out where they were coming from.

'But he isn't a ghost,' remarked Honey. She did not voice that if he was, she would have him exorcised.

'This hotel will be littered with ghosts once Mary Jane's presented her ghost story session. Everyone will be claiming to have seen them.'

'You could be right,' said Honey. She groaned as her knee made contact with a splodge of chocolate gateau. What a waste!

Lindsey changed the subject. 'I see that there are now fifty reindeer sporting red noses around the city. The artists aren't well pleased. I wonder who's doing it?'

'And why,' added Honey. 'What's the point?'

'A grudge, perhaps?'

'Could be. I also have to ask myself where they're getting that many red noses.'

'They've obviously got a stash of them. Either that or they're making them themselves.'

'The super glue is a problem. It's hard to get off, besides which, they can't keep up with them. As fast as they remove one, another five appear. It's proving an unending task.' Honey sighed. 'And so is this. How can seventy civilised people make this much mess when they're eating?'

'Never mind. Not much more,' said Lindsey.

'Amen to that. Not much more. Great things, office parties. And the best thing about them is the money they generate. The worst thing is clearing up the morning after the night before.'

She eyed the bin liner as though she would like to rip it to pieces, which wasn't far from the truth. They'd filled two and it would take another two to accommodate the remaining detritus of the night before.

Splashes of gravy and splodges of Baked Alaska and Christmas pudding were mopped up with industrial strength kitchen roll. Christmas crackers, empty wine bottles, screwed-up napkins, and a pair of fishnet stockings was consigned to a black plastic rubbish bag.

Lindsey held up a pair of scanty bikini briefs between finger and thumb. 'Hope they've got a spare pair.'

'Or a good disposition,' her mother added. 'It's two degrees below freezing outside.'

'Hardy types. The lot from Mallory and Scrimshaw certainly made the most of it. They were drinking until three, determined to get their money's worth. Sounds as though their boss wasn't known for going overboard at Christmas — or, if they're to be believed, overboard at any time.'

Honey tied the end of the bulging black bin bag. 'Well I've got a lot of time for Mr Clarence Scrimshaw. He's done the finances of the Green River Hotel a lot of good. Never look a gift horse in the mouth.' She couldn't quite explain why a reference to a horse had entered her head. 'They were well behaved last night and I'm not expecting them to be any different on Christmas Day. Everything is plain sailing from now on,' she declared with a lilt to her voice and a touch of renewed energy.

The first sign that this was wishful thinking and that a horse was involved caught her unawares.

Anna waddled in from the bar and stood politely waiting to be noticed. Her blonde hair was tied back with a pink and white checked bow and a pink cardigan was straining at the buttons over her very pregnant belly.

'Mrs Driver,' she said calmly. 'There is a dead horse in the bar.'

Anna was a Jill of all trades and her first language was understandably her native Polish. Although her English had improved, she did get the odd word wrong. Honey assumed this was one of those times and smiled an understanding smile. 'Say again?'

'It is a horse,' said Anna, a slight frown denting her fair brow. 'It is definitely a horse. It has four legs, a tail, beady eyes, and a red hooter.'

'Hooter?'

'Nose.'

'Right.'

Sticking to the view that her first assumption was right and that Anna was a bit awry on the language front, Honey took her time going to investigate. Besides last night's party had been pretty wild. The fallout was subtle but in need of attention, i.e. she was presently disengaging a vol-au-vent from between two brochures advertising an event at the Roman Baths.

While wending her way between dining room and bar, she was stopped in Reception by one of last night's guests. She recognised the woman as being one of the Mallory and Scrimshaw party.

'Mrs Driver. If I could just have a word . . .' Her tone was soft and her expression was one of concern. 'Our boss, Mr Scrimshaw; I'm a little worried. I didn't see him last night so I presume he arrived late. Is he down yet?'

'No, I'm afraid I haven't seen him. Anna must have checked him in last night. Sorry.'

The woman was of a comfortable size, the type who rarely missed a meal and enjoyed her food — not that Honey held that against her. In fact, she had instant empathy.

It was likely the woman hadn't overindulged on booze the night before. The rest of the party had done their utmost to drink the cellar dry, and few were likely to be up for the full breakfasts on offer so early in the day. The lady, Mrs Finchley if she recalled correctly, would likely be one of the few diners.

There was something resembling vain hope in Mrs Finchley's eyes, a yearning to lasso Mr Scrimshaw before breakfast might explain it, but there could be something else.

Mrs Finchley frowned while fiddling with the strap of her handbag. 'I wonder where he might be?'

'Sleeping it off perhaps?'

Honey said it with a friendly smile. After all it was the usual sort of thing people said after having a party.

But Mrs Finchley was not amused.

'Mr Scrimshaw does not indulge!'

Now that was news. Last night it had seemed to Honey that everyone had been overindulging. On the other hand, she wasn't sure what Mr Scrimshaw looked like. He'd paid the bill over the phone. She'd not met him face to face and she hadn't been able to locate him in order to give him a free drink for organising the party.

'I'm sorry if I was speaking out of turn. I only presumed . . .'

'Mr Scrimshaw has *standards*. He is not a man to drink or eat to excess.'

Or anything else, Honey thought to herself deciding that Mrs Finchley, a dried-out divorcee if ever she saw one, was living in hope that he might indulge himself with her.

It was politic to offer an explanation — which she did.

'Well seeing as he seems to have had a late night, perhaps he's decided on a lie-in anyway. If you care to go on into breakfast, when he appears I'll send him in to you. How would that be?'

Mrs Finchley took on a pinched expression, sucking in her pinched lips. 'I'm not even sure he arrived for the party. He may have fallen asleep in his room. He has been working very hard of late, and I was worried when I saw . . .'

Honey decided she didn't have any time for this. There were more rubbish bags to be filled. Even during the serving of breakfast, she could see herself kicking the odd bread roll into touch.

'Well, there you are then. He found the bed very comfortable and decided to take advantage of the situation. Everyone needs a break from work.'

'Can you get someone to check? Can you ring his room? I need to speak to him about a very important matter . . .'

'I can if you wish, though I would point out that he might not be too pleased. As you yourself have just pointed out, he has been working hard. Isn't it likely that he could well be having a lie-in?'

'That's true.' Mrs Finchley jerked her head in something that passed for a nod, but she didn't look happy. The moment she'd disappeared through the double doors into the dining room, Honey put the 'ring the bell' sign in place and headed for the bar with Anna. Investigating a dead horse seemed eminently preferable than dealing with a doomed love affair.

'Poor lady,' said Anna. 'She looks very unhappy.'

'The poor lady is a blossom unplucked,' said Honey.

Anna looked puzzled. 'Plucked? She is like a flower?'

Honey nodded. 'Just like a flower. No man has plucked her — well, not recently anyway.'

'I have been plucked,' said Anna, smiling.

Honey stole a quick glance at Anna's belly. 'Yes. You certainly have.'

CHAPTER NINE

There was a Christmassy emptiness to the bar and the smell of scattered peanuts and stale beer was balanced with that of pine needles and chocolate. Dropped crisps scrunched into the carpet beneath her feet. All pretty normal.

The only out of place thing amongst the holly, ivy, and red velvet bows was the purple horse with yellow spots.

Anna stood with hands resting on what remained of her hips — which wasn't a lot.

'You see?' She pointed an accusing finger.

The horse had its rear end perched on a Chesterfield sofa. Its front half sprawled on the floor, its head on the opposite sofa. It was definitely a horse — a pantomime horse.

The colours clashed with the traditional décor of dark wood and green upholstery. It even out-glared the shiny glass balls and sparkling tinsel.

'I need to vacuum now,' said Anna firmly. 'This horse must go. It is in my way.'

Honey was totally in agreement. Anna was a good worker who liked to get on with her job. Honey felt obliged to make things as easy for her as possible. Number one priority was getting rid of the horse. To do that she had to rouse the people who were evidently inside it.

Perhaps it had something to do with being cruel to animals, but although she raised her foot and thought about it, she just couldn't bring herself to give it a kick. Then it snored. It was a recognisable snore. She'd definitely heard it before.

She landed a smack on the spotty rump with the end pole of the vacuum cleaner. 'That's it! Stop horsing around and get out of here.'

Loud groans and muffled expletives were accompanied by an infrequent juddering of the saggy legs as the two inmates attempted to get to their feet.

Somebody muttered, 'Where am I?'

'You're a horse's arse.'

'Don't call me that.'

'You *are* a horse's arse.'

Honey folded her arms. She'd had this idea in her head to have a slow run down to a peaceful Christmas, guests, friends and family only at Christmas Day lunch. Once this horse was out of the way . . .

'Right. Disrobe. Now.'

An exclamation of surprise came from within the purple and yellow suit.

'Off! Now!'

Head chef Smudger Smith had hair the colour of corn and the fair skin of someone of Scandinavian descent, though he actually came from Nottingham. As he emerged, Smudger's face was pink and crumpled and his hair stuck up like the bristles of a worn-out toilet brush. His sous chef, a young lad named Dick, looked just as pale, perhaps paler but that might have something to do with his dark brown hair.

Both of them were obviously the worse for wear.

'So.' Honey crossed her arms over chest. 'Where did you get it?'

The two chefs looked at each other, then at the horse outfit. They exchanged shrugs.

The smell of a spent Christmas celebration — a scent heavy with whisky and beer — was suddenly replaced with a cloud of Chanel No.5. Honey's mother, Gloria Cross, had arrived. On seeing the horse and two half-naked men, she stopped in her tracks.

'What . . . ?'

'It's a horse. A pantomime horse,' Honey proclaimed.

'Well. It's certainly not a contender for the 2.15 at Lansdown, is it,' said her mother. 'By the way, dear, why the hat?'

'I had an accident with my hair.'

'You should get it professionally styled. I'll get you an appointment with Antoine.'

'I'd rather you didn't,' Honey shot back.

Antoine was a slinky Latvian with slim hips and a tight bottom who pretended to be Italian. He wore black satin trousers, and a series of steel combs dangled from a belt around his hips. Women of her mother's age loved him. Antoine didn't just style their hair, he smothered them with oily attention. He knew how to turn the old girls on all right, and was a dab hand with wedge cuts and beige and pink rinses. Outwardly Antoine appeared undisputedly gay, though she'd heard through the grapevine it was far from the case.

'He flirts with men,' muttered Casper, the chair of the Bath Hotels Association, 'but it is a persona, dear Honey, a front for his business. Old ladies feel safe with him.'

'So what is his bag?' asked Honey.

'Older women. I think he likes being their pet. Cheaper than a dog. And he does their hair.'

Honey patted the crown of her head, deciding she'd prefer to wear a tea cosy for the rest of her life rather than endure a session with Antoine.

Her mother, however, did not insist on dialling Antoine and demanding he fit her daughter in for a total treatment. Her attention was now firmly fixed back on the horse.

'I want him,' she said, her eyes bright, her voice a breathless hush of wonderment.

The sous chef and Smudger exchanged nervous glances.

'The horse,' said Gloria. 'I want that horse.' Her tone was resolute as she pointed a red-painted fingernail at the mass of yellow and purple. The red nail varnish was a perfect accompaniment to the outfit she was wearing, a grey tweed ensemble with red suede inserts on the cuffs and collar. Her boots were the same shade of red, with little bells hanging from the sides which jingled as she walked. When it came to taking the prize for senior citizen style, Gloria Cross won it hands down.

'It isn't mine and I don't think I can let you have it,' said Honey. 'I think the boys, here, should return it to where they got it from. Right boys?' She gave them a pointed look.

Her two chefs were in the process of disentangling their limbs from the suit.

Smudger and Dick, the sous chef, frowned and looked shifty.

'The truth is . . .' Smudger began. 'We can't return it, because we can't remember where we got it from in the first place. You see, we were a bit . . .'

Honey held up her hand in a 'stop right there' gesture.

'No need to explain. You were drunk. Can you recall the last pub you went in?'

'I remember going in the Saracen's Head,' said Dick.

'I don't,' said Smudger. He made the mistake of shaking his head and groaned. 'Some bender,' he said. Covering his face with both hands he collapsed onto the body of the horse.

'Then I'm sure whoever owns it won't mind me looking after it,' Gloria said brightly. 'Someone has to.'

'I don't know about that,' said Honey, surprised about her mother being so insistent over a pantomime horse.

'I've made up my mind. I'll look after it until the rightful owner turns up. It'll have to work for its keep of course in our pantomime, but I doubt whoever . . . *mislaid* him will mind.'

'Mislaid? Hang on, Mother, it's not mine to give you. The correct thing to do is to report its whereabouts to lost and found!'

Her mother waved her aside. 'Phooey! The police haven't got time to bother with a mislaid pantomime horse. It's not as though there are two dead bodies inside there and a serial killer of pantomime acts on the loose. It's just a pantomime costume. Nobody's going to mind a group of pensioners using it for their Christmas pantomime, now, are they?'

Honey pointed out that the innards of the horse could be scouring the street looking for it. Her mother was unmoved.

'Anyway, the police wouldn't have room for something that big. I've made up my mind and will take total responsibility for Galloper until his owner shows up. Book a taxi. Get him sent round to St Michael's.'

'*Galloper*?'

Gloria nodded. 'I think it's a good name for a horse.'

Nobody would dare go against Gloria Cross when she was determined about something. Honey certainly wouldn't. She recognised this as one of those moments when she had to give in. Her mother had made up her mind. She'd decided at what point it would appear in this year's pantomime produced, directed and performed by Bath Senior Citizens' Drama Group.

Honey gave in. She was too busy to argue. The chefs, who were just getting up off their knees, had a lot to do too and there was no way she was about to send them off around the city trying to locate the owner. She could phone the police, but on reflection, would they really want to be bothered with that at such a busy period?

'OK,' said Honey, 'I'll do as you say, but that doesn't mean to say I'm a party to the theft of this animal — panto horse . . .'

'*Galloper*,' said Smudger, and managed a smirk.

Honey rolled her eyes. What with her hair, the horse and her mother . . .

'Honey, you're a treasure!'

It wasn't often her mother hugged her and called her a treasure. She decided it must be the time of year, and if the pantomime costume caused her to do that, then why not let her have it?

'It should definitely fit into the back of a taxi,' Gloria went on, tilting her head from one side to the other. 'I'll call my usual man. He'll be around to collect it.'

Gloria made her way to the door, where she paused and turned on her heel.

'And Honey. No chocolates for Christmas, please. I saw a silk Hermes headscarf in the House of Fraser. It's got the Mona Lisa on it in red, blue, and green with a touch of gold. That should do nicely as a present.' Then she was gone.

A *Hermes* scarf. Honey grimaced. Chocolates and a nice bunch of seasonal flowers would have been much cheaper.

Free of further encumbrance, Smudger and Dick made for the door, heads bowed, shoulders slumped.

'As for you!' Honey's accusatory followed the two chefs to the door. 'I'll be speaking to you two later.'

Somehow or other and with the help of Gary, the barman, she bundled Galloper into a manageable mass and shoved him behind a sofa. His head still sprouted over the top, but she couldn't do anything about that.

Gary wore a pin-striped waistcoat over a sparkling white shirt and tight-fitting black trousers. Galloper, the horse, was wearing his birthday suit of yellow-spotted purple and outrageously long lashes over black googly eyes.

The two eyed each other like desperados in a Mexican standoff.

It was Gary, of course, who broke the stalemate. 'I suppose someone will claim him.'

'I should think so. He must belong to somebody.'

Gary folded his arms and heaved a sigh. 'But what if they don't? What happens then? In fact, it's got me thinking — what does happen to pantomime horses once the pantomime season is over?'

Honey threw back her head, closed her eyes, and made a heartfelt wish that when she opened them again, the horse would be gone. Unfortunately, the fairy of heartfelt wishes must have been on an all-inclusive sunshine break in the

Caribbean, because when she opened them again, the horse was still there.

A heartfelt wish was replaced with a heartfelt sigh. 'Just keep him here until the taxi comes. That's all I ask.'

She didn't voice the fact that she was going to defy her mother's wishes and get in touch with the police. No need to go through the lost property department. She'd get in touch with Doherty and ask him to run a check on the loss of a pantomime horse.

Unlike the fairy of heartfelt wishes, the fate fairy hadn't flown to warmer climes. Doherty phoned her.

'I need to speak to you.'

He'd got in fast and she pre-empted what she thought he was going to say — telling Lindsey about his proposal.

'I haven't told her yet.'

'This isn't about that. I hear that employees of Mallory and Scrimshaw stayed at the hotel overnight. Are they still there?'

All thoughts of reporting the whereabouts of Galloper trotted out of her mind.

'Yes?'

'Well, I'm guessing their boss didn't turn up to the party last night. He's pinned to his desk — in a manner of speaking.'

CHAPTER TEN

Seven days before Christmas. Looking perplexed, shocked, and hung over, the ten employees of Mallory and Scrimshaw were huddled in a group in the bar. Doherty's intention was to carry out preliminary interviews while the trail was still hot — though Clarence Scrimshaw's body was now stone cold.

David Longborough squeezed the bridge of his nose between finger and thumb.

'Do we have to do this now? We all have things to do.' His impatience was obvious.

'Yes. We do.' Doherty's tone was sharp and to the point. Ordinarily he could be as laid-back as anyone, but when it came to his profession he was deadly serious.

Although the oak-panelled walls usually lent warmth to the ambience of the room, the employees — or rather former employees — of Clarence Scrimshaw added an air of melancholy, even of guilt.

Honey stood by the door, watching as they fidgeted and exchanged nervous glances. Mrs Finchley was hugging her handbag to her chest, staring at her feet. Unsuccessful in his challenge to Doherty's authority, Longborough now harboured a blank look. Across from him, Samantha Brown looked terrified.

Just before they'd come in, Honey had fired up the coffee machine behind the bar so at least everyone had a drink in front of them.

She hung around at the end of the bar. There was something she wanted to say to Doherty.

Their eyes met. He got the message and joined her.

She kept her voice low. 'Mr Scrimshaw never turned up for the party. His bed was never slept in.'

'Did anyone try to find out where he was?'

'Not that I know of. But they all acted like they hadn't noticed that he hadn't turned up; either that or they didn't care whether he was there or not. Nobody seemed that concerned.'

Honey saw Doherty glance at the pantomime horse peeking over the edge of the sofa and took the time to explain its presence to Doherty. 'It's lost. A taxi is coming to collect it later. If that toothy smile and googly eyes are going to put you off your job, I'll have it removed now.'

He shrugged and smiled. 'I'm used to it. I've had lawyers sitting in on interviews that looked like that.'

The woman with the dyed black hair job, no longer able to shift further, asked if the horse had to stay where it was.

'Yes,' said Honey. 'Galloper forms part of an ongoing missing property mystery.'

She knew the remark would attract a querulously raised eyebrow from Doherty. She took a glance at his face. Yep! There it was. His eyebrow was almost sky-high.

'I'll explain later. First things, first. Yes?'

'Right. I'll stick to the case in hand. When's Cool Cat Casper likely to come clawing at my tail?'

'I've informed him.'

Whenever some heinous crime occurred, it was Casper who stepped forward like some latter-day Knight of the Round Table, determined to seek and destroy — or in this day and age, lock up — the perpetrators of serious crime. Nothing, absolutely nothing, should, in his opinion, be allowed to sully the reputation of the fairest city in the world.

Bath had been declared a World Heritage City some time back. In Casper's opinion, the accolade fell something short of the mark. Bath, to him, was the centre of the universe.

He'd been surprised when she'd phoned to impart the bad news.

'Honey! You're going to tell me how much you admire my Christmas decorations and wish to make a return visit? Am I right?'

She hated to ruin his good mood. 'Not exactly.'

She'd visited him two days previously and had, of course, been stunned by the aesthetic superiority of his Christmas decorations. Everything, from the swathes of silk festooned over the windows, to the angels hanging in a celestial flight over the stairwell, were colour co-ordinated in subtle shades of violet, mauve, and silver.

In contrast, the decorations at the Green River Hotel looked outdated and store-bought. Her predominantly red and green decorations were randomly festooned to fill gaps rather than to declare any kind of fashion statement.

Casper, on the other hand, adored fashion statements. He also adored handmade clothes, flirting with young men, and clocks. Reception at La Reine Rouge was full of clocks.

When she told him about the murder of Clarence Scrimshaw, he'd sucked in his breath and for a moment she almost believed he was going to cry '*woe is me*'. He didn't, but he did take a moment to collect himself. In her mind's eye she could imagine him genuflecting and raising his eyes to heaven.

At last he surfaced.

'How *very* inconvenient for this to happen now. And the employees of this man were staying with you?'

She'd confirmed that indeed they had been staying with her.

'Then you have to give the police all the assistance possible. Nothing else matters. This terrible occurrence must not be allowed to fester over the Christmas period. We must do all in our power to wrap this case up before the New Year, mustn't we?'

'We?'

His meaning wasn't lost on her. He expected her to work the case with Doherty despite it being a holiday and despite her having a hotel to run.

'I will, of course, be available to lend you support. Now, where did this event occur?'

'The event — the murder — happened at his office, so I understand. No one else was there. As I've already told you, his staff were all here.'

'How terribly convenient for you with regard to their interrogation.'

There were times when Casper St John Gervais sounded like the Grand Inquisitor.

'Every avenue will be investigated.'

'A very untidy affair in my estimation. Doubly so as I knew the man professionally,' he added. 'He'd admired my poetry. Said it had languorous appeal.'

This was the first Honey had heard Casper declare himself a poet, and whatever languorous appeal meant, it sounded pretty positive.

'Did he publish your poems?'

'No.' He sounded disappointed. 'Mr Scrimshaw said poetry doesn't sell, but I didn't kill him for saying so. I wouldn't want you thinking that the fact that he rejected my work might cause me to end the man's life. I am of the opinion that he may have been a little too hasty in rejecting my work. I think that on publishing a small tome of my select sonnets he may have been pleasantly surprised.'

'Do you want to know what Casper said?' she asked Doherty once she'd hung up.

'I can guess. Hang around. You might be able to vouch for the alibis of these people. They may not be able to remember much due to intoxication. I understand they were a bit drunk.'

'*Merry*,' returned Honey, unwilling to admit that she might be running a rowdy bar and therefore attract the attention of the licensing justices.

Doherty gave her a knowing look.

'You don't need to sit in, okay? Just be on hand if required.'

She said that she would be. There were plenty of things that needed doing before the holiday. One thing she still hadn't ticked off her list was collecting a sausage supply from her favourite butchery in Green Street. She'd do that as soon as Doherty was gone.

It was one of those times when she needed something physical to do in order to take her mind off things.

In the meantime, she took over the vacuum cleaner while Anna went for a lie down. She'd questioned whether Anna should be in at all.

'The baby is due soon.'

'Not yet. Not for two months.'

Honey could barely believe it. Anna looked fit to burst. 'Are you sure?'

'The doctor say now. I say no.'

Privately thinking that the doctor was more likely to be right, Honey scooted around the dining room, music from her iPod deafening the sound of the suction.

Once the dining room was done, out she went into Reception, moving furniture, vacuuming up pine needles, and setting discarded party hats onto the window ledge for future use.

Lost in Dire Straits belting out 'Going Home' and the noise of the vacuum cleaner, she was totally unaware of the world outside her mind.

Then a hand landed on her shoulder.

She jumped. The vacuum shot forward. A plant stand wobbled and a blue and white Chinese-style vase fell sideways.

She shouted an expletive as the vase landed in her arms. Her earphones dragged at her ears and twisted tightly around her neck, ending up drooped around her shoulders.

'I'm so sorry, Mrs Driver. Please, let me relieve you of this. Not broken is it? No. I can see it's unblemished — like its owner,' a man said, his voice as smooth as his looks, his teeth white against the healthy tan of his face.

She pulled her hat down onto her head with both hands and took deep breaths.

'Professor Truebody! You really shouldn't creep up on people like that.' It was the first time she'd spoken to him face to face and close up.

He didn't look even slightly abashed. He seemed more amused. One side of his wide mouth lifted in a smile that was both cynical and triumphant.

'I'm sorry. Look, I just wanted to say that if you see your daughter, can you tell her that I've gone on ahead?'

'Lindsey?'

'Such a lovely girl, Lindsey. Just like her father. Great guy. Shall I put this back for you?'

'Great guy' was not how Honey would have described her ex-husband. At times she wondered what she'd ever seen in him. But she'd been young. Youth had a lot to answer for.

She told herself that it cost nothing to be courteous and pasted on a smile that was as uncomfortable as ill-fitting shoes — too tight to wear for long.

'Yes, please do,' she said in answer to his offer to replace the vase. She handed it to him and watched as he placed it back on the pedestal. Professor Jake Truebody was well built — athletic for a professor of history — and he moved like a sportsman, not like a man who browsed books and dealt in things long dead. She remembered that Carl had moved like that.

'Do you sail, Professor?'

He turned round and seemed genuinely surprised by the question.

'No. I don't. I don't like water much.' Maybe his tan was fake.

'That's unusual for people from Maine, isn't it? I thought they all liked the water.'

'Only those who live near it.'

His style was smooth and easy. She guessed he could charm the pants off any woman he wanted. And apparently it was Lindsey who was off out with him, Lindsey whom he appeared to charm.

'So where are you and my daughter off to today?' She tried to sound casual, but the worry that he might charm her daughter's pants off sat like a gremlin clinging onto the back of her head.

'Sightseeing. I thought it best to keep out of the way with all this going on.' He jerked his chin in the direction of the bar. 'Have you any idea when they're likely to be finished? I realise that it's necessary, but it is slightly disruptive . . . I think under the circumstances that it's best I keep out of the way.'

Honey was very much aware that only personal details — names and addresses — would be taken. Any statements likely to be needed would be done down at Manvers Street. She explained this to him and added, 'I shouldn't think it will take too long. A couple of hours. No more.'

'All the same . . . I've got a lot of territory to discover.'

As long as it's not Lindsey's body you're aiming to discover, she thought to herself. But mothers shouldn't interfere and she'd never been like that. Lindsey had always been left to work things out for herself and advised when advice was requested. Not like Honey's mother, who didn't so much offer advice as give orders.

And Truebody was a guest. She had to remain courteous.

'This is a murder investigation, Professor. I'm afraid I have to ask for your forbearance.'

'Of course.' His smile remained the same, but the look in his hazel eyes was searching. This man, she decided, was trying to read her — just as Doherty read her. But Doherty could get beneath her covers and read her chapter by chapter any day of the week. Truebody was a different matter.

'You don't mind me dragging your daughter off with me, do you?'

She was right! He had read her. Was she that much of an open book?

'Of course not. Anyway at her age, it's up to her.'

She congratulated herself on sounding so incredibly sincere. Inside she was seething.

'We must get together and talk about old Carl,' he said in that languid drawl of his.

'Yes,' she said, her smile so forced now she spoke through gritted teeth. 'We must.'

Was he kidding? Didn't he realise that she and Carl had parted on less than friendly terms?

Even if Jake Truebody had been a celibate priest, she still wouldn't trust him. And anyone who'd been a close friend of Carl's wasn't likely to be very trustworthy, and certainly not celibate.

The same question she'd asked from the moment she'd read the letter was whirling around in her head. What are you doing here, Professor Truebody? Why turn up now claiming to know my husband and taking my daughter away from me? It made her want to hold fire on speaking to Lindsey about her engagement — or proposed engagement — to Doherty.

She watched surreptitiously as he stood there, six feet tall or more, winding a thick woollen scarf around the lower half of his face. After pulling his hat down more securely, he adopted a pair of dark glasses. She wanted to ask him why he was bothering to do that. The sky outside was leaden, not a streak of blue or a puffy cloud in sight.

'Adios,' he said, and raised a gloved hand.

'Have a nice day.' She didn't mean it. Hopefully, if he did have a nice aspect to his day, it would take him away from her hotel and her daughter.

'That man is very . . . orange,' said Anna. Her belly had rounded the corner from the residents' lounge before the rest of her. She was waving a feather duster in one hand and rubbing her back with the other.

Honey agreed with her. 'Perhaps he might get mistaken for an amber traffic light, as in get ready to *go*.'

'I do not think he likes it here.'

'Well, I do not like him here, so I really don't care if he dislikes it here. He can leave any time he likes.'

Normally, Honey took it personally when somebody proclaimed that they didn't like the Green River Hotel. Some visitors loved the traditional décor, the fat sofas in the bar, the tester and half-tester beds, the cornice running around the walls just a few feet from the ceiling, the chandeliers, the dado rails, and the eighteenth-century wooden shutters and brocade curtains at the windows.

Out-and-out complaints were usually addressed with calm consideration and the offering of soothing extras, like a free bottle of wine or tickets to whatever was on at the Theatre Royal. The latter were sometimes available at a knockdown price, or even free, though this only occurred on those rare occasions when one of the stars or production crew was staying and handing out freebies.

Sometimes it was a professional moaner, somebody who made a point of complaining to get something — or preferably everything — knocked off the bill. They were just part of the scene and a professional hazard.

Anna was shaking her head. 'No, Mrs Driver. Not that. He does not like the police, I thought. Then I thought, it is not them he does not like, it is you.'

'Me?'

'Yes. You, Mrs Driver. You come in. He goes out. He went to his room after breakfast when he saw the police come in, but you came in at the same time. Now he has left the building. He goes when you arrive.'

'Are you sure?'

'There was nobody else around to frighten him. Only the people who stayed and the police, but he is trying to avoid you, I think.'

The last piece of information related to the employees of Mallory and Scrimshaw. Truebody wouldn't know any of them. Anna could well be right and the professor was trying to avoid her. Well, she had made it plain that Carl drowning at sea had been no great loss to her. She certainly hadn't welcomed the professor with open arms and an invitation to chew over old times. And there was the matter of Lindsey. He'd obviously taken a shine to Lindsey and her daughter was responding in a friendlier manner than her mother.

'This is news,' murmured Honey, her eyes immediately going to the double doors that had closed so resolutely behind the man who was trying to steal her daughter.

* * *

She didn't care if Jake Truebody didn't like her. She didn't care that he'd known her husband — as long as he didn't bring up the past. The past was dead.

All she cared about was Lindsey. Perhaps if she had a word, point out that they really knew nothing about him? Not easy. Lindsey was so independent. Her mother rarely interfered with what she did; to do so now might cause trouble.

CHAPTER ELEVEN

Lindsey Driver had promised her mother to oversee the consigning of the pantomime horse to the care of her grandmother's pet taxi driver.

While awaiting his arrival, she manned Reception at the same time as doing a little job for the chef. She was also singing a daft ditty to herself and wearing a pair of plastic deer antlers that blatantly advertised the fact that she was well and truly entering the spirit of Christmas. Like her mother she was relieved that the office parties were over and childishly excited that from now on it was food, fun, and whatever else happened along the way. No more turkeys to stuff, no more slobbering youths armed with sprigs of mistletoe chasing her around the hotel, and no more dancing to old songs from the seventies provided by a DJ wearing a blonde wig and a gold lamé waistcoat.

'No more birds to stuff,
No more jokes to swallow,
No more singing silly songs,
They'll be gone tomorrow.'

The tune was hardly original and the words made up on the spur of the moment, but Lindsey didn't care. The countdown to Christmas proper had begun.

Hidden by the reception desk, she was rolling pieces of streaky bacon around the chipolata sausages that would be served with the turkey on Christmas Day. She wouldn't normally be doing this but as Anna was close to giving birth to her second child she'd needed yet another break from her duties. At times there was little point her coming in at all.

'I might give birth here,' Anna had quipped, beaming brightly to Lindsey and her mother. 'I wonder if I will get gifts from wise men and a nice sheepskin rug from the shepherds. I would like a sheepskin rug. I could put it in front of my coffee table.'

Honey had reminded her that this was the Green River Hotel, not a stable, and the first aid kit didn't amount to much more than plasters for cut fingers and, a little against the rules, a supply of headache tablets.

Anna wasn't the only one who was slightly indisposed. Head chef Smudger Smith was also feeling less than one hundred per cent fit, though this had nothing to do with pregnancy and everything to do with entering the spirit of Christmas with too much enthusiasm. He always tended to get involved in the office parties, dancing along with them until his legs gave way and he was reminded he had a job to go to in the morning — or rather that he wouldn't have a job if he didn't quit the festivities and get to bed, sharpish.

Banning him from getting involved had not worked. He'd got caught up in other parties outside the hotel, hence the acquisition of the pantomime horse, though he still couldn't remember where he'd got it from.

Due to the way the reception desk was constructed — a high counter for guests checking in and out, a lower one for whomever was manning reception — it was easy for Lindsey to get away with the job she was doing.

Their one and only resident who talked to ghosts and entertained a long-dead ancestor in her room had fully entered the Christmas spirit too. Mary Jane was as bright as any Christmas decoration, due mainly to her chosen outfit which today was a red padded ensemble that made her look twice the width she was. The outfit was termed a 'lounging suit' — her favourite attire; it was made of a shiny velour. The coat she wore over it closely resembled a patchwork quilt; Mary Jane was into recycling.

'I'm off to do a little shopping at the Christmas Market,' she declared, her voice louder than usual, possibly because her deafness was increasing with her years. She was well into her seventies, if not more. Not that she would admit to it.

At this moment her hearing was further impaired because she was wearing a pair of white fur earmuffs in the shape of rabbit ears. 'I just love that old-time feel of the little shops down in the alleyways, don't you?'

On receiving no response, plus noticing the vague look on Lindsey's face, Mary Jane paused.

'Anything wrong, honey? You look as though you've seen a ghost.'

'Well,' said Lindsey. 'It's that time of year, isn't it? A time for dragging up ghosts from the past — whether you want them dragged up or not.'

Mary Jane held one earmuff away from her ear in order to hear more clearly.

'If you're talking of ghost stories, I've pinned a poster up on the notice board. Ghostly Tales at Christmas. A few friends and I will be telling ghost stories in the lounge on Christmas Day. We could repeat the event on Boxing Day as well — after you Brits have held your boxing bouts, that is.'

Lindsey allowed the ghost of a smile to cross her lips. 'Historically, Boxing Day has nothing to do with boxing bouts. Boxing Day was the day following Christmas Day when the Lord of the Manor placed gifts of coin and other things in a box as a thank you to his serfs and servants. Then it was shared out amongst them.'

Mary Jane raised her thin eyebrows which looked as though they'd been drawn on with a pencil. She was genuinely surprised. Genuinely interested too.

'Oh really. Sir Cedric would have done that, I'm sure. He was very generous with his favours.'

'So I hear,' muttered Lindsey.

According to what she knew herself and what Mary Jane had imparted, Sir Cedric had liked the ladies, which was, according to legend, how he'd met his doom. Pistols at dawn. His last duel had been the death of him. He'd only been injured and had managed to get back to the hotel — which at the time had been his town house. His opponent, the cuckolded husband, had arrived soon after and finished the job with a brass poker. Ignominious, but deserved.

'Excuse me, miss.'

This time she looked up into an open pale brown face. He had a pencil-wide strip of beard on his chin and wore a gold ring in one ear.

'You have a passenger to go to St Michael's Church?'

She looked at him blankly but managed a smile. For a moment she thought a guest had booked a taxi and somehow she'd forgotten about it. But that couldn't be. The office party guests not required by the police had all left and those booked in for the Christmas break — an all-in price for accommodation, food and seasonal festivities — had not yet arrived. The party from Mallory and Scrimshaw would be back later.

'I'm not sure . . .' she began — and then it came to her. He wasn't talking about a human passenger.

'Ah. Yes. Come this way. You'll need a hand.'

'I don't take drunks. I think you should know that.'

'The passenger isn't drunk, just helpless.'

She led him into the bar where Gary the barman helped slide the sofa forward. The garishly coloured pantomime horse flopped onto the floor.

The taxi driver looked bemused. 'That's the passenger?'

Lindsey assured him that it was. 'Gary will give you a hand.'

The horse was large and cumbersome and difficult to get out of the door.

'It doesn't wish to leave the bar,' the taxi driver remarked wryly.

Gary grimaced. 'I've had worse. Two pints and some folk turn into a horse's arse. It's par for the course.'

Lindsey grudgingly accepted that the term 'horse's arse' was the in joke of the moment. Probably would be until New Year.

The horse was bundled into the back seat of the taxicab, its front legs folded up behind its head.

Lindsey braved the chill and watched the taxi pull away. The horse seemed to be waving a painted hoof, its goofy grin and big black eyes gazing out through the taxi's rear window.

* * *

Jake Truebody watched her from his bedroom window.

He rubbed at his chin, certain that she'd swallowed his story, and planned what to do next.

Her invitation to act as his guide around Bath was welcome. Not that he'd stick with her all the time. There were some aspects of this visit for which he had to be alone. Still, he thought, she was slim and pretty and if being here was only about pleasure, he would have concentrated full time on seducing her. As it was, he had ulterior plans. He had a debt to repay, though neither Lindsey Driver nor her mother would know that.

Nobody knew that, only him.

CHAPTER TWELVE

Lindsey Driver knew she might be a bit late for her 'date' with the professor, but he could wait.

She was presently sitting at her laptop in her bedroom, staring at the result thrown up by the Google search engine.

There were a few entries for the name Truebody, though only one for a professor matching Jake's description. What brought Lindsey up short was the fact that Professor Jacob Truebody had disappeared just two months ago. An academic, he'd met her father, a wealthy businessman and yachtsman, after Carl Driver had bestowed a large endowment on the professor's university department a few years before his death.

Leaning closer to the screen, she lightly tapped her upper lip as she digested the information. Once digested, her thoughts spilled into words.

'Curiouser and curiouser, said Alice as she fell down the rabbit hole. Now if you're not who you say you are, Professor Jake Truebody, who are you and what are you doing here?'

She quite often spoke to her computer screen when there were questions to be answered, though mostly when she was alone, and generally in the still of the night. This was most definitely one of those occasions — but today it was in broad daylight.

'Now shall I tell the Queen of the Castle about this, or should I keep it to myself?'

She pondered the question and let out a deep sigh before talking to the screen again.

'My mother says she's never met this man. OK, she may not have met him, but did she recall this man's name ever being mentioned by my dad?'

Normally she would ask her mother outright, but something made her hesitate.

No, she thought. I think I can handle this myself. I am not a child.

The screen blinked from one page of information to another.

'But who is he?'

The screen stayed focused on the details of the missing man. Professor Jake Truebody had indeed been a history professor, though his tenure at the state university and other venues seemed short-lived.

Still, there were glowing reports about him, a man known for his work in the prison system, his membership of the local church, and his work with the poor and destitute.

'Overall, a good egg,' she murmured. 'But my instinct tells me he might be a wicked troll.'

The photograph was fuzzy, the image indeterminate. It could be the Jake Truebody they had staying here, or maybe not. It was hard to tell. Then she reminded herself that she'd checked his passport. Everything had checked out.

Reading on, she came across the details of his death, or rather his disappearance, presumed dead. His sister had posted the details. Lindsey took a note of the sister's name and the email address to which any information about his whereabouts could be sent. Mrs Darleene Van Der Velt, his sister, implored anyone with details of his last known whereabouts to get in touch. His body had never been found but his car and clothes had been left at the edge of the sea.

'*Our family want closure,*' said the sad missive.

Her mouth was dry and she tingled with excitement. Taking a deep breath she typed out an email.

'Can I send you a photo of a man claiming to be Professor Jake Truebody? I need to know he is who he says he is. I must stress this is very urgent. Please respond asap.'

She pressed send. The screen flashed blue. Email sent.

'This is my case,' she said defiantly. 'I'm the one who fell down the rabbit hole and found all this out; therefore I'm the one to give it a go.' She paused, arms stretched above her to be brought down to rest on her head.

A message came up in her inbox.

'Please do so. I look forward to receiving it. So kind of you to oblige.'

Now all she had to do was take a decent photo and send it off. Either she had to get her hands on his passport and use that photograph, or take one herself. The latter seemed the one least likely to arouse his suspicion.

She told herself that she could. 'Everything will be OK.'

Taking a deep breath, she sat back in her chair with her hands on her head, shut her eyes, and began to plan. It was going to be fun, she told herself. First the photo; at the same time she had to get under the man's skin, ask questions that made her sound interested rather than probing.

'I can do it,' she said to herself. 'I can do it very well. Honey Driver is not the only crime solver around here. I want to know who you really are, Professor Jake Truebody. And I'm going to find out.'

* * *

Lindsey's mind was buzzing as she counted sheets, table-cloths and pillowcases before they were stuffed into green canvas bags. Usually she gave every task she undertook her undivided attention, but today was different. Her mind was whirring. Her stomach was fluttering.

It seemed likely that Professor Jake Truebody was not actually Professor Jake Truebody. This was something she wished to keep to herself.

Laundry count finished, she went through into her mother's office and set the dockets needed for laundry collection on her desk.

'All done.'

'Thank you.'

'I'm off out shortly.'

Her mother looked up. 'I know. The professor said he would meet you as arranged.'

'That's right.'

'He seems quite taken with you.'

Lindsey could hear the caution in her mother's voice. Tossing her hair back from her face, she stayed non-committal, pretending to make an alteration to the laundry list.

'Uh huh.'

She waited for the million-dollar question she was sure tingled on her mother's tongue. It was coming. She could see the pensiveness in the way her mother was twiddling a pen between her fingers — not writing anything, just twiddling. And her lips were moving, her head twitching.

At last it came. Her tone was hesitant.

'Ummm . . . so there's nothing going on between you two that I should know about, is there?'

Lindsey hung her head in order to hide her smile. Honestly, but mothers could be so damned predictable. However, she'd made her mind up. The professor was in her sights. This was a Christmas gift to herself. She was going to find out who he really was if it killed her. Or, at least, just exhausted her.

'I think I'll take the camera today. Take a few shots of the Abbey and Pulteney Bridge. Is it in the usual place?'

'Yes. It is,' replied her mother.

Lindsey knew that was not the end of it. Her mother was dying to know more.

'Well?' Honey prompted. 'Is there anything going on between you?'

'That's my business.'

Her mother squirmed. 'I didn't mean to pry. What I meant was . . .'

'What you meant was, is he out to bed me, wed me, or merely have me provide the service of tour guide.'

Honey tried to look unperturbed, but Lindsey wasn't fooled. 'And?'

'He's a professor of history. Right?'

'Right.' Honey nodded. 'Right,' she said again.

Lindsey could see that her mother had hit the buffers about what to say next. What she did next confirmed it. Typical of her mother. She opened the right-hand drawer and picked out a chocolate marzipan. When in doubt, eat.

Lindsey carried on with what she was doing. There was no way she was going to give anything away unless further investigation revealed Jake Truebody as a convicted axe murderer. Then she'd have to get help.

Honey went back to checking the bookings for next season. 'These bookings are slow in coming. Shame. We could do with the deposits to see us through January and February. The exchange rate's got a lot to do with it. So has the price of fuel. Ditto the fact that some volcano's erupted somewhere and people are being cautious — as though the eruption is likely to last for the rest of the year.'

Lindsey gave her mother a direct look that said it all. The words that followed finished it off. 'Forgetting to book an advert with the English Tourist Board has a lot to do with it.'

Honey coloured up. 'You're blaming me?'

'Aren't you blaming yourself?'

Honey pulled a face. She really should have made the deadline but didn't like bearing the blame.

'OK,' she said, pen flung down on desk. 'When business is slow, that's the time for creative thinking if we want to fill those rooms. Perhaps we could do themed weekends. They're the in thing, aren't they?'

Lindsey shook her head, 'You don't really have a clue about themed weekends, do you?'

'Of course I do. Murder weekends. Wine-tasting weekends. Cookery weekends. We could invite a famous TV chef to run a course. It's bound to be popular.'

Lindsey thought it only fair to point out to her that their head chef was likely to run amok with a meat cleaver should another chef be allowed in the place. 'Not with Smudger.'

Honey's face dropped.

'OK, perhaps not cookery weekends but there's bound to be a right sort of weekend for the Green River.'

Lindsey bucked up at that. 'We could offer Roman weekends, Georgian weekends, Jane Austen weekends — we could do guided tours. And we don't need to pay for a guide. I could take people round. Then there's that one-woman show, the one married to a vicar who collects antique underwear. She's very good, so I hear. I'm not sure, but I think the show's called *Knickeragua*.'

'I'll look into it.'

Lindsey made a big show of straightening her skirt and fluffing up her hair. 'Right. That's the laundry list completed. Time I was going. I've got time to change into trousers and boots. It's cold outside.'

Honey hesitated, obviously still on the fence about saying more about her date. 'There's something about him . . .'

'Leave Jake Truebody to me, Mother. I can take care of myself.'

CHAPTER THIRTEEN

Concentrating her mind on what was happening in the bar helped Honey control, if not forget, her concerns about her daughter. Murder didn't sit well with the season of 'good will to all men'. She wondered if Mr Scrimshaw had figured on anyone's present list. Had he bought presents for friends and relatives? Did he have any friends and relatives?

The questions came thick and fast. Leaving the placing of more baubles on the tree to one side, she scribbled them down.

1. Where did Clarence Scrimshaw usually spend Christmas and who with?
2. Did he send Christmas cards, and if so, to whom did he send them?
3. Did he receive Christmas cards, and if so, from whom?
4. Did he give or receive Christmas presents?
5. Did old friends drop by to wish him season's greetings?

She ran her pen down the list she'd made and decided there was a sixth question to be added, a very important question. Why had he booked into the Green River Hotel this year for both the office party and Christmas Day lunch? His employees had categorically stated that it was out of character; that he was tight with money; in truth, that his surname should be Scrooge!

She looked over to the bar door. Jeez, if Doherty didn't come out soon she was liable to wet herself with excitement.

The bar door was still closed and willing it to open by psychic willpower — a feat much praised by Mary Jane — did no good whatsoever.

This was just a preliminary thing. The main questioning would go on down at the station but there was no point in having everyone down there. The interview rooms couldn't take the strain. The prime suspects — if there were any — would be cherry picked out from the rest of them.

Her ongoing concentration was broken when her mother arrived, dressed in a brown suede jacket with fur trim around the collar and cuffs. Hopefully it was fake fur, but there was a price to pay for top class fashion — and it was the farmed mink that likely to be paying the price in this instance. Her entrance was reminiscent of a movie star treading the red carpet between hordes of loyal fans.

But in reality, the reception carpet was blue, and Honey was hardly a fan; purely a blood relative.

'What gives?' asked her mother. She jerked her impeccably exfoliated chin towards the policeman guarding the closed bar door.

Honey explained about the murder.

'Clarence Scrimshaw was a publisher.'

'Clarence Scrimshaw? I knew him. Short little man with even shorter arms and very deep pockets.'

'Ah,' said Honey in response. She knew what her mother was getting at. Clarence Scrimshaw had been a miserly cuss. 'You didn't date him, did you?'

'Certainly not. I've just told you. He was as tight as . . .'

'A duck's arse. And that's watertight,' said Honey with good humour.

'There's no need for vulgarity, Hannah.' Gloria sniffed. 'I had a writer friend who went along to Mallory and Scrimshaw with a book to publish. That mean old cuss offered to print it on a fifty-fifty basis. Imagine! He wanted my friend Alfred to pay half of the price of publishing his own book!'

Honey breathed a sigh of relief. For one dreadful moment she thought her mother was going to say that Clarence Scrimshaw had enrolled on her dating site for the over-sixties. What a can of worms that could have turned out to be!

'Now! Fred says that I've put too many details on Snow on the Roof, but I think people like to know people's marital and relationship history before committing, don't you?'

'I don't know. I've never used a dating site.'

'Well you'll be pleased with my profile. It's bound to get a lot of hits. Fred is certain of that. I think you should participate.'

Honey shook her head vehemently. 'Mother. Your dating site is for the *over-sixties* . . .'

Her protests fell on deaf ears. Her mother was racing away with her plans.

'Photographs are all very well, but I do think a video would work even better. Of course before, we start filming, you'll have to sort out something decent to wear for the promo. And have your hair done,' she said with a cursory glance at yet another all-encompassing hat Honey had found in the lost property closet. 'You can't wear that hat, that's for sure. Men are likely to mistake you for a garden gnome.'

'Mother, I'm the best judge of that! I will not fall in with this. Haven't you heard that the internet and dating sites in particular are targeted by conmen and perverts, all preying on gullible females?'

'Perverts?' Gloria gasped and grabbed her handbag. 'I won't stay to listen to such language!'

Her mother held her head high, as though something smelly was wafting under her nose. With great deliberation, she readjusted a pair of pale gold leather gloves, totally deaf to Honey's protests.

Honey counted to ten, telling herself not to get hot under the collar, not to forget the time of year, or that this woman was her mother and should be treated with respect.

'Have you got all your presents?' Even to her own ears, her voice sounded surprisingly calm.

'Everyone's! Except for *him*!' Her mother's apricot-coloured lips clamped into a tight line. 'Your *boyfriend* is very difficult to buy for. And before you say just get him a bottle of whisky, the answer is no. I will not encourage a man to drink to excess. Now I must rush.' She took a step in the direction of the main entrance then turned suddenly. 'However, I will do my utmost to rescue your policeman from his total lack of fashion sense. And, by the way, Fred is the right man to dress up as Santa Claus this year.'

'Doherty's offered.'

'He's too thin,' her mother said. 'So that's that. And Fred has his own white beard. Anyway, your beau is too busy to play Santa Claus. He has a murder to investigate on top of this vandalism of the Reindeer for Bath display. He should have caught the culprit by now. For both crimes.'

'Reindeer aren't his department,' Honey murmured.

Her mother wasn't listening. 'Now you mustn't keep me chatting here any longer. I've got shopping to do.'

Honey had no chance to advise her mother on what Doherty was likely to wear or not to wear. It was a vain hope, but maybe she'd simply buy him a pair of socks or perhaps a necktie or a plain cashmere sweater from Marks and Spencer. She raised her eyes in prayer.

'Please, God, anything but garish socks with reindeer on the side.'

She hoped that God would take the prayer from his in-tray and act on it. He'd have an uphill task. Her mother was single-minded. She would do as she pleased. She always did.

But the mention of Doherty playing Santa Claus set her to daydreaming. In her mind Doherty was wearing that Santa outfit — him the trousers, and her the tunic and nifty little hat. Her legs were good. So was his six-pack.

When Doherty arrived he looked deadly serious, nothing like a guy likely to don the red and white outfit of the

Green River Hotel's very own Jolly Saint Nick — alias Father Christmas.

Brow furrowed in thought, he settled in a chair, leaning forward, flipping over the pages of his notebook.

Honey sat opposite him with her own list. But she'd let him go first.

While she waited for him to speak, she plied him with coffee and two chocolate chip cookies. Not saying a word, he dipped each one before eating them. Honey sipped a hot chocolate.

'Everyone confirms what you've already told me,' he said at last. He sat back resignedly as he slapped his hands together to dislodge the crumbs. 'Nobody can recall actually seeing Mr Scrimshaw either beforehand, at the party, or afterwards. And you say he definitely had a room booked?'

Honey confirmed that he had. 'It was part of the deal. The team are also booked in for Christmas Day lunch and the ghost story session afterwards.'

'So what was he like when you spoke to him?' he asked her.

She shrugged. 'I don't know. I've never met him. Everything was done by telephone. I never saw him. I only heard him.'

'What did he sound like?'

She turned her mind back to the day she'd received the phone call. 'There was nothing special about it. He was curt but courteous. Every so often he cleared his throat — you know a prolonged cough — as though his throat was dry.'

Doherty nodded. 'Did he collect his key?'

'I would think so. I checked in most of the party from Mallory and Scrimshaw, then Anna took over.'

'Is she here now?'

'No. She's at home. I'll check if she remembers anything. She's got a pretty good memory.'

Except when it came to naming the father of her children. Her first child lived at home with her mother in Poland. Anna had always been very reticent about her private life.

Dumpy Doris, the breakfast cook, had once overstepped the mark, insinuating that Anna opened her legs for anything in tight jeans with a well-stocked lunch box. Once Doris's back was turned, Anna shoved the end of the vacuum cleaner between her large buttocks when it was turned on full power. Doris had been shocked. Anna had been angry and told her in no uncertain terms to mind her own bloody business.

Honey relayed the details Anna had given her.

'She recalls giving him his key but can't recall that much about him because she had a sudden stomach cramp and had to rush to the loo. She's getting near her time.'

Too bloody near! Hopefully Anna would hold off giving birth until the second of January. Honey had told her to take the leave she was entitled to, but Anna was very sensitive to accusations of milking the system.

'I will work until I drop, Mrs Driver,' she'd resolutely declared.

Honey had responded that dropping from overwork was one thing. Dropping a new born infant before the ambulance arrived was far more worrying.

'Did he return the key?' Doherty asked.

'It's here, so he must have.'

'You mean you didn't see him return it?'

She shook her head and pointed to the slot in the counter and the notice asking that keys be posted into it. 'It was in here. He didn't need to present it personally.'

Honey felt a need to explain further. 'Scrimshaw paid his bill in advance, including drinks at the bar, the meal, and the rooms. All he had to do was return the key following the party, which is what he did. Any likely suspects yet?' She clutched her notebook to her chest, waiting for the right moment.

Doherty shook his head. 'Scrimshaw died between six and eight last evening. Six of the staff were in the bar at the time. One got called to the car park to shut off his car alarm, one went shopping, one had to go to the hairdressers, and one popped home to see her mother who was having trouble with her toddler son. Three of those in the bar popped out for a smoke — not really long enough to nip back to the office and stab a letter opener into someone's ear.'

Honey pulled a face. 'Nasty. That also means that he can't have been the one to return his key — as he never made it here at all.'

He ran a hand over his face which made a rasping sound; Doherty wasn't keen on shaving, especially in cold weather.

'I've made a list,' Honey declared. She passed him the notebook.

Doherty perused it.

'What do you think?'

'All very relevant. Let's give it a try.'

She followed him back into the bar where the party from publishers Mallory and Scrimshaw were getting ready to leave.

They looked resigned to their fate when Doherty re-entered the room.

'Just before you go, folks, there are a few questions my colleague here wishes to ask.'

David Longborough looked pissed off. 'Hey! Not more questions. What the hell's this about?'

'Just a few questions,' said Honey firmly.

'You're not a police officer.'

It was left to Doherty to explain. 'Mrs Driver is Crime Liaison Officer on behalf of Bath Hotels Association. This city thrives on its tourism. Those who employ people and entice tourists to Bath take an active role when a crime is committed — especially such a serious crime as this. Now, sit down.'

It might have been Doherty's no-nonsense tone, or it might equally have been his stance, but David Longborough was the first to sit back down. The rest followed suit. They always did, thought Honey She'd realised from the start that Longborough was a ringleader, and an arrogant one at that. The rest of them followed where he led.

Doherty nodded at Honey. She asked the first question.

'Can you tell us where Mr Scrimshaw usually spent Christmas and who with?'

David looked at Samantha Brown who was fidgeting nervously. 'You know the answer to that, don't you, Sam?'

Samantha's blonde hair had been glossy and bouncy the night before. Today it hung, lank and lazy, around her face.

'He used to go away to a hotel in Ilfracombe. The Bay View.'

'Why Ilfracombe? Did he have friends there?'

She shook her head. 'I don't think so. I think he went there because it was cheap.'

Honey didn't bother to read out her next question. She knew it by heart.

'Did he send Christmas cards, and if so, to whom did he send them?'

This time more than one person answered, mostly with a short burst of derisive laughter. 'No. He didn't send any. Too tight for that.'

'Did he receive any?'

'Of course he did,' snapped Mrs Finchley who was dabbing a tissue at her red rimmed eyes. 'Some people remembered him.'

Doherty gave her a piercing look. 'And who might that be?'

David Longborough sniggered. '*Her* mostly. I wouldn't be surprised if she sent him the lot herself.'

'I heard that!' Mrs Finchley glared at him. 'You have an attitude problem, David Longborough, and are out for your own ends. You always are.'

'Stupid bitch!'

'Less of that!' Doherty's voice boomed over them all. 'We'll collect the cards that are there and go through them.' He looked at Honey. 'Next?'

Honey took her cue. 'Did he give or receive Christmas presents?'

Again David Longborough sniggered in the direction of Mrs Finchley. 'Only one as far as I know. A little box of handkerchiefs. Is that right, Freda?'

Freda Finchley turned bright red.

'That's not true.' Samantha Brown's voice was high pitched and doll like. All eyes turned in her direction.

'Someone did send him a present?' Doherty asked.

She nodded. 'It arrived a week ago. He seemed extremely pleased about it.'

'Do you know what it was?'

She shook her head and lowered her eyes. 'No. I don't. He just looked over the moon. I remember it was quite heavy. That's all. Look, can I go now? My mum's been looking after my son. I need to see that he's all right.'

Doherty's voice turned softer though like a velvet glove, it covered a sharp interior motive. 'One more question and then you can go.' He turned back to Honey. 'Next?'

'Did old friends drop by to extend the season's greetings?'

Nobody answered. Most people shook their heads. Mrs Reid, another employee, looked uncomfortable. Freda Finchley looked down at her hands as though she suddenly didn't want to look either Honey or Doherty in the face.

Doherty rolled his gaze over each in turn. 'Nobody?'

Longborough shook his head. 'Nobody. Nobody of any consequence that is — unless you count the window cleaner in pursuit of his money.'

Mrs Reid interrupted. 'Some of his authors dropped in, though not to extend the season's greetings. He was behind with the royalty payments. They wanted their money too — though the last one dropped in weeks' ago. No one's been by lately.'

'OK,' said Doherty. 'You can go . . . Wait, just one thing.'

Everyone paused in reaching for their coats and overnight bags.

'As you've already intimated, booking this office party and Christmas lunch was totally out of character for the deceased. Any idea what may have triggered a change of heart — if there was one?'

Longborough grinned. 'Must have been visited by Mallory's ghost.'

Once everyone had dispersed, Doherty and Honey wandered back into Reception. Carly, the new receptionist, was on duty. Honey checked that everything was running smoothly before escorting Doherty to the door.

Out of sight in the vestibule that separated the external doors from the internal ones, he kissed her.

'A fine job you did there. How about you pick up the Christmas cards left at the scene of crime and follow up any that strike you?'

'And look for that present?'

'It's worth a try. If it isn't in his office, it might be in his flat. He did live above the business. Just try not to get in the way of the lab boys.'

'I'll pop in tomorrow after stocking up at the sausage shop.'

'Sausages! My, but you're a girl with priorities!'

She grinned. 'Aren't I just.'

CHAPTER FOURTEEN

It was after lunch on the following day and six days before Christmas when Honey finally got her chance to escape, though not before her head chef had forced her to taste his brandy sauce. After two tasters, she was warmed through and her eyes were playing hopscotch.

Unblinking he waited for her approval. 'Good?'

'Too good.'

She went on to point out to him that the emphasis should be on cream rather than brandy.

'It can't be that bad. You had two tastings,' he said, wearing a hurt expression in his red rimmed eyes.

She was tactful. Good chefs were hard to come by.

'Well, I need it. I'm off out and it's perishing outside. Everyone knows brandy keeps out the cold. That's the whole point of a St Bernard dog carrying a barrel of it around his neck. A little more cream, chef.' She paused. 'However, our guests for Christmas lunch will be warm enough already and you admitted yourself that the plum pudding is bursting with rum, brandy, and whisky — besides the usual sultanas, currants, and candied peel. To my mind, a contrast in tastes is needed in order that they can appreciate the heady content and aromatic pleasures of your pudding. Your pudding deserves that, don't you think? But, of course, I'll leave the final ingredients up to you.'

Being tactful and flattering was necessary when dealing with a chef. Each meal was an artistic masterpiece in every chef's eyes. They craved praise and got high on the discerning palates of people who wrote restaurant reviews though couldn't boil an egg for themselves.

She had to get him to go easy on the brandy in the brandy cream. Most of the guests would be well oiled enough by the time they reached the pudding stage. Brandy-soaked fruit plus a cream sauce heavily infused with brandy would likely lay them out for the rest of the day, or at least have them snoring through Mary Jane's ghost story session.

Outside was cold and misty when she made her way muffled to the ears in a purple pashmina and a black knitted hat that vaguely resembled the top half of a truncated balaclava. The cloche hat had gone the same way as the knitted tea cosy affair. A head of obnoxiously coloured hair certainly raised her level of hat-wearing.

She popped into a few hairdressing salons along the way, hoping against hope that somebody might have cancelled their appointment; nobody had.

The white mist was persistent, blanketing the old buildings of Bath with a ghostly veil. Viewing her surroundings was like gazing through a fine gauze curtain, blunting the edges, dulling the Christmas decorations seen through fuzzy windows.

The city was drenched in the sights, smells and sounds of Christmas. There were lights, Christmas trees and red-robed Santas everywhere. The smell of roasting chestnuts, hot pies and fresh fudge lay heavy on the air.

In Abbey Churchyard the Salvation Army Band was belting out 'Hark! The Herald Angels Sing'. A carousel of golden horses whirled around where the old fountain used to be.

The fountain had been moved into a side street to accommodate a development, a bad mistake as far as Honey was concerned. People used to congregate at that fountain but now it was just a big open space between shops selling the same stuff being sold in every high street shop in the country — in the world for that matter.

The carousel was a definite hit. Kids were screeching with delight, noses nipped to rosebud pink.

The reindeer standing beneath the Colonnades was sprayed gold and dark blue in thick waves across its body. The title was printed on the notice next to it: *Aurora Borealis. Northern Lights*. The red plastic nose was an added extra. People were pointing and laughing at it. She had to smile too.

The sausages were weighed and divided between two bags for ease of carrying. She'd bought enough to see them over both Christmas and New Year.

Seeing as it was mid-morning and therefore coffee time, she treated herself to a hot chocolate piled high with whipped cream. The chocolate drink was accompanied by two Amaretti Virginia biscuits, the soft ones that melted on the tongue.

Sitting alone gave her time to consider how lucky she was. Mr Scrimshaw had apparently been a lonely old soul with no friends, no family, and a frugal way of living.

It made her glad — very glad that she had a family. OK, there was that old saying about being able to choose your friends but not your relatives. Even the closest of families had problems. If she really considered the matter, there were few problems with her family. In fact she could count the present problems on one hand, so that wasn't so bad, was it?

Firstly there was this business of telling Lindsey about Doherty's proposal. No problem. Sooner said, soonest mended! That's what she told herself. That was before she called herself a coward.

A thick moustache of chocolate-flavoured foam on her upper lip remained untouched as she thought about Professor Jake Truebody. She hadn't recognised the name and she hadn't recognised him but then of course, she hadn't known all of Carl's acquaintances.

Her thoughts turned to presents. She'd bought her mother the Hermes scarf as directed. She'd bought Lindsey a year's gym membership plus a year's subscription to *British History* magazine. Doherty was getting a weekend away in the New Year, all expenses paid. She would be with him, of course, so it was a present they could share.

Honey licked the mix of foam and crumbs from her lips. Her mother was coming to lunch on Christmas Day. No doubt she'd be cornered again regarding the dating website.

'I will not submit to being videoed,' she muttered to herself.

It came out a bit too loud. She looked swiftly around her for anyone who might have heard and wondered at her appetites. No one seemed remotely interested, everyone wrapped up with their own lives, their own little Christmases.

Her thoughts went back to Mr Scrimshaw lying there with a letter opener sticking out of his ear. No goodwill to all men there, then!

Following his murder, the possibility of a little sleuthing had checked her rushing around. Christmas was receiving a more measured approach than per usual.

She was shaken from her reverie by a deep Scottish accent.

'A Merry Christmas to you!' A kiss landed on her chocolatey lips from a mouth surrounded by hair.

'Alistair!' She started. 'Good to see you. Can I buy you a coffee?' She looked up into a beard that almost matched the colour of her hair.

Alistair said that he'd love a coffee, but only if it was laced with whisky — Scotch whisky. 'I'm a Scot, so I don't do Irish, hen.'

He sipped the drink when it arrived. Honey must have looked surprised that he didn't knock it back in one when he explained that it was too hot.

'I take it you're involved in this murder case? Poor old Clarence. Skewered in the ear with his own letter opener.'

'Did you know him?'

'I spoke to him a few times.'

'Socially?' asked Honey, her lips frothy from her second cup of chocolate.

He shook his head. His big arms were folded and took up half the table. 'Business matters. He used to buy old books at auction. The old devil never liked parting with money. I had to chase him for it.'

Honey told him that a booking had been made for an office party and for Christmas lunch. Alistair raised his bright ginger eyebrows. 'Well there's a surprise. And there was me thinking that a leopard never changes its spots.'

Tucking a stray strand of hair beneath her hat, she eyed him questioningly. 'You don't think it likely that he had a change of heart and wanted to reward his employees?'

Alistair threw back his head and laughed. His orange mane was long on his shoulders.

'Not him. He only paid what he had to pay — to the penny. Take this place for instance; if he came in here to partake of a hot drink — which is pretty unlikely — he would tender the exact amount from his purse.'

'His purse?'

'A small leather purse that fitted in the inside pocket of his jacket. He'd have the exact amount in there — probably phone up beforehand to find out the price. Oh, and he didn't give tips. Not him. Basically, on those rare occasions when he did eat or drink out, it would be in company.'

She nodded in understanding. 'When the company was paying the check? Though not his firm.'

'Absolutely.'

She thought about it. It seemed old Scrimshaw might well have been plucked direct from Dickens's *A Christmas Carol.*

'Did he have any friends that you know of?'

'That was a grand drink. Thank you.' Alistair placed his mug on the table and wiped his whiskers with the back of his hand. 'I don't recall talk of him having friends, though there was talk of him being a bit of a boy when he was younger.'

'Really?'

The divorced Mrs Finchley came to mind. Perhaps her unrequited love wasn't as misplaced as she'd thought.

'There was talk of family at one time — a sister — dead by now I shouldn't wonder. His business partner of course, Eamon Mallory, though of course we all know he's been dead for some years.'

'How did Mallory die?'

'Eamon Mallory?' Alistair's lofty brow wrinkled into a thoughtful frown. 'Well, let me see now.' He threw back his head and closed his eyes. His fingers were still around his cup as though if he didn't it might grow legs and run away. 'I heard tell that he died in a house fire. That's basically all I know.

'There might be relatives,' Alistair continued. 'As I mentioned, there were rumours of him being a bit of a ladies' man. They both were, funnily enough, though age might have dimmed the urge in old Scrimshaw.'

'The dirty old goat.'

'Now, now,' said Alistair, his loud trumpet of a voice causing heads to turn in their direction. 'Everyone is driven by the procreative urge for a while in their lives. Even you, eh, hen?'

Honey feigned embarrassment. Alistair knew her well. She'd known the big Scotsman from the auction house for quite some time. He was a great contact, tipping her the wink when a particularly interesting item of underwear was up for auction.

She turned her thoughts back to Scrimshaw.

'On the other hand,' she said, 'he couldn't be so tight all the time. At Christmas he used to go away to a hotel in Ilfracombe.'

Alistair pulled a face. 'Nice enough in summer. A bit drear in winter.'

'Perhaps he got fed up with its dreariness. Perhaps that was why he decided to Christmas at home — in the bosom of his workforce if not his family and in a city that always has something going, no matter what the season.'

Alistair shrugged. 'You've a rose-coloured view of Clarence Scrimshaw, Mrs Driver. The man lived to make money, not to make merry. Now you must excuse me,' he said, half-rising from his chair. 'I've a train to catch for Edinburgh. I'll leave you to your Christmas. I'm off to do what all Scots do at this time of year — head for the homestead and Hogmanay.'

She wished him a prosperous New Year and a fine time with his folks in Scotland. Although they celebrated Christmas north of the border, the true making-merry didn't happen until New Year's Eve when a rendering of 'Auld Lang Syne' was accompanied by a skirl of bagpipes, a stuffed sheep's stomach, and a lot of drinking and reciting of Robbie Burns.

Alistair had confirmed what she'd already been told, and yet according to young Samantha Brown, someone had sent Scrimshaw a present. She hadn't specified it being wrapped in colourful paper, complete with ribbons and bows, but a present was a present at this time of year.

Her chocolate drink finished, Honey's boots took on a mind of their own, and promptly made their way to Cobblers Court.

The sky was leaden, the air as cold as a snowman's nose, and people were scurrying round in a fever of last-minute shopping. The whole thing was like a scene from a silent movie, when women in big hats and men in bowlers moved in double-quick time, their speed of movement detached from reality.

A crowd had gathered at the alley that led into Cobblers Court. Inquisitive eyes peered through steaming breath. The usual daft things were happening. A few people were wearing reindeer antlers or fur trimmed red hats. Three young men, obviously the worse for wear, had linked arms while singing an upbeat version of 'Silent Night'.

'Nothing going on here now,' stated a uniformed policeman standing in front of the crime scene tape. His stance and voice were heavily authoritarian. 'If you're got no official business here, go home. The excitement is over.'

An elderly couple turned round abruptly, bumping into Honey as they did so.

'Oh, so sorry, miss.'

'No need to apologise.'

'Are you English?' Their tone was incredulous, as though Bath was only filled with people visiting from elsewhere. Like a kind of giant Disneyland.

Honey confirmed that she was.

'Well I just have to tell you that I think your policemen are wonderful.' The accent was pure Tennessee.

Honey got in quick before the police officer got chance to tell her to shove off.

'Is Doherty here? I need to see him.'

He began shaking his head. 'No members of the public or press . . .'

'I'm his fiancée.'

The word was out before she could stop it. The woman from Tennessee stopped in her tracks and offered her congratulations.

'Fancy that, Cecil. This lady is marrying a policeman.'

The policeman immediately held up the tape, murmuring to her so the tourists couldn't hear, 'He's back there, miss.'

'Thanks,' said Honey as the officer held up the tape so she could pass under. With hindsight she regretted saying 'fiancée' out loud. It could have been because word travelled fast in Bath, or it could have been a premonition of problems to come.

CHAPTER FIFTEEN

'There,' said Lindsey, feeling very pleased with herself. She was speaking to the Christmas pot pourri design she'd just created and set at the end of the reception desk against the wall. Red poinsettia, pine cones, and dried apple shavings all mixed in a scooped-out piece of tree bark.

Hands on hips, she admired it from various angles. Yes, it was just right. It looked a treat and smelled it too.

A blast of cool air preceded a policeman coming through the door into Reception. Two plastic carrier bags were swinging from his fingers.

He had a rustic complexion, probably pinched there by the cold. His top two incisors loomed large when he smiled.

'Bacon and black pudding. Asked if I'd drop them in. Reckons she's still got sausages to get. Busy time Christmas. Your mother and the guv'nor are grabbing a quick lunch. Seems they've got a lot to talk about.'

'Oh yes. The murder of Bath's very own Mr Scrooge, so I hear.'

The policeman's round face broadened with a knowing smile and a wicked wink. 'And the impending marriage. I expect they've got a lot of personal stuff to sort out.'

Lindsey frowned. 'Beg your pardon?'

'Your mother said she's the guv's fiancée. Straight from the horse's mouth.' He paused in response to the look on her face. 'Was it supposed to be kept a secret?'

'No. No,' Lindsey said, automatically. 'Of course not.'

'Cheerio, then. Merry Christmas.'

'Merry Christmas.'

Lindsey felt a wave of heat flood her face. Was she the last to know this happy news?

Anna was totally enraptured by the news. 'How wonderful.'

'You knew?'

Anna shook her head. 'No. But it is lovely, yes?'

Lindsey didn't commit. Yes, it was lovely. *Lovelier if she'd been told about it first.* What was going on here?

Once she'd secured the peace and quiet of an unoccupied room, she punched in her mother's phone number.

'What's this about you and Doherty getting married?'

There was a stunned silence on the other end.

'I was going to tell you,' her mother began falteringly. 'But you know how busy it's been . . . How did you find out?'

'A stranger. A complete stranger wearing a police uniform and bearing a bag of sausages.'

'Nothing's been agreed . . .'

'No doubt I'll be the last to know about it when it has been agreed.'

She closed the connection abruptly. She'd not been so bolshie towards her mother since she was fourteen and finding her feet like all young adolescents do. Rebellious teenagers are par for the course — not that she'd been that rebellious. She decided this might be a delayed reaction.

'Perhaps I'm a late developer,' she muttered, and headed for the kitchen.

She stormed in, the door slamming behind her, her eyes blazing.

'Right. So who knows about my mother being engaged?'

Smudger backed up against the hot range and shook his head vehemently.

'Nothing. Nothing at all. I'm just the engineer in the engine room. OK?'

No, it was not OK, but Lindsey left the kitchen staff to get on with their work and didn't stop until she reached a handy alcove in which to brood. Alcoves were deep and abundant in the Green River Hotel. She stood there with her eyes closed and her heart racing. She was feeling angry. So angry! To think a local bobby had told her the news before her mother had done so. It wasn't right. It wasn't right at all.

She returned to Reception to find Mary Jane looking excited and in need of an ear to bend in her direction.

'I thought I might hold a séance on Boxing Day. The ghost story session is fully booked. I thought some of the guys attending — well not just guys — girls as well, might like to come to a séance too. What do you think?'

Lindsey thought about it. 'Have you ever had anyone come through?'

'Of course I have. There was this Hispanic woman whose husband was suspected of murdering her, and then there was this highwayman up in Lincolnshire who was hanged, and then, best of all I think, there was a Regency gent who shot himself after he lost everything at cards . . .'

'How about more recent deaths.'

Mary Jane looked at her quizzically. 'I don't see why not. Anyone in particular?'

'My father.'

* * *

At Cobblers Court, Doherty came down the stairs from where the murder had taken place, his hands in his pockets and his chin close to his chest.

Honey detected a twitch of a smile when he saw her.

'Office, first front,' he said. 'You can take a look when the boys in crackly suits have done their thing. The flat is on the top floor. I've taken a look. No cards. Not one. No parcel either.'

She guessed by his grim expression that the method of despatching Clarence Scrimshaw had been particularly nasty and that he hadn't told her everything.

'And the ones in the office?'

'Mostly from suppliers.'

'Hmm,' she said thoughtfully. 'Probably trying to keep on the right side of him in order to get their money.'

'Probably.'

They waited until someone came out to say that they'd finished with everything except for the actual crime scene in Clarence Scrimshaw's office.

Honey followed Doherty up the stairs.

The walls of the room were of painted plaster. There were about four desks in the general office. Christmas cards were pinned onto the screens that divided one desk from another. A few sat on the mantelpiece of a white marble fireplace.

'Are there no cards in Mr Scrimshaw's office?'

'Not one. That bloke Longborough said that Scrimshaw opened the cards himself then handed them into Sam Brown's keeping. She was the one who placed them on here.'

He picked one up that showed a fat robin sitting on a log. 'It's initialled, not signed.'

Honey took a look. It said, '*To Clarence.*' Underneath was the imprint of a pair of red lips and the initials FF.

'We could get a DNA fix on those lips,' said Doherty.

Honey put the card back on the mantelpiece. 'Don't bother. I know who sent it. The love-sick Mrs Finchley. She was wearing that same shade of lipstick for the party the other night.'

'Oh, yes. Of course she was. Not a suspect, I take it?'

Honey shook her head. 'Just a woman in love.'

'What's she like?'

'Quite big. Why do you ask?'

'Mr Scrimshaw was small. About five one.'

'Odd bedfellows. Not that I think things went that far.'

'Height doesn't matter much when you're lying down,' Doherty quipped.

She continued looking through the cards while Doherty went off to liaise with the people in white suits. Most of the cards were from recognisable companies that would deal with a publishing house; printers, computer technical support, stationery suppliers. Their greetings were printed and overwritten with an incomprehensible scrawl that may have been the signature of company director, though the post room boy was just as likely to have been employed to do it.

It was exactly as they'd expected; Clarence Scrimshaw's popularity certainly did not run to receiving Christmas cards from old friends and relatives — possibly because he never sent them himself — or just didn't have anyone worth sending one to.

There was no sign of any unopened or opened parcel. If Scrimshaw had received a present, then it hadn't been left in the office.

'It had to be someone he knew,' Doherty said on his return. He scraped his fist over the stubble on his chin as he thought about it. 'You say he was coming to you for lunch on Christmas Day?'

'The whole workforce of Mallory and Scrimshaw, including the boss. Surprising to get them all here on Christmas Day, but it was a novel experience for them, generosity was totally out of Scrimshaw's character according to our friend Mr Longborough and his colleagues. Sam Brown said that he always booked into the Bay View Hotel in Ilfracombe.'

'He did this year,' said Doherty. 'I've just had it confirmed.'

Honey frowned. 'So he booked two hotels? That doesn't make sense, though he didn't book any rooms for Christmas Day at the Green River. Perhaps the plan was to stay in Ilfracombe on Christmas Eve, drive up to us for lunch, and drive back again.'

'He'd booked an all-inclusive deal. Apparently he did it year-on-year.'

Honey frowned. The more they investigated the life of Clarence Scrimshaw, the more she wondered whether he'd instigated the booking at her hotel in the first place.

Doherty was obviously on the same wavelength. 'Why would he book with you if he was already booked somewhere else? You're sure it was Mr Scrimshaw who made the reservations?'

Honey rubbed at her forehead as she tried to remember. 'I'd never met him before, but his voice was quite memorable. A bit Laurence Olivier-like. But all that concerned me was that his debit card checked out — and it did. How about his will? Who will inherit?'

'Her Majesty's Treasury. As far as we know he didn't have any close relatives left, and he never made a will, so it becomes the property of the crown. I presume he was too mean to die — or thought he never would. Further enquiries will be made.'

'What a turnip! A very dead turnip,' she added in a more muted tone.

Doherty stroked the nape of her neck as he voiced his thoughts.

'Being there on Christmas Day is going to be useful. I've got some questions to ask Longborough and the rest of them. They've already admitted that their boss wasn't one for kicking his legs up and splashing out with his money. By the looks of this place, I believe them,' he said, frowning at the dark oak panelling and the avenue of doors along a higgledy-piggledy corridor.

'Still no sign of that present they mentioned. It must be somewhere. Sam Brown was specific. It was heavy — like a book?'

'Perhaps upstairs in his flat. Someone's coming in with the key. We'll take a look then. I don't think Forensics will need to look around. It's becoming more and more likely that the victim was killed here.'

He looked tired. She promised him some rest on Christmas Day.

'You'll still be working, but you'll be well fed, and you snooze in front of the TV as long as you don't snore during the Queen's speech. It's not respectful.'

'HM won't know if I doze off.' He smiled.

'Will you?'

'No. And I'll get out the best brandy.'

'I'm all yours.'

'And then you'll have the joy of attending Mary Jane's ghost story session. Oh, come on,' she said in response to the face he pulled. 'Everyone enjoys a good ghost story at this time of year.'

'How could I resist?'

His smile held the promise of good things to come, but she wasn't fooled. Once a case bit him, Doherty was like a dog with a bone; he kept with it, rarely getting more than a few hours' sleep per night. She'd slept with him, literally. But she knew he'd be there on Christmas Day — albeit for the employees of Mallory and Scrimshaw as much as for her.

CHAPTER SIXTEEN

Two days before Christmas and Honey was just leaving Doherty and Cobblers Court when she spotted a sign. *Bee in the Bonnet — Under New Management.*

A fat bumble bee appeared to be shooting from a black and yellow arrow. The arrow pointed up a narrow staircase.

She could barely contain her excitement. A Christmas wish had come true; she'd come across a fairly new and well-hidden hairdresser. A place called Bee in the Bonnet couldn't be anything else. Her heart didn't exactly miss a beat, but her hair at least seemed to bristle with excitement.

After she'd explained the problem, a girl with sleek black hair confirmed they could fit her in. 'You're in luck. Ariadne will be working on you.'

Ariadne had hard eyes and beaded blonde tendrils rattling around her shoulders.

'Problem?' she asked without bothering to say hello.

Honey whisked off her hat.

'I've had an accident. Can you do something with this?'

Ariadne eyed her hair disparagingly and asked the million-dollar most embarrassing question. 'Who did this colour?'

'A friend.' Ruining her hair was stretching friendship to the limit, but Honey wasn't going to admit too much.

'Did she do the colour test first?'

'I think it was past its sell-by date. I'd really like it sorted. It's just not my colour.'

'I quite agree. Neon orange only suits orangutans, though in your case even they might need to reach for their sunglasses.' Her voice was devoid of emotion. Honey suspected that if Ariadne did get excited, it never showed in her voice.

'It shouldn't have been this colour, and I wouldn't have let her do it if I'd had more time and could have got an appointment — somewhere.'

'Excuses, excuses, excuses! You have to be careful with colour. Older women especially. But, yes. It's not impossible, but we are busy. I don't usually do colours myself. I'm a stylist. But I'll sort you out as long as you promise never to do anything so stupid again.'

Honey gulped. Had she heard right? If she had then Ariadne would have been better named Jo Blunt.

Honey felt obliged to point out the error of Ariadne's ways.

'Excuse me, but aren't you supposed to make me feel at ease by asking if I'm doing anything special for Christmas? Failing that, you could ask me whether or not I'm going to brave airport chaos or the possibility of striking traffic controllers in Spain.'

Unfazed by her obvious sarcasm, Ariadne picked at Honey's orange locks.

'I could do if you like mindless drivel. Personally, I couldn't care less what people are doing over the holiday as long as I've got some time off, but if you insist, what are you doing for Christmas?'

'Working.'

'Well that's something I don't want to know about!'

'This is a very busy time in the hotel trade. I've got a lot still to prepare and I can't sit here all day talking rubbish. I would appreciate it if you could get a move on.'

'Suits me.'

Wearing dye-stained rubber gloves, Ariadne's brush strokes and folding of tin foil did not cease. Her fingers flew with as much dexterity as when Smudger was stuffing a turkey. Although the tin foil was cut into little squares for her hair, the turkey kept popping into her mind. Even now her chef would be preparing the Christmas bird, soaking it in butter, covering its bulging breast with tin foil. The whole exercise got her wondering how Ariadne was at making stuffing balls or foil-wrapping anchovies.

Ariadne threw a steel tailed comb and the brush she'd been using into a plastic bowl.

'Done!' she finally exclaimed.

Honey eyed her reflection and decided that she vaguely resembled a pile of foil-wrapped sandwiches. Her head looked twice the size it actually was.

'The colour should take OK, though anything's got to be better than looking like an exploding bunch of carrots. Now if you'd like to come over here.'

Being compared to carrots was beginning to wear thin. Never mind carrots exploding; she was pretty close to exploding herself.

Calm down. Think how great it will look.

As though she were blind and had to be protected from objects and other people, she was guided to where a chair had been placed immediately in front of a special drier. She settled herself down, comfortable beneath the nylon cape protecting her shoulders.

The view through the window was of the building opposite — the one occupied by Mallory and Scrimshaw.

She could see Doherty and the people in white suits. They looked like snowmen; very white against the dark walls as they recorded and bagged evidence, even down to the desktop which four burly assistants were attempting to take out of the door.

The brusque Ariadne was forgotten and the warmth from the dryer was making her doze. Her eyelids began to droop. This murder was a terrible thing, but she had to think positive. What if the outcome of the case did affect her hotel bookings? Could she really help that? One man's meat was another man's poison — or in this case one man's letter opener was another man's lethal weapon. She wasn't really being mercenary, just practical.

She made herself a promise to visit a hair stylist more often, though not necessarily this place. Ariadne was bearable only in small doses. But there were other hair stylists in Bath — very good ones — discounting, she reminded herself, her mother's hairdresser Antoine of the snake hips and slender hands.

All the same, there was considerable thinking time to be gained when sitting in a chair, head warm and nothing else to do.

She narrowed her eyes at the view opposite. There were four windows on the same floor where Scrimshaw had been murdered. The room to the far right was bright with light. She could just about see the last of the Forensics team working there. The one next to that was less busy but looked interesting and the one immediately opposite her was Mr Scrimshaw's office with its dark panelling and masculine furniture.

Suddenly someone switched the light off. The effect was instantaneous, as though the curtain had come down on a stage, as though nothing over there was real but just a drama.

Ariadne came over to check that her new colour was drying evenly and peeled back one strip of tinfoil.

'Ah! A professional finish.'

'I suppose this is going to cost me a fortune.'

She sniffed. 'Your own fault. You should have sought professional help in the first place.'

The inference that her own efforts — or rather those of Mary Jane — were amateur was obvious. But she wasn't going to take this lying down.

'I couldn't find a decent hairdresser — not one that was *recommended* anyway.'

She saw Ariadne's lips curl up in a snarl, bristling at the inference that she hadn't come recommended.

'Never mind. Shall we go back to small talk? Let's see. Where shall I start? I know, how about I ask you if you've been admiring the view?'

Honey turned up her nose. 'You don't have much of a view. Just offices.'

'Not just offices now, though. A drama has been unfolding. There's been a murder,' said Ariadne with an air of outright smugness. 'The police are still over there investigating. Right load of clodhoppers. Should scare the mice out from the woodwork if nothing else.'

Doherty was over there. She felt obliged to defend him.

'Oh, I don't know. One or two of them are quite cute.'

'Can't say I've noticed,' sniffed Ariadne. 'I only notice *really* attractive men.'

'So do I, but I'm lucky. I have twenty/twenty vision.'

Ariadne pursed her pale pink lips as though swallowing whatever she'd been about to say.

'Have they been over here to ask you questions?' Honey asked.

'Yes. Stupid questions. As if any of us saw anything. Too busy. Hairdressing is a busy trade at this time of year, besides being very skilled. It's imperative that a stylist concentrates on what he or she is doing.'

'Then I should be grateful that you managed to fit me in, but then you're pretty new here aren't you and kind of tucked out of the way. It can't be easy for a newcomer to build up a clientele.'

She knew the moment she saw Ariadne's turned-up nose turn up that bit more that the tone would turn icy.

'We've done very well since we opened, thank you very much! I only managed to fit you in because of a no-show.'

Honey grimaced as a sliver of tin foil was peeled roughly from her hair, the colour examined between Ariadne's sharp eyes before she was rewrapped.

'Am I done?'

'You are as far as I'm concerned.' Her tone was abrupt. 'I'll allocate a junior to sort you out.'

The wheels on the chair and heaters squealed in protest as she was pushed closer to the window.

Was she being oversensitive in thinking that she may have been placed with her back to the salon on purpose — like a naughty schoolgirl being forced to stand in the corner?

Calm down. Concentrate on the job in hand.

Ariadne was a bit of a shock to the system. Hairdressers, like hoteliers, usually adopted a courteous persona when dealing with clients. All was sweetness and light, worn like a well-padded ski outfit when dealing with the public, if not when in the bosom of family and friends. In Ariadne's case she hadn't adopted the ski suit in the first place. Her attitude seemed to be: *take me as I am, like it or lump it!*

Honey stared across at the brightly lit windows of the building opposite. The bay window she was sitting at jutted out from the main wall of the building, like a little turret, separate but still remaining part of the whole.

She looked around her. A woman sitting in front of the next window, her head as parcelled up as her own, gave her a reassuring smile.

Turning back to look across the road, she watched Doherty standing at the window, his arms braced, hands resting on stone ledges. He was looking down at the yard, raking it from side to side with his eyes, upwards and, more importantly, across in her direction.

Much as she adored the guy, she didn't want him to see her unadorned — without her new hair, or at least with it covered up like a piece of poultry set for oven ready roasting. She slunk lower in her chair, legs splayed out in front of her — lower still when he craned his neck and appeared to notice her.

Unfortunately she hadn't seen that one of the power cables from the drying monster had tangled around the heel of her shoe. The dryer slid forward, the centre oblong toppling, its bright red element landing on her head.

The smell of burning filled the air.

'My hair!' she shrieked.

'She's on fire! She's on fire,' screamed the junior allocated to look after her. It was pandemonium.

A woman close by was having her hair blow-dried. She leapt from her chair. Another woman spun round in hers sending a hair stylist toppling and a hairbrush flying off into space like a delinquent missile.

The sniffy Ariadne lost her cool for a moment, though she soon regained enough control to tell the hysterical girl to shut up.

Landing in a heap as soon as she was extinguished, Honey felt an instant rapport with a Golden Retriever puppy she'd once seen cowering beneath a shower of well-meant patting.

A lady whose waistline was hidden somewhere beneath her ample bosom, her belly sitting comfortably on her thighs, leaned forward. 'You could sue.'

At the mention of litigation, even the stuck-up Ariadne looked momentarily panic-stricken.

The woman's eyes glittered at the prospect of an insurance payout.

'Tallulah. Make some fresh coffee,' barked Ariadne. At the same time she tossed her head sending the beads of her hairdo rattling like hell stones on a glass roof. 'Come on, girl. I haven't got all day. Coffee! Make coffee,' shouted Ariadne.

Thinking this was Ariadne's one and only attempt to offer an apology, Honey waved her hand. 'I'm fine. I don't want coffee.'

'It's not for you,' snapped Ariadne. 'It's for me.'

'Then make it yourself!' barked Tallulah. 'My lady here needs my attention.'

Honey smirked. It was nice being referred to as a lady.

'I could do with some fresh air,' she said.

Tallulah helped her back into her chair and pushed her closer to the window.

After touching her hair to make sure it wasn't singed, she took deep breaths.

Tallulah checked where the glowing red heater had landed on her head. 'Your hair's OK. The tinfoil protected most of it. I can cut the tiny bit that's burned out for you.'

'Will it show?'

'I shouldn't think so.'

'I'm fine with that as long as the carrot colour is gone.'

'It's gone. Sorry about the electricity cable. I should have noticed. Can I get you anything?'

'I'd like a drink of water. Can you manage that?'

While she was gone, Honey leaned forward so she could better see down into Cobblers Court and across the way. There was a good view of the main entrance and of the offices on the floor directly opposite. She could see Doherty speaking to someone before he finally moved out of sight.

Tallulah came back with the water she'd asked for.

'So how long have you worked here?' Honey asked.

'Three months.' Tallulah began taking out the pieces of tinfoil one by one, laying them in a plastic dish perched on a spindly trolley.

Honey kept her eyes focused on events happening — or not happening — opposite.

'Are you enjoying it — I mean, do you enjoy those days when the customers' hair doesn't catch fire?'

Recognising that her 'lady' had a sense of humour, Tallulah managed a hesitant smile. In answer to Honey's question, she shrugged in that unsure way that teenagers think makes them look grown-up. 'It's OK.'

Honey judged the girl's confidence was returning. A little *focused* conversation went a long way.

'You sound very informed on colouring. Is that what you specialise in?'

'I do most of the colouring, except when it's busy, then we all have to do it. Ariadne prefers to stick to styling. Most hairdressers hate colouring. It can be messy and can even go wrong . . .'

Tell me about it, thought Honey. A quick peek in a mirror to her right indicated that her hair colour was back to normal.

'Not much of a view,' she said, changing the subject from hair and incompetent colourists.

'It's nice when the weather's warm. I see visitors come and go all the time over there.'

'Anyone in particular — anyone famous, I mean?'

The teenage shrug again. 'Nobody I know. I recognise the people that work there, of course. They don't change that much.'

Honey tuned in to what she was saying. 'Is this the colourist's permanent station? I mean; is this always where you colour peoples' hair?'

Tallulah confirmed that it was.

'Do you see many people go past the window?'

'There's always someone. People use Cobblers Court as a short cut.'

'How was it the night the man opposite was murdered? Was it very busy?'

'Dark and misty. Really spooky. Everyone looked like a ghost, all grey and hard to recognise. The only things you could see were sparkly things — like tinsel, Christmas decorations, and people wearing jewellery . . . especially one piece of jewellery — big jewellery that someone was wearing . . . funny you can see things like that through the fog.'

The apparent intimacy of their conversation did not escape Ariadne's eagle eye.

'Tallulah! I'd like madam's hair ready for rinsing before Christmas please!'

'Ever thought about working somewhere else?' murmured Honey.

Tallulah whispered her answer from the side of her mouth. 'Many times.'

The woman with the rounded belly and the non-existent waistline had got up from her chair. Hair still wet and dripping, she waddled over, her plump hand landing on Honey's shoulder. She was beaming as though she'd just won the lottery.

'I've just realised who you are. You're Mrs Driver, the Hotels Association Crime Liaison Officer. I suppose you're working with the police on this murder. I'm June Weller. I run the Rose Posy Bed and Breakfast in Bathwick. Pleased to meet you, I'm sure.'

June Weller went on to inform her that her bookings for next summer were coming in very nicely and from all over the world. To Honey's ears it sounded as though she were the most successful hotelier Bath had ever had — even though it was only a bed and breakfast that she ran.

A few questions from those who'd overheard were only to be expected. Honey fielded them expertly, explaining that it was her job merely to liaise with the police at times like these.

Wanting very much to leave now, Honey paid up swiftly, and gladly. Her hair looked better than normal: glossy, thick and not a grey hair in sight. There were definite perks about having your hair dyed professionally.

She gave Tallulah a five-pound tip. 'And here's another tip — leave and get yourself a better boss.'

She got to the bottom of the stairs when she realised she'd left the sausages behind. On re-entering she saw that the door to the coffee room was closed. On the other side of the glass she could see a red-faced Tallulah and Ariadne, quivering like an angry porcupine. Whatever was being said wasn't nice, but it wasn't her business.

Honey stood out on the landing; certain that pretty soon Tallulah would come out to use the ladies' cloakroom.

She was right.

'Tallulah?'

She could see the girl was on the brink of tears.

'Are you OK?'

She lowered her eyelids and nodded. 'I'm fine. It's just her, asking me questions . . .'

'Just like me. Sorry about that.' She said it jokily.

Tallulah lowered her voice. 'That's just it. When she heard that you work with the police, she went mad. She told me I'm not to discuss anything that happens across the way. Nothing. Nothing at all.'

CHAPTER SEVENTEEN

Although her hair was sorted, the weather was cold, so Honey kept her hat on.

Tallulah had impressed her; so had Ariadne, though in a different way. Why had Ariadne warned Tallulah not to talk to her about events over the road?

On leaving the hairdressers, she checked over the road to see if Doherty was still there, but was told he'd already left.

She left a message on his mobile then phoned Lindsey, desperate to know how she was getting on with the professor.

There was no response. Various worrying visions darted around her brain. Lindsey and the professor in a lustful clinch. Lindsey and the professor booking into a room at a Travelodge. They were cheap, and even though they declared they didn't let rooms by the hour, there was nothing stopping people from booking in, sleeping together, and checking out again.

On the way home, she popped into the bank, gave them a sob story about next year's bookings. Turned out it was the wrong thing to say. A sudden concern flash onto the accounts manager's face, so quickly backtracked.

'But we've picked up some good business from elsewhere,' she said hastily. 'A big firm of equity agents will be holding regular conferences with us next year prior to relocating.'

Equity agents? What were they and where had they come from?

It may have been the season, or it may have been that there really were such creatures as equity agents, but the accounts manager was seriously impressed. Honey reminded herself to look up equity agents as soon as she got back home.

Fearing her lie might be discovered, she exited the bank quickly. On the way she passed a number of decorated reindeer, some with wings, covered with psychedelic swirls of purple and pink; others with zebra stripes, and one reindeer with gold tipped horns and 'Harrods' painted in swirly letters along its flanks. All of them sported large plastic red noses.

Normally there might have been some council employee attempting to remove the offending articles with hot water and some kind of paint thinner. There wasn't. Even council employees had different priorities at this time of year.

When she got back to the Green River Hotel, Steve Doherty was outside leaning on the roof of his car. He looked cool, unflustered; evidently, he hadn't been there that long.

She kissed his cheek. He smelled of aftershave, which was funny considering he hadn't shaved. His bristles were soft, at that length between unshaven stubble and furry bear.

She linked arms with him. 'You got my message?'

'About the hairdresser opposite Mallory and Scrimshaw? Yes, I did.'

'It may be nothing, but it could be something. She was rattled.'

He shrugged. 'It could be just about keeping the hairdressing banter on the usual subjects: the weather, shopping, and where you're going for your holidays.'

'You've known a few hairdressers?'

'I've known a few women. And I've listened in on some of your conversations.'

Honey couldn't help smiling.

Hooking a finger beneath the front of her hat, he lifted it and took a peek. 'Yep. You look good. I could forgive that hairdresser anything.'

'I called in at the bank on the way here.'

'And I thought you'd dressed to please me.'

'It pays to put on a good show for one of the most important people in my life.'

She wasn't kidding. Bank visits were about as welcome as visits to the dentist, but unlike with visits to the dentists it was imperative to make a good impression. At least the dentist was friendly and keen to do anything to ease the patient's pain, no matter what they looked like. Bank officials were under no such obligation. She'd gone along dressed up to the nines hoping to impress. Her mother was to blame for that.

'Always wear the most expensive outer garments possible. Give a well-heeled impression from the skin out and you'll get what you want.'

With an increase in her overdraft facility in mind, she'd squeezed into an Artigiano lambswool dress. A few things bulged beneath its clinginess but the grey and cerise jacket she added skimmed her hips nicely.

She was half-admitting to herself that her mother's advice might have worked. On the whole her visit hadn't worked out too badly. Besides the rubbish about the equity agents, she'd assured the account manager that the Christmas takings were looking good. She'd added that her trading account should remain in the black until at least Easter. The spick-and-span woman behind the desk usually pursed her lips when Honey told her a tale like that. Instead her plump lips had jerked into a hesitant smile. 'I'll believe you, Mrs Driver.'

Honey had thanked her and silently blessed the time of year that had made her so amenable. On the way out she also promised God that she'd poke her nose into midnight Mass. It wouldn't hurt to thank him too.

'Any developments?' she asked Doherty. She was, of course, referring to the murder case.

Doherty shifted, about to answer, when they were interrupted by a traffic warden.

'That your car?'

Doherty flashed his warrant card. 'Police business.'

The traffic officer sniffed and marched off to pastures new.

Doherty suddenly planted a kiss on her cheek.

'That was nice.'

'I've a reputation for being a good kisser.'

My, but he could be so over-confident at times!

'It wasn't that much of a clincher.'

'We *are* in a public place. I came here to ask you what you want for Christmas.'

A number of items flashed across Honey's mental wish list. First place went to Doherty's body but she'd probably get that anyway. There were a few other possibilities further down the list but none nearly as enticing.

She played along.

'Well you know the old saying about diamonds being a girl's best friend.'

He grinned. 'I did give them some thought but then I know the overheads of a privately run hotel, especially the insurance premium. You wouldn't appreciate me buying you diamonds. Much too expensive — insurance . . .'

'There's some logic in what you say. How about you? What's your Christmas wish?'

His grin turned to a grimace and a touch of the serious policeman invaded his cool good looks — cool as in rugged and scary — depending on the situation that is.

'On the personal side I'd like you covered in brandy cream on Christmas morning.'

'There's a lot of me. It might take a while.'

Their eyes locked.

Honey shook her head and smiled. She wasn't going there so Doherty carried on where he'd left off.

'On the professional side I'd like to find out whoever skewered Scrimshaw to his desk after killing him.'

'*After* killing him?' Honey's eyebrows shot upwards.

'He was poisoned.'

'Before being knifed?'

'Yes. And between the two he was suffocated.'

'That's what I call overkill. So which actually did it?'

'The poison worked first. He might have been half-dead when he was suffocated and totally dead when the knife went in.'

'The letter opener.'

'A knife, then the letter opener. That's what I'm being told.'

Honey knew enough about pathology to work out that his heart had stopped pumping before the knife speared his ear drum. There would not have been too much bleeding.

'Someone wanted to make sure?'

'I suppose so. Someone must have hated him a lot to make sure like that!'

'So what next?'

'I have a plan. In the meantime . . .'

There was an alluring intimacy about the way his eyes snaked over her body before finally fixing on her face. She felt herself colouring up as she waited for the compliment she was sure was coming.

'You've got your hair back, and that calls for a celebration. That hair colour was awful. Promise me you won't ever go back to that particular hairdresser — Mary Jane should stick to what she knows — which isn't much.'

'Come on. It wasn't that bad.' She took off her hat and tossed her head so he could better see her hair's shimmering glossiness. A little flattery was good.

'Oh yes it was.' One corner of his mouth was already raised in a smile.

'Bright colours are modern.'

'Do I get a coffee?'

'I've got a lot to do.'

'If I help make the coffee, do I get brownie points?'

'A lot more than that if you play your cards right.'

He grinned. 'The Queen of Hearts.'

He left the car there complete with a 'Police on Call' notice in the front windscreen.

Honey breathed a sigh of relief when she saw that Lindsey was back. Her relief was lessened considerably when she saw that her daughter was sitting in an armchair, with Professor Jake Truebody sitting in the chair opposite her. There a coffee table between them; hardly a barrier, but better than nothing, thought Honey.

'Did you get to take some photographs?' Honey asked her daughter.

'Not many. The light wasn't good.'

It seemed a poor excuse. The camera was modern. Light levels didn't matter. And Lindsey seemed overly nervous. Why was that?

Doherty waded in. 'Hi Lindsey. Mind if I ask you some questions?'

Lindsey's face was poker straight and her response was muted. 'Now? You want to speak to me now? You've hardly had a word to say to me about you and Mum getting hitched, and NOW you want to speak to me?'

Surprised by her sharpness, Doherty turned to Honey. 'What did I do?' he whispered.

'Nothing.'

Jake Truebody had already got to his feet and was making a move to leave the hotel.

Anna was right, thought Honey. Truebody left as soon as the police appeared. Or was it when she, Honey, appeared?

'I'll leave you all in peace.' He nodded at Honey and Doherty, at the latter just a shade too abruptly. 'I have to pay a visit to the ATM — get out some cash to see me over the holiday.'

Lindsey's eyes flickered as he got up, posted his key into the keep box, and headed for the exit. A small frown appeared on her face. Honey saw it and wondered what it meant. But she wouldn't ask. Her daughter's personal life was her own. Besides, come the New Year, Jake Truebody would be heading back across the Atlantic and out of their lives.

Doherty pulled up a chair, the same one the professor had been sitting in.

'OK. Let's make a start. Some of the Mallory and Scrimshaw party left the building just before the party on the night in question. A car alarm went off. Somebody went out to check on it. A young lady went home to check on her child and another couple — Mr and Mrs Emmerson — said they left to check on an aged parent, but were seen having one hell of a ding-dong in Reception and then departing in different directions so they couldn't both have been going off to see that aged parent. Is that right?'

Lindsey linked her hands around her knees. 'I'm not sure which alibi belongs to which of those people, but I saw all of them go out. David Longborough went to check the car alarm, one was in tears, two were arguing, and the fifth left in a flurry of fretfulness. Mary Jane was here too. She spoke to Mrs Finchley and David Longborough.'

'I take it that Miss Brown was the one who was crying.'

'I think so.'

'The Emmersons went to visit their aged relative and Mr Longborough went to shut off his car alarm. Is that right?'

Lindsey frowned. 'Those were the reasons they gave . . . I couldn't vouch as to whether any of them were telling the truth.'

There was nothing else Doherty could think of. He thanked her and went with Honey for a coffee.

Lindsey waited until they were gone before doing what she'd steeled herself to do. Making sure nobody else was around, she emptied the key box. There were only three in there. She easily found the one she wanted; number thirty-six, the key to Jake Truebody's room.

Anna had returned from lying down and took over Reception. Key hidden in her hand, Lindsey made an excuse to go upstairs.

'I just need to check that we've got enough laundry to last us,' she explained.

It was a poor excuse and Anna looked a little surprised. They'd gone through the laundry list together. Everything had been in order. Anna did exactly what Lindsey had feared she would do and took it the wrong way.

'I did it right. Honestly, I did,' said Anna sounding as though she could be on the verge of tears.

'I know you did,' said Lindsey reassuringly. 'But perhaps I didn't. Won't be long.'

She didn't look back in case Anna saw the guilt on her face. Not guilt about lying with regard to the laundry list, but guilt at what she was about to do.

Jake Truebody had refused to be photographed. The only other course of action was to borrow his passport. Hopefully the photograph would scan OK, but there was no guarantee.

Everything was quiet in the first floor corridor. Lindsey glanced up and down. Nobody appeared. There was no sound except for the television in Mary Jane's room. Mary Jane didn't admit to being a little deaf. She had a tendency to sleep with the TV going full blast. It was usually downright annoying, but on this occasion Lindsey welcomed the noise.

Nobody could possibly the key being put in the door and turned. Nobody could have heard the door squeak as she pushed it open, but she was careful — very careful.

The room was in darkness. The curtains were drawn. If she were to discover anything about this man, she either had to draw back the curtains or switch on a light. She decided to switch on a light.

A single piece of luggage, a brown leather holdall sat on the foldable luggage rack. For someone who'd crossed the Atlantic, this man travelled light.

She searched for his passport, but couldn't find it. She guessed he'd taken it with him. He'd definitely had a passport stating he was Jake Truebody. They'd checked him in. She'd taken a photocopy and made a note of the passport number.

Yet his sister had posted him as missing, presumed dead.

It occurred to her to contact that sister telling her that her brother was spending Christmas at a hotel in Bath. Not yet, she decided. Not until she was totally clear who he was and why he was here.

There were no tell-tale pieces of paper in the bag, no newspaper clippings, no files. She knew her father had been rich and dealt in companies. She also knew that rich men were not always honest. It wasn't beyond reason that the American federal authorities might be going over a cold case. She needed to know. She needed to find something. But all she could find was his laptop.

Her fingers itched to take it out and log in. But could she log in? It would take an age to find the right password. If he was FBI, there was probably some device not only preventing her from logging in, but also recording her attempt. She couldn't risk it. Not until she knew more about him. All she did know for sure was that he sure as hell was not a professor of history.

CHAPTER EIGHTEEN

Honey led Doherty into the dining room where boxes of crackers were piled up waiting to be placed on tables. It was five days before Christmas and there were a few more office parties to go. Sick of the sight of Christmas decorations, she kicked an escaped balloon aside, poured coffee, and set it down on a table.

'Was that balloon your ex-husband's head?' Doherty watched it float across the floor.

'What made you say that?'

He shrugged. 'Just a joke — I think.'

Carl was like a nasty taste on her tongue this morning, and she didn't want to talk about him.

She handed Doherty a bag of balloons. 'Blow them up and put them in the net. Once it's full we can fix it to the ceiling.'

He lost the serious look. 'I know a game using balloons. It's best done naked, though.'

'I bet you do.' Her imagination went into overdrive when he returned her own knowing smile. She knew that game too, passing a balloon up between bodies.

'This is kids' stuff. Lindsey should be doing this,' he exclaimed suddenly.

'Some kid!'

Lindsey was closing on twenty but Doherty was right. Usually she would be helping but she was in a mood.

'So?'

Honey knew what the questioning tone meant. Calling Lindsey a kid had been a leading comment. He knew things weren't running too smoothly and being a policeman he just had to ask questions. At Honey's request, he had not mentioned the engagement to her daughter. He asked her about it.

'She knows,' she said and told him how a police constable had spilled the beans.

'That's not good.' He frowned. 'He should have kept his mouth shut. It's that time of year. Nobody is concentrating on what they should be doing. How did she take it?'

'She's been very off and not terribly helpful. I would prefer that you didn't mention it to her.'

'I won't.'

In sympathy, he stroked her cheek. It should have soothed but it prickled. The fact was, it hurt that Lindsey was being so off with her.

It was as though a big sheet of glass had been placed between them. She could see Lindsey clearly but couldn't touch her. In one split second everything had changed, and that was difficult to deal with, especially at this time of year. Since Honey had first bought the Green River Hotel, a massive investment for her at the time, her daughter had been totally supportive.

Anna was also proving to be a bit of a worry. She had presented herself for work despite the baby being due. 'It is mostly sitting down work today, I think,' she'd said in her soft voice. 'I will write up the name cards for the dinner tomorrow and the ghost story people. That will be no problem. I tell you, I have two more months. Two months. I know better than the doctor.'

'But the doctor said . . . ?'

Anna pulled a face. 'He is wrong. I am not ready. Baby is not ready.'

There was no way Honey was going to insist. Being firm might upset Anna, she might go into labour then and there. Very apt for the time of year, but the Green River Hotel was not a stable and she, Honey Driver, was not a midwife, and Anna, bless her little cotton socks, was not a virgin. Apart from that, it might be quite a crowd-puller if it made the front page of the *Chronicle*.

Honey came back down to earth, applying herself to the job in hand. Doherty was also applying himself. One big puff and he had a fully blown-up purple balloon.

'So what do you think is happening between Lindsey and the professor?' he asked as he knotted its end.

'How do you know he's a professor?'

He shrugged. 'Stands to reason. He looks like every film or television's fictional ideal of a professor I've ever seen.'

Thinking about it, she had to agree that Steve was right. Jake Truebody was indeed stereotypical of every professor she'd ever seen in movies. She should have noticed herself.

'Now you mention it, he does look what he is. On top of that, he doesn't look like the type that Carl usually associated with.'

'Too academic?'

'Could be. Carl mixed with movers and shakers and people out to have fun. I'm not saying the professor is a party pooper, but he doesn't strike me as a party animal either. And I keep asking myself, why did he come here?'

Doherty heaved a big sigh, wrapped his arm around her and gave her a hug.

'Some people are not born sensitive. He probably thought that Carl Driver's wife would be happy to see someone who'd known him; chew over old times and all that.'

'Strange.'

'What is?'

'That I feel so jealous of him. He's got Lindsey's attention and I can't figure out why.'

'Has Lindsey ever been rebellious? Run away? Got blind drunk, taken drugs?'

'No. Nothing like that.'

'Then perhaps she's making up for lost time.'

Honey took a deep breath. 'No good dwelling on it. There's work to be done.'

He nodded. 'Right. I'll blow up more balloons.'

Honey was only half listening. 'I could make mileage out of this for next year's bookings. I know the actual murder didn't happen here, but there is a connection. And people love murders — the whodunnit kind, like Agatha Christie.'

She ran the idea past Doherty.

'Would you think it a little mercenary if I use this murder in my marketing campaign for next year?'

'It didn't happen at the Green River.'

'No, but the employees are suspects, right? People love stuff like that.'

'Ghoulish, but you're right. People do love stuff like that. Now if you could arrange a murder . . .'

'Blood everywhere? No. I'll pass on that one. Getting the carpets cleaned costs an arm and a leg. So have you got any leads?'

He shook his head. 'None that are leading anywhere special. I'd like to talk to the employees again, though in a more relaxed environment. This ghost story session on Christmas Day could be just what I'm looking for — mingle and mix; get close up and unguarded. I shall look forward to it.'

'Not so much as Mary Jane.'

'Mary Jane doesn't count.'

'I don't think she'd like to hear you say that.'

'Mary Jane has one foot in the real world and one in the hereafter.'

'True.'

'Do you believe in ghosts?'

Honey sucked in her bottom lip while taking a moment to answer. She recalled one particular incident when it had been pouring with rain in a particularly historic alleyway in the centre of Bath.

While bending down to tie her shoelace someone wearing shoes with shiny buckles had passed by, yet when she'd looked up — there was no one there.

'I keep an open mind. How about you?'

'Irrelevant. You've got a full house for ghostly storytelling, so obviously a lot of people do believe in ghosts.'

Honey nodded. 'You're right there. Ghost stories are popular. My mother's coming too.'

'Great. She can get in some practice.'

She gave him a look. 'You're being facetious. Better still, you're not crying off.'

He shook his head and took on his policeman face.

'Personal feelings don't count. In this instance I'll be forbearing. This is police work and I'm taking advantage of a useful situation. The Scrimshaw crowd have all given statements but I figure they'll be more relaxed in a party environment.'

'And by that you mean you hope they're a little drunk.'

'That too.'

Honey puffed just once on a balloon, then paused. 'My visit to the hairdresser turned out lucky.'

Misunderstanding, he looked at her hair. 'They did a good job. Beats wearing a paper bag over your head.'

'That wasn't what I meant. They had a good view of the Scrimshaw building. It may be that Ariadne, who I presume is the owner, was warning the girl off as a matter of course; she was a bit paranoid.'

'It could be something, it could be nothing, and we did question them. According to Sergeant Catchpole, the officer I sent over, nobody seemed to have noticed anything.'

'Tallulah mentioned something about a big piece of jewellery someone was wearing that was still visible even through the mist. She didn't say they looked suspicious. She just noticed.'

The balloon expanded as Honey gave it another big puff.

Two figures walking close together, laughing pleasantly, passed on the other side of the dining room doors. Lindsey and Professor Jake Truebody. Honey felt her face muscles harden.

Doherty saw her looking. 'Stop grinding your teeth.'

'I wasn't.'

'I heard you.'

'Jeesh!'

She felt Doherty's eyes on her, scrutinising, evaluating the thoughts in her head purely by reading her body language. Doherty was good at body language. Good with bodies full stop, in Honey's opinion.

He tilted his head, his hair flopping forward, giving him that boyish look, the one that sometimes filled her dreams when she hadn't seen him for a while.

CHAPTER NINETEEN

Four days before Christmas. The idea of using the murder to boost next year's marketing campaign had stuck in her mind. She was still considering the prospect when attending the auction rooms and was to blame for her failing to win a very nice pair of 1920s camiknickers.

On her way home she called in on Casper.

Le Reine Rouge was an elegant hotel with an exquisite interior. When it came to presentation, Casper and his friends certainly knew how to fling things together — though the posse of beautiful boys who worked for him as waiters and greeters *never* flung; they chose, they prevaricated, they had eclectic stripes running down their backs.

Casper's great passion was clocks. Not for him the odd grandfather clock shoved in a corner, clanging the quarters with a resonant twang. Casper's clocks were of such pedigree that some of them should really have been holed up in a bank vault or a museum. One of them, a great white porcelain thing, of putti, naiads, and bunches of grapes, and nineteenth century, had been exhibited at the Great Exhibition in Paris.

Her feet sank into the thick Turkish rugs scattered around Reception as she made her was to Casper's office.

First off he wanted to know everything about the murder case.

'And this red nose thing. I disapprove. I think you should get involved.'

She didn't like to tell him that she'd already got herself involved and that it had been a case of mistaken identity on two different counts. She'd mistaken a plumber for the vandal and a ballcock for a red nose. On reflection, there was a third case of mistaken identity; the plumber had presumed her loaf of bread to be a baseball bat.

She promised him that she'd do what she could.

She had not mentioned running murder mystery weekends on the back of her connection to the case.

But I could, she thought to herself as she walked back to her own hotel. I could give talks on what it's like being Bath's Crime Liaison Officer. Even once she was back behind her reception desk, visions popped into her head like multicoloured bubbles.

Her mother phoned and burst the bubbles — all of them.

'I've got a confession to make,' Gloria said, without preamble. 'When Fred set this website up for me, he asked me for the details of someone to use as a guinea pig, so I put your details online.'

Honey groaned. The last thing she wanted was to be offered like an auction item on a dating website — correction, a dating website for the over-sixties. She pointed this out to her mother.

'When did you do this?'

'About two months ago.'

'I'm too young for your website. It's for the *over-sixties*.' A website called *Snow on the Roof* could hardly be anything else, thought Honey.

Her protest was ignored. Her mother was nothing if not persistent.

'You ought to check it out. I've pulled no punches. I know you'll be pleased when you see it. I've used a few photos of you that I already had.'

Honey rolled her eyes and mouthed, *Give me strength!*

'Mother, I've already told you that I've got a man in my life. I don't need another.'

Her mother wasn't really listening. 'Things are really going well and your details did attract interest. I've put them in the pending folder for now until you get chance to have a look. They seem keen; well-heeled too.'

Honey was mortified. 'I feel like a set of crockery on eBay: "a bit chipped, but useable".'

Her comment was totally ignored. 'I've got a counter on it that measures the hits I receive. Fred set it up that way. He's very good. He learned all about computers at U3A.'

U3A was University for the Third Age. The over-sixties were well-catered for in Bath.

Honey scrunched up her features and squared her shoulders. She felt ready for a fight. All to no avail of course. Her mother was blind as well as deaf when it suited her.

'Take a look at the site. I'm sure you'll change our mind,' she was saying.

'I will when I can. I'm a little busy right now. We've got a full complement for lunch tomorrow and the kitchen is in need of help.'

'And there's still lots to do for Christmas Day,' Honey added.

At the mention of Christmas Day, her mother changed the subject.

'I've got a great dress for Christmas Day. It's silver. I look svelte in it and I have to stay that way. We don't give our last performance until the fifth of January, so I can't eat much. I have to be able to get into my costume. I can't possibly disappoint my fans. Now just remember not to be late for tonight's performance.'

Being beautifully turned-out was very important to Gloria Cross. Honey would be wearing a little black dress on Christmas Day. It clung in all the right places and happily avoided the wrong ones. A simple set of large pearls would set it off. It was all she'd have time for.

Honey promised she would not be late for the opening night of *Cinderella*. Her mother was starring in the title role. OK, she was a tad old for the part, but so were the rest of the cast. Bath Senior Citizens' Drama Society made up for lack of youth with oodles of enthusiasm.

She would be at the panto and Doherty was going with her — though he didn't know it yet.

In the meantime, she made the decision to keep her finger on the pulse of this murder and not just because of her plans. Being murdered once was gruesome; getting murdered three times over was downright unusual. She mentioned the fact to Mary Jane, at the same time swearing her to great secrecy.

'I've heard of something like that before,' said Mary Jane. 'The ancient Britons used to do it. They did it to Pete Marsh.'

Honey frowned. 'Never heard of him. When did that murder happen?'

'Round about the time when Queen Boudicca went on the rampage.'

Honey didn't ask why the man had been called Pete Marsh. She had enough on her mind, though she was open to any theory, however outlandish.

The ultimate in best laid plans entered her head; what if she was the one to solve this crime? She could see the headline now. *Hotelier Nabs Scrimshaw Slayer.* What a boost to earnings that would be!

* * *

John Rees phoned to ask if she'd like to pop in for a pre-Christmas drink. 'I have sherry. I know you Brits like sherry.'

She said she'd be right round, but she didn't tell him that she didn't like it. Sherry was very sweet, but so, for that matter, was John.

Cobblers Court was not far from John's bookshop. She decided to call into the bookshop first, then wind her way to Cobblers Court.

Huddling deep into her coat, she ventured out into a wintry evening. The mist was coming down again like a piece of damp muslin. The air was getting colder, the moon was coming up, and a heavy frost was promised.

The shop windows were still blazing with light, prettiest when those windows were bow fronted. Narrowing her eyes, she imagined that the shoppers peering into window displays were wearing crinolines and poke bonnets. The task proved a bit difficult seeing as even the prettiest young women were dressed in black leggings, heavy boots and padded jackets.

She sighed. Oh well. That was progress for you.

Cobblers Court was a different matter. Was it her imagination, or was it darker and mistier here?

Two policemen were standing to either side of the door to Mallory and Scrimshaw. There was a fair chance that they'd be standing guard duty all over the holiday, stamping their feet to keep the blood circulating.

'Merry Christmas,' somebody shouted.

As if on cue, a light flurry of snowflakes fluttered like confetti from the narrow strip of sky between the buildings.

A figure hovered at the bottom of the stairs leading up to Bee in the Bonnet, bearing two steaming cups of tea. The policemen needed no encouragement, stomping over to cup their hands around the hot mugs.

The odd pedestrian wandered past, but the initial interest in the murder had waned. Last-minute shopping had a lot to answer for, as did the signs going up for the January sales.

Just as she was debating whether to sneak into the Mallory and Scrimshaw building, she became aware that she was not alone.

Another figure was standing at the entrance to the alley leading into Cobblers Court. Tall and broad shouldered, she thought at first that he was watching her. On further observation, she realised he was watching the policemen, standing quite still and pensive, as though chewing through his thoughts.

Then Lindsey joined him. The man was Professor Jake Truebody.

The urge to rush out and warn her daughter that this man wasn't right for her was very strong. But she couldn't do that. On the other hand she didn't want to be here and be accused of being the interfering mother. For goodness' sake, she knew how it felt to have one of those.

She saw Lindsey was holding her camera. Judging by her actions and the little she could see and hear, her daughter was trying to take Jake's picture. The professor wasn't having it. She saw him mouth no; heard him protest, his refusal louder now.

This time Lindsey seemed to accept that he was unwilling to be photographed. Her daughter looked disappointed. Truebody was unruffled. He looked confident, triumphant.

Preferring to remain unseen, she drifted away down the short alley that sprouted off the main one. Narrower than the main alley, it ran between the buildings and felt as though it were being squashed even smaller by their presence. She'd get to John's bookshop that way — a little longer but needs must.

CHAPTER TWENTY

Lindsey had done her best to take a photograph, but Jake would not allow it.

He was looking up at a battalion of starlings sitting high above on a stone parapet.

'It's very Dickensian,' he said loudly. His voice echoed around the old stonework that surrounded them. It was like being inside a very large box with very high sides.

The starlings on the ledges rustled their wings and shifted at the noise. A few dropped baggage. He saw it coming and stepped smartly aside.

Lindsey Driver was perusing the guidebook. 'It dates from much earlier than the reign of Queen Victoria. Years ago it was an Inn of Court.'

'Hell, you don't say. What does that mean?'

Not totally surprised by his ignorance, she looked at him, her expression blank. Her mind was not blank.

'A place where lawyers had their offices.'

He was standing there with his hands in his pockets gazing upwards, still apparently studying the starlings.

'Is that so?' He smiled when he looked at her. 'You're a smart kid.'

She frowned. 'I'm not a kid.'

'No insult was intended. You have a youthful countenance. Don't knock it. Even in old age you'll still look young. How good is that?' His tone, along with his smile, could charm the pants off an aged grandmother. Lindsey suspected doing the same to her was very much part of the plan, but Jake Truebody was out of luck. He'd met his match but just didn't know it yet.

She threw him a forced smile. 'Thank you.'

Entering and searching his room hadn't been as successful as she would have liked. The real man beneath the name — she was pretty certain it wasn't his real name — was locked in the laptop he carried in his bag. She was sure of it.

Basically, he could tell her pretty much what he liked about Carl Driver. She wouldn't know if it was true. She hadn't known her father for that long or that well. Most of the details she had were second-hand, passed down by those who had known him — mostly her mother.

And he'd turned up at Christmas. Why Christmas? Why here? Why had he homed in on them? And why had she been so accommodating, offering to give him a guided tour.

The fact was that he'd turned up just before the news about her mother and Steve Doherty. OK, there was an element of pique here. She'd gone out of her way to accommodate his request for a tourist guide, firstly because of his connection with her father, then because her mother had not told her about her and Doherty. Not that she really minded — not deep down. It was just that she felt a need to prove herself, to make them see that she was not a child.

They descended the steps at the side of Pulteney Bridge and strolled along the towpath. The night was drawing in, but people were still out and about, some the worse for drink, others overburdened with shopping.

Jake sighed and looked up at the stars. 'Look at all those stars. Tonight reminds me of a Christmas in my childhood. I was seven. It was just me and my mom.'

'And your father?'

'They'd parted. I'm not sure how old I was when he left, but according to my mother I was about five.'

'Did you ever see him again?'

'No. He died. Some kind of accident. Right on Christmas. Pretty dreadful, huh?'

She agreed with him that it was pretty dreadful.

'So you lived in Maine?'

'Sometimes.'

'Not all the time?'

'Depended on work and relatives around to take care of me. Not that my mother left me alone a lot.'

'She cared for you.'

'Very much so.'

'How did you manage for money?'

He shrugged, attempting nonchalance. 'We managed.'

Up until this moment, she'd prodded without seeing any adverse reaction. Now she sensed he was clamming up. The last thing she wanted was for him to be suspicious. There was so much still to find out.

Hopefully he wouldn't guess what she was up to. She couldn't afford to lose his trust — not if she wanted to uncover his secret.

'So you're a professor of history,' she said, changing the subject. 'What's your speciality?'

'American History, of course! Especially Native American. I just love that whole period from the landing of the English at Plymouth Rock to the defeat of Custer at the Battle of the Little Bighorn.'

'Is that so?'

'It is indeed.'

He went on a bit about Jamestown and the Native American princess, Pocahontas.

'How far is Gravesend?' he asked suddenly. 'Is it close by?'

She explained that Gravesend was on the eastern side of the country close to the mouth of the River Thames.

'I expect you're wondering why I'm asking.'

'Yes.' Actually, she knew very well why he was asking, but he went on to explain anyway.

'Pocahontas. That's where she was buried when she came to this country with her husband, John Smith. She died of smallpox. I personally think that her body should be returned to her people.'

Lindsey hid her twitching lips in the comfort of her high collar. She was almost laughing. She knew the history and he'd got it wrong; Pocahontas, or Rebecca as she came to be known, had married John Rolfe, not John Smith. The latter was the man she'd rescued; the former the man she'd married.

In fact there had been excavations around the church where Rebecca Rolfe — Pocahontas — was said to have been buried. No trace of her was ever found.

She didn't voice the real facts to him. It occurred to her that now might be the right time to tell her mother of her misgivings, but something was holding her back. Perhaps curiosity was passed through the genes; her mother had a mind for sleuthing. Perhaps she did too.

They circled back up and walked again through Cobblers Court. Everything was quiet now.

'This place is pretty old,' she said. 'A murder happened here the other day.'

'Is that so?' he replied. 'Well, it's damned cold here, I'll give you that.'

Jake Truebody was presently feeling the benefit of a long grey coat, a thick grey scarf, and a black hat with a broad brim. The latter was not exactly a Stetson. The curved crown and broad brim was more Deep South preacher than Midwest cowpoke. The scarf was held in place with a shiny pin shaped like a leaping buffalo. When she'd admired it he told her it had been a gift form a Native American.

'Shall we move on?' His voice sounded as though it was growling from the back of his throat.

'Why not? Though I must inform you that most museums are closed at this time of year, so I'm afraid we're here for purely the architecture. And fighting our way through the last-minute shoppers.'

'I'm descended from a long line of pioneer types. I'm sure I can handle a bunch of intrepid shoppers, old thing.'

I was a young thing five minutes ago, Lindsey thought to herself, though she smiled and made things seem perfectly normal.

'So what's the smile for?' asked Jake Truebody.

Lindsey latched on to a reasonable excuse.

'It's the time of year. Everyone's happy at this time of year, aren't they?'

'Some of us are,' he said, 'but there are always ghosts of Christmases past. Bittersweet memories some of them.'

* * *

Christmas greetings rang around the tiny bookshop. The shop frontage was only about ten feet wide, but inside it sprawled like a narrow and very deep cave. One section of books followed another, the width of shop diminishing with each section traversed.

John Rees kissed her cheek and pressed a schooner of sherry into her hand.

'Harvey's Bristol Cream,' he said, nodding at the blue glass he had handed her. 'Only the best.'

'So I see. The glasses too. Very nice.'

'Bristol Blue. I bought them from a shop in Bristol.'

He handed her a vol-au-vent topped with green cheese and a solitary prawn. 'So how goes life?'

'Fine.'

'How's your policeman? Are you still going strong?'

She knew he'd ask. At one stage John Rees had been a definite contender for her affections. Sadly for him, Doherty had got there first.

'Yes. We are.'

'Shame.'

His expression dropped in mock sadness. Perhaps because of the shape of his beard and his head, he resembled a mask from a Greek tragedy.

Yes, there was a time in the not-so-distant past when John Rees had been in with a chance. The warm-voiced American was tall and lean, and his dress sense wasn't far removed from that of Detective Chief Inspector Steve Doherty. A denim shirt of one colour worn with denim jeans of a different shade. The look was confidently masculine, casually thrown together to be comfortable rather than to impress.

'I heard about the murder,' he said. 'Poor old Clarence Scrimshaw.'

'You knew him?'

'Sure I did. He came in here now and again, though quite frankly he was way out of my league. Big collector. Big money.'

Honey was instantly confused — and just a little curious. She stopped thinking of what John might have been like in bed and skipped to a question.

'You mean he actually spent money on something? His staff and everyone else who brushed his way portrayed him as the skinflint to end all skinflints. Scrooge with a capital "S".'

John sipped at his drink then wiped his top lip with finger and thumb before continuing.

'He collected Bibles.'

'I'm listening.'

'Very old Bibles.'

'Should I twin old with valuable here?'

'You bet you should!'

'Ball-park figure?'

He shrugged. 'Anything from ten thousand pounds to well over a hundred thousand. It all depends on the rarity. Tyndale's 1537 Bible fetches a good price, though there are rumours of older and rarer. Take Wycliffe. It's said that his manuscript Bibles were enough to get a contemporary, John Hus, burned at the stake. It was him that forecast the coming of Martin Luther. Now if you could find one of those Bibles, the sky's the limit . . .'

'Do you know anything else about him?'

'A little. I know where he lives. I even know a few of his authors.'

She finished her glass of sherry. 'How about I return the hospitality and you come around after lunch on Christmas Day? A drink or two? A mince pie or some butter-rich Scottish shortbread?'

'I'm a pushover for shortbread, but I'm afraid I'll have to pass. I have a date.'

'Shame.'

He used his thumb to gently wipe a crumb from the corner of her mouth.

'But if Starsky ever dumps you, remember where there's a shoulder to cry on.'

She smiled. 'It's a deal.'

On her way back to the hotel, she phoned Doherty.

'Guess what? I know what was in that parcel.'

CHAPTER TWENTY-ONE

Doherty had acted on the information she'd given him. His men had done a thorough search of Scrimshaw's flat but nothing resembling the parcel had been found, certainly not a Bible.

Doherty had put it to her that a collector would keep something that valuable under lock and key. Honey admitted that he was probably right. But where would that be?

So here she was, sitting in Reception and licking her wounds, or at least the end of her ballpoint pen. Honey was making quite a meal of it when she remembered she had something better to put into her mouth. Chocolates. Foil-wrapped marzipan, bought on a whim to celebrate the time of year when diets flew right out of the window — at least until New Year.

Anyway, she reasoned, eating chocolate was traditional at this time of year and her lumpy bits didn't matter until she attempted to squeeze into a bikini sometime in May.

Once the chocolate was in her mouth, she set to with the list again. Her nose had to be to the grindstone if she were to solve this murder.

The list was a start, though she was having trouble getting her head around it. Under the word motive she'd written, 'money, sex, jealousy, blackmail, theft, unrequited or requited love, outright hate'. Under the word 'suspects', she'd written the name of every person employed by Mallory and Scrimshaw, plus the names of authors published by the company. Lindsey had gone online to get her their names.

Despite wracking her brain, the list on the left side of the paper hadn't grown much. The list on the right side was huge; it seemed the world and his wife could have killed Clarence Scrimshaw.

And now there was a Bible to consider.

Her mother popped in for coffee, her mind whirling with ideas for her dating site venture. Honey's ear was bending under the weight of it all. An idea popped into her mother's head, and she just had to run it past someone — usually Honey.

'I thought I could give a discount for the over-eighties — seeing as they need to hook up with a partner PDQ.'

She caught Honey's dropped jaw and went on to explain.

'For the over-eighties, time is of the essence in affairs of the heart.'

Nobody could argue with that.

'For their hearts, period,' remarked Honey. 'Are you providing defibrillators?'

Her mother sucked in her breath. 'I shall treat that comment with the contempt it deserves. My new business is going to be run on very professional lines. For instance, I've got it in mind to arrange dinner parties for my clients. Equal numbers of male and female members will be invited. No more than ten people, I think; any more than that and it's no longer an intimate dinner party. I've arranged one for the day after Boxing Day. Care to come?'

Honey declined the invitation and fended off the impending pressure with a ready-made excuse.

'There'll be a lot of clearing up to do, plus arrangements to be made for New Year.'

'You've got staff to do that.'

'I'm the boss. I have to be here. Anyway, I don't need to look for a man. I've got Doherty.'

Her mother pursed her lips and looked visibly disapproving. 'So, you've landed a catch. But is he the right catch? Who knows how many other fish are out there waiting to be landed?'

'Yeah, yeah. I'll throw in my line for a salmon and end up with a stink fish,' Honey muttered.

'There's no such thing as a stink fish. And anyway, I think you could be making a big mistake. You don't have to marry Doherty.'

'Yes, I do.'

'You do?'

If Smudger hadn't come barging in, hammering on about the Dover sole starter for Christmas dinner, she might have taken more notice of her mother's expression. As it was, Smudger's contentment was far more important than discussing her mother's dating website for the over-sixties.

* * *

Mary Jane found Honey's mother sitting in the residents' lounge, looking stunned.

She touched her shoulder. 'Gloria. Is something wrong?'

Honey's mother's mouth hung open when she looked up at her.

'I don't know that I should tell you.'

Measuring the gravity of the occasion by the look on Gloria's face, Mary Jane sat down beside her and took her hand.

'Now come on, Gloria. I'm your friend. You can tell me.'

Gloria thought about it. She came to a decision. 'You mustn't breathe a word,' she hissed, leaning close to Mary Jane's ear. 'I think I'm going to become a grandmother again.'

'Aw, right,' said Mary Jane, not quite getting it. 'Your other child is becoming a parent?'

'Other child?' Gloria Cross drew in her chin until the wrinkles sagged around her neck, — something she usually avoided like the plague. 'Mary Jane, I haven't got any other child!'

Mary Jane's eyes widened as the truth hit her. 'You mean . . . Honey? Are you sure?'

Gloria nodded. 'I've counted how many chocolates she's been eating. It's a lot. Too many to be normal.'

CHAPTER TWENTY-TWO

Honey was perusing the list of party bookings detailing deposits paid and final sums once the booze and food had been added in. The sum total of Christmas parties was building up nicely — and there was still Christmas Day to come.

The archaic method of record keeping was something she insisted on, despite Lindsey's assurances that the computer was totally dependable.

Lindsey was scathing about it. 'Handwriting is a great skill, but technologically you're still in the Stone Age when it comes to keeping bona fide records.'

Honey had stood her ground. 'Yeah, yeah.'

No matter how much Lindsey assured her that the computer would not digest the details, pass it on to third parties, or jumble it up into an incoherent mess, Honey backed the computer records up with a written record. OK, she admitted to being old-fashioned, perhaps even a bit lazy. Also, why learn the ropes when Lindsey and the computer were bosom buddies? Not that she'd voiced that particular kernel of truth.

Paper records could be referred to any time, any place, and were crumb-resistant. The computer was less so, bits of stray debris getting trapped between the keys.

She ran her finger down the list of dates, companies, and payment details. She paused when she came to Clarence Scrimshaw. At first sight there didn't seem to be a problem, but the man was dead, and before he'd died he'd been acting out of character. It wouldn't hurt to do a rerun, so she checked the records again, at the same time reaching for another chocolate.

The booking had been made only days before the poor man had been murdered. At face value, there was nothing wrong with that; no discrepancies there. Mr Scrimshaw getting himself murdered before enjoying the party was pretty bad luck, but life goes on, and he'd obliged her by paying his bill before shuffling off his mortal coil.

Running her finger across the company name and the total cost she came to the payment details. He'd given her the correct debit card details. No problems. The bank hadn't stopped the payment for any reason, and money had been swiftly transferred from his account to that of the Green River Hotel.

'Good old Clarence Scrimshaw,' she said to herself. 'He may have been a skinflint, but he paid up on time.'

'You what, dear?'

She looked up to see that Mary Jane had paused on her way to wherever she was going.

Honey relaxed against the back rest of her chair, hands folded on top of her head. The right-hand drawer of the reception desk was open. She spotted another box of rum truffles.

'This guy who got murdered was rumoured to be a skinflint, yet he paid his bill up front. Now if he was that much of a skinflint, surely he wouldn't have done that. Would he?'

'Just because he was careful, didn't mean that he wasn't honourable,' Mary Jane stated.

'And to die like that at Christmas. What would his relatives say? That is, if he had any relatives. None have been found so far, but that doesn't mean he hasn't got any. If he did then they would no doubt remember him at the same time every year and shed a tear — that's if his passing brought tears to their eyes. If they considered him an old skinflint they probably wouldn't care. Probably raise a glass in a toast and thank him for leaving them his money.'

'The way of the world,' Mary Jane said sagely, and headed for the residents' lounge.

Honey stopped chomping the last sliver of truffle. She licked a few stray bits from the corner of her mouth. Call it woman's instinct but she couldn't help thinking that somebody had thought to benefit from his death. But who and what would they inherit? That, she decided, was the million-dollar question.

Two rum truffles had been devoured. She considered eating a third but resisted.

She told herself that if she focused on the subject matter, she wouldn't feel the need to eat chocolate — or anything.

She set the last chocolate to one side and vowed not to have lunch.

By lunchtime, her stomach was rumbling in protest, but her head won the battle. Never mind what her stomach wanted; the murder of Clarence Scrimshaw was a very serious business.

Her attention was drawn back to the details she had scribbled down. The debit card was in the name of Clarence Scrimshaw and was issued against his bank account. All the details checked out. It was only to be expected. Clarence Scrimshaw wasn't short of money apparently, but he was extremely careful with his spending. So there was one big question in need of answering: why had he suddenly splashed out?

She jotted down several reasons. First among them was that he was dying from a terminal disease. Second that he'd had a visit from the Angel Gabriel advising him to stop being such a miserable old sod. Thirdly . . .

Honey didn't get chance to write the third possibility down.

A delectable smell that cost plenty per ounce made her look up. Her mother was smothered in winter white — or was it off white? — like whipped Jersey cream. The outfit was Aran, no doubt hand-knitted by some elderly islander with gnarled fingers and poor eyesight.

'Hannah! Wipe your mouth.'

'Just a rum truffle,' said Honey opting for the singular and trying not to look guilty.

Her mother eyed her accusingly. 'More than one, knowing you. Still. Under the circumstances . . . Now listen,' she continued before Honey had chance to question her meaning. 'These flyers about my dating website are for you to place in Reception. I'm sure there are plenty of people looking for love.'

'They're not staying here.'

'How do you know that?'

'Because . . .'

Honey couldn't think of a single reason why she should be so sure about that.

'Precisely. Take Mary Jane for a start. There she is, single at her age, and talking to ghosts. A man would do her the world of good, don't you think?'

Honey shook her head. 'No. I think Mary Jane prefers ghosts.'

'Give me one good reason why she would prefer a ghost to a red-blooded man.'

'No socks to wash.'

Her mother tutted. 'Here are the flyers.' She plonked them down on the desk. 'I need a few more men to include on my "Men Available Page". Who do you have working here that might be interested?'

'Nobody over forty-five.'

For one mad moment, Honey imagined getting Smudger dragged into this. It didn't bear thinking about.

'How about Dumpy Doris?' she suggested.

A nervous tic began to pulse beneath Gloria 's left eye. Dumpy Doris was built like a champion wrestler.

Honey guessed her mother was seeking something tactful to say.

'She's not . . . photogenic.'

'As good an excuse as any.'

'You could become a partner in my business. At least it would take the weight off your feet. Think what you'd be buying.'

'What would I be buying?'

'A future. Now this is the score . . .'

Gloria took the grey suede folder she was carrying from beneath her arm. 'As I've already told you, this all started back in the summer. A few of us got together and talked about men. Then Fred showed me how to operate a computer. I thought I should look into it more deeply so I enrolled into night classes. But Fred is far better at it than I am. Fred is top totty when it comes to computers.'

Honey wondered if Fred was also top totty in other departments, or whether her mother had compromised. After all, eligible men of seventy-plus were thin on the ground — largely because they were mostly dead.

Her mother leaned across the reception desk, her voice dropping to a whisper.

'Now listen, owning a hotel means being on your feet all day. With this business, you wouldn't be doing that.'

'No, I'd be sitting on my rear and it would get wider by the day.'

'But you have to consider the future, Hannah. A woman of your age . . .'

'My age!'

Honey flopped back so heavily in her swivel chair that it over-swivelled, and she fell backwards and was wedged against the wall.

Her mother rushed round and began fussing over her. Honey stared at her, this was most unlike Gloria.

'Oh, my word, Hannah. You really do have to take care of yourself. It's not like when you were expecting Lindsey, you know.'

Honey felt a whole series of emotions wash in, out and over her . . . What was going on here?

'You don't have to marry Doherty, you know,' her mother said soothingly.

'I know I don't. I don't have to do anything.'

Her mother looked at her aghast. 'It may be old-fashioned but think of the shame!'

Honey frowned. 'Beg your pardon?'

'The baby,' said her mother, pointing at Honey's stomach.

'Baby! What baby?'

Gloria Cross now looked affronted. 'You mean . . . I'm not going to be a grandmother again?'

'No. Of course not!' Honey almost laughed. 'Whatever gave you that idea?'

Her mother patted her chest as though she'd been about to faint.

'My, my. Thank goodness for that. I had it in mind that we should get a well-heeled father to adopt the unborn, but seeing as there isn't any . . .'

'Of course there's not!'

'Oh well. Never mind. I'll go and speak to my granddaughter, see what makes the younger generation tick. Maybe I can apply some of her modern wisdom to my blog — once I find out what a blog is. Is she around?'

'No. She's out with the professor.'

'A new beau?'

'Hardly.' She said it through gritted teeth.

'Good. Professors don't rate too highly on the salary scale, and their dress sense is terrible.'

Honey covered her eyes with her hand. Her mother's point of view was predictable. In Gloria Cross's estimation, men should be well-blessed with both cash and taste if they wanted to attract a woman. Charm made the list too. But even a Mafia godfather could be charming and have a great taste in clothes . . .

'Mother, I'm a little busy . . .'

'Did I say I wanted your help this very minute? We can talk again when you're looking more presentable and don't have smears of chocolate around your mouth. You've been eating a lot of chocolate of late. Are you sure you're not expecting?'

'One hundred per cent.'

'Then that's it. There's no need to exclude you from my website. In my opinion, you're not spoken for, and who knows what nice man might be out there for you.'

Honey turned away so that her mother wouldn't see her roll her eyes. There had to be a better time for this. There were portions of pudding to control, wine glasses to be inspected and the final presents to be wrapped. Roll on New Year.

A neon light flashed on in Honey's brain. That was it.

'How about we leave it for a week or so? New Year, new beginning! We'll all be feeling in the mood for making a new start. That should pep a little energy into your scheme.'

Honey's tone was enthusiastic, though quite honestly she didn't feel that way. She was putting off the dreadful moment and entertaining a faint hope. With a bit of luck her mother might find a more willing guinea pig between now and New Year. It was worth a try.

Judging from the flickering of her mother's eyebrows — she avoided frowning in order to ward off wrinkles — she was giving the suggestion due consideration.

'Well . . . I guess there's some mileage in that. And I have put some stuff online already. I just need to pad it out, I think.'

There were times when miracles happened and surely the best time for them happening was Christmas. A miracle happened now. Mary Jane had finished drinking her hot chocolate in the residents' lounge. Honey was pleased to see her crumpled, aged face, which vaguely resembled a ten-month-old crab apple. Her eyes were bright. A froth of chocolate clung to the peach fuzz on her upper lip.

'Just checking that everything's ready for my ghost story session,' she said to Honey, then turned to Honey's mother. 'Hi, Gloria.'

Honey confirmed that everything was ready. 'You've got a full house.'

Mary Jane clapped her hands. 'Great.'

'I wonder,' said Honey following the flowering of an idea. 'Do you still do readings — you know — astrology and tarot?'

Mary Jane's face turned serious. 'Free of charge to you, Honey. You're good to me. I'll be good to you.'

'My mother could do with it for her new business venture. Is it possible that you could advise her on an auspicious date for getting things going?'

Luck, miracles, and Michael and all his angels must have been on Honey's side. The deal was done. Gloria and Mary Jane went off together, chattering excitedly, one outlining her scheme and the other assuring her that the heavens knew best.

CHAPTER TWENTY-THREE

Doherty popped in around lunchtime. She'd arranged for the two of them to have lunch in the coach house.

'Just leftovers,' she said.

'You, or the food?'

'Ha bloody ha!'

They went into a clinch the moment they'd closed the door on Honey's private accommodation.

'Can't stop long,' she said to him. 'I'm wanted by a sack of Brussels sprouts.'

He backed her against the kitchen units and did what he could to make the lunch break worthwhile. For a moment the sprouts took a back seat. Once they had a breather and broke for lunch, she told him about checking method of payment for the Mallory and Scrimshaw office jamboree.

Between mouthfuls of smoked salmon, she said, 'If he was that tight with his cash, why not get his employees to pay for it themselves, like a lot of firms do?'

Doherty frowned. 'I agree with you. Seems out of character.'

Honey took a bite of her sandwich. The salmon was left over from the last party but was still tasty. The bread was fresh and baked with nuts and crushed olives.

'It occurred to me that someone else might have used his bank card. Was it with his personal effects?'

Doherty got out his phone and punched in a shortcut. 'Casey. Refresh my memory as to the contents of Scrimshaw's wallet.'

The response was fast. Doherty looked over at Honey as he repeated what had been said.

'He used a leather purse. It was empty except for a library card and membership of the Automobile Association. He didn't have a wallet.'

'And no debit card? There had to be one. He paid me with it.'

Doherty asked the question of Sergeant Casey, the man in charge of recording that kind of thing. 'I see. So all he had on him was a bank debit card. Where was it found?' He nodded as he took in the details, his eyes still fixed on Honey who was silently munching on. 'In his coat pocket. Outside pocket or inner pocket?'

Honey waited.

'I see.' He nodded in response to what was being said on the other end of the phone. 'Thanks, Casey. How's the hip?'

Charlie Casey was an aging sergeant who had been dragged back from retirement to keep the records in order. He was a dab hand with both computers and paperwork. Nothing dared slip out of place under his watch.

'Keep going, buddy,' Doherty said before severing the connection. 'Coat pocket. Outside.'

He took a bite of his lunch and chewed slowly. Honey regarded him thoughtfully, knowing for sure that the bread and leftover smoked salmon didn't deserve the amount of scrutiny he was currently giving them. Doherty was chewing over more than salmon. He'd made a judgement and was taking his time sharing it. Patience was far from being her greatest virtue. Her fingers started to tap dance along the table.

'So. Where do you keep your bank cards?' she asked him.

'I have a wallet.'

'And if you didn't?'

'Inside breast pocket. Safe place.'

Their eyes met. 'Clarence Scrimshaw was careful with money. He'd also be careful with his bank card,' Honey remarked.

There was no need to say anything else. Clearly, Clarence Scrimshaw had not booked or paid for the meal of his own volition. Someone else had done it.

'So they stole it, paid for the hotel, then returned the card to his pocket.'

'That's about the size of it,' Doherty agreed. 'So was the card returned to his pocket while he was still alive or once he was dead?'

Honey scrutinised what was left of her lunch with one eye closed. It helped the thought process.

'Someone had to have lifted it. The phrase "over my dead body" springs to mind before Clarence Scrimshaw would willingly hand over his bank card.'

They knew the reservation had been made before the murder, but by whom? It could just as easily be an employee as anyone else, though making the reservation would have definitely been to the murderer's advantage. In the absence of evidence to the contrary, he — they presumed it was a male — would have wanted everyone out of the way. No point in having an audience around to witness the deed.

CHAPTER TWENTY-FOUR

She'd told Doherty that John Rees had mentioned Scrimshaw being a collector of old Bibles. None had been found at the office.

Before night fell and the snow got heavier, Honey made her way back to Cobblers Court for the last time. Her hair was back to its normal self and for that she felt she owed a debt of gratitude to the staff at Bee in the Bonnet. At this time of year chocolates would say it all.

Armed with two boxes of Thorntons' seasonal selection, she headed up the creaking staircase.

The air in the salon was thick with the scent of conditioner and the heat droning in waves from the hi-speed hairdryers. Bee in the Bonnet was living up to its name; it was a hive of activity. Every stylist's chair was taken; busy hands were skilfully weaving the dryer in one hand, a circular brush in another.

Honey paused for a moment, admiring the deft way they handled their tools. It all looked so easy. She'd bought a circular hairbrush herself, thinking she could ape their actions. Ape was the right word. Her dexterity was no match for the flick of their wrists, the synchronisation between twirling brush and buzzing dryer.

The pink faces that jerked in her direction said it all. *No more work. We're all worked out!*

'I just came to thank you,' she said boldly and loudly. 'My hair is great. Happy Christmas to you all.'

First she gave a box of chocolates to Ariadne, the salon owner of steely countenance and rattling hairdo. Ariadne's initial surprise was swiftly replaced with abrupt efficiency. She had a brush in one hand, a dryer in the other. 'Put them on there, will you?'

Ungrateful bitch, thought Honey, but in view of the hectic time of year, she decided to believe it was all a front.

The dangling multicoloured beads of Ariadne's shoulder-length hair clattered like clogs over cobbles as she nodded towards a place next to a pile of hair style magazines.

'Thanks. Can't stop. Too busy.'

She carried on blow-drying her customer's hair.

The friendly junior, Tallulah, was checking a head full of hair dye wrappers in her spot by the window. The dark circles beneath her eyes were a dead giveaway that she hadn't slept well. What with Christmas parties, a busy salon, and the bullying from Ariadne, it was a wonder she was still on her feet. Her eyes, bright blue in their pools of purple eyeshadow, brightened when she saw the box of chocolates.

'Oh, Mrs Driver!'

It was a pleasant surprise that Tallulah actually remembered her name; nice to think she might have made an impression.

'Thanks for giving me my hair back, Tallulah.' She handed her the box of chocolates.

Tallulah grinned with delight. 'It was no bother. Anyway, it wasn't just down to me,' she said shyly, though judging by the colour of her face she relished the praise. 'Look. I have to give you a Christmas card,' she added, laying down her brush and her pot of colour.

'You really don't need to. I was just grateful you sorted me out.'

'It's no bother. I have to sign it first. Just wait a minute until I can find a pen.'

While she waited for Tallulah, her attention flipped to the office windows across the way.

The windows were casement and set in stone mullions. Their panes were pitch black, though that was no big surprise. The place was empty. The staff had been banned from entry until the police said they could re-enter. Time of year dictated that wouldn't be until the first few days of January. The employees had no problem with that. They were still being paid, though how secure their jobs were now the boss was dead and gone was anybody's guess. Someone was bound to take it over. There had to be an heir — somewhere.

The light from the old gas lamp hanging on the wall flickered on the lower corners of the panes. The light was constant, never leaving that position — at least, that was the way it seemed at first. Then, suddenly, the light moved, but not outside — not the old gas lamp. Someone *inside* the building opposite was using a torch.

Narrowing her eyes, Honey made a snap judgement. If either Scrimshaw or Mallory had come back as ghosts, they wouldn't be using a torch. Someone was in there. Someone who shouldn't be in there. Anyone legit would have turned on a light.

Tallulah thrust a card into her hand. 'Here you are, Mrs Driver, and a Merry Christmas and Happy New Year to you.'

Honey smiled, distracted. 'Same to you.'

'And thanks for the chocolates.'

Honey's heart was hammering and her feet were twitching. She took a step back, then another, desperate to discover who the hell was mooching around over the way. She was sure the police had vacated the premises. Someone else was in there.

'Thanks for the card. And a happy New Year to you, Tallulah. To all of you.'

Most of the staff returned the greeting, Ariadne in her usual offhand manner. Honey wondered what Ariadne's regular clients thought about her. She was hardly top of the tree when it came to interpersonal skills. What a woman would do for a good hair cut!

The night was closing in. A few footprints blemished the light smattering of snow. One set led into the porch of Mallory and Scrimshaw.

The police officers supposed to be guarding the door were nowhere to be seen. The scene-of-crime tape was unbroken. Honey ducked underneath it.

The door to the building was deep set within a stone porch graced by a pair of Doric columns. The columns were a later addition to the building. Someone in the Georgian era had tried to bring the old place up to date. Still, she counselled, it could have been worse. The Victorians would have simply knocked it down.

Just as she'd expected, the door was unlocked. Familiarity with police procedure told her that they would not have left it that way. It was possible that the policemen had come inside out of the cold. It did cross her mind that the torch might have belonged to one of them.

If Honey's curiosity hadn't been so all-consuming, she would have reported the possible intruder to Manvers Street police station. She hesitated in the darkness of the porch in front of the main door. Common sense told her not to venture in. Did she want to get herself killed — by three different methods like poor old Clarence Scrimshaw? But her curiosity was too strong.

The porch door opened into a dark hallway. The light from a wall-mounted alarm system blinked intermittently. Shapes and shadows moved around her, on and off with the blinking of the light; one moment everything was well-defined, and the next minute gone.

Suddenly the light seemed to flicker even more. Perhaps something was reacting to her presence; that was before she realised that she was blinking in time with the blasted thing. If only she'd brought a torch.

Whoever had divided the fine old rooms into offices had done it some time ago. Nowadays they would never have got listed building consent. Glass-panelled doors interspersed with heavy mahogany doors Scrimshaw, it seemed, had changed nothing if he could help it.

Honey mused on the skinflints she'd known in her time. Thinking of something else helped keep the heebie-jeebies at bay. There was Rigby, that grotty man who used to own a five-storey Georgian building down in Green Park. How he'd ever afforded the place was a riddle in itself. Though on second thoughts, the fact that he wore the same clothes year-in-year-out and drove a vehicle that could easily earn the title 'Rustbucket of the Year' might have had something to do with it. He'd never spent money on anything, and that included the building he owned. Like a lot of multi-storeyed properties of historical importance, the spacious rooms had been divided up into bedsits, the bottom of the barrel in the letting market. Apartments had a movie-star connotations; flats were perfectly acceptable, but bedsits? Bedsits were small rooms with a bed, a chair, and a kitchen in the corner, and a tiny, shared bathroom at the end of a corridor.

In Rigsby's case (they'd named him after Leonard Rossiter's dodgy landlord in *Rising Damp*), the hot water heater over the sink had been positively medieval, and the gas fire downright dangerous. The décor could best have been described as *severely* decrepit.

Skinflints! She'd known a few. There'd been a bed and breakfast owner who . . .

The sound of creaking floorboards from upstairs brought Honey round to the job in hand. She had decisions to make. Firstly: should she flee or fight? The latter was definitely a last resort. She could run far better than she could fight, though she didn't do either particularly well.

Assumptions came thick and fast. There was a maniac shuffling around upstairs. Thinking of the intruder as a maniac caused a sensation similar to cramp in her feet. The cramp was crimping her toes, making her feet seem as if they would make for the exit by their own volition.

Alternately, the intruder might be someone with a right to be there, but scared of upsetting the police. There were various innocent possibilities. Someone could have left their lunchbox behind, and wasn't keen on leaving limp lettuce to slither into sliminess over the Christmas period. Slime and mould wreaked havoc on lunchboxes.

Dim as it was, Honey glimpsed a flight of stairs to her left. Like a lighthouse it signalled her. The meaning was clear; someone was padding around upstairs, so upstairs was where she had to go.

Feeling a fluttering in her chest, she took a deep breath, then reached out and folded her fingers over the newel post.

She found herself imagining how many hands had worn it smooth. Lots. Hundreds. Thousands. And it was warm. It might take only one hand to make it feel warm. The intruder . . . ?

Her imagination went into overdrive. Blood was warm. Her common sense kicked in at that one. Blood was wet. With her heart in her mouth she took off her glove and fingered the wood. Much to her relief the newel post was dry; no blood there.

She let out a big sigh, counted to ten, and drew in her breath. 'Here goes.' She placed one foot on the bottom stair.

It creaked, or at least it seemed to. No, she decided. It wasn't her. The sound was too muffled. Too distant.

Honey's gaze fixed on the top of the stairs; not that she could see that far. The darkness up there was complete. But that sound? It couldn't have been her foot. It had to be whoever was upstairs.

The footsteps continued.

It wasn't easy to determine but a sneaking suspicion crept into her mind. The suspicion was probably caused by her applying Murphy's Law to her circumstances. The law was: that if the worst is going to happen, then it'll happen to Honey Driver! The footsteps were coming along the landing and towards the stairs.

She slunk back, meaning to flatten herself against the wood panelling and hide herself in the darkness, when old Murphy struck again. There was one spot in that smooth wood that wasn't so smooth. A splinter of wood embedded itself in her hand.

'Ouch!'

She couldn't help it.

'Hello! Is anyone there?'

The voice came from the top of the stairs — a woman's voice.

Excepting Lizzie Borden and her axe, no infamous female maniacs sprang immediately to Honey's mind, so she advanced into the light of the woman's flashlight. Mercifully, there was no axe to be seen.

'I didn't think anyone was here,' she called.

'Right back at you. Who are you?' The woman's tone was aggressive. It reminded her of Ariadne.

Honey glanced over her shoulder, wondering if perhaps the rude hairstylist from across the road had followed her in.

'No one's supposed to be in here. I saw your flashlight from across the road and came over to investigate.'

'You sound like the police. Are you police?'

'Not exactly, but I work with them from time to time and . . .'

'Then you have no business being here.'

The flashlight was bright and shining into Honey's face. In an effort to diffuse its strength, she raised her hand to eyebrow level. She found herself level with a pair of thrusting bosoms.

'I could say the same about you.'

The woman had frizzled red hair and prominent teeth, and jangled when she moved. The jangling was due to the trio of chains hanging around her neck. The chains all differed in design. The one thing all three had in common was that the links of each were the size of saucers. The appendages hanging from them appeared to be blobs of turquoise, set in what might or might not be gold.

'I have every right to be here. I'm Patricia Pontefract. I'm an author. Published by Mallory and Scrimshaw, who, you should be aware, own this building.'

'A novelist? What do you write, romance perhaps?'

Patricia Pontefract huffed and puffed, swelling in size. 'Certainly not! I write about historical artefacts. I doubt the likes of you would know anything about the subject.'

It was Honey's turn to puff up and be counted. 'I think I would surprise you,' she declared, straightening up enough to avoid the exceptionally bosomy view. This mainly depended on her standing on tiptoe.

Her boast was not entirely without foundation. Her daughter Lindsey knew lots about history. If this woman was at all famous, Lindsey would know all about her.

'Never mind what you write,' she continued. 'What are you doing in here? Didn't you see the police tape?'

'I did, but I've come a long way. I've just returned from a book signing in Maine.'

'So why sneak in and creep around in the dark? This place is old but it does have electricity.'

'Sarcasm is the lowest form of wit.'

'And flashlights are the stock in trade of criminals.'

'A fuse must have blown. Hence that thing.'

'That thing' was obviously the emergency light. It was still flashing.

'What were you doing here?'

'None of your business.'

Her abruptness again brought Ariadne to mind. It helped harden Honey's resolve.

'Tell you what, I'll phone the police and get somebody round here. You can answer to them.'

She adopted the sort of look TV cops take on when they mean business. Her phone beeped as she opened it. It sounded kind of threatening. It wasn't really. The reason it did that was because it needed recharging. With all the work she just hadn't had the time. Still, Patricia Pontefract wasn't to know that.

The bluff worked.

'Alright. I'll tell you. I wanted to see Clarence. He owed me. He always owed me.'

'He's dead.'

'I know that *now*. Samantha phoned me. I hadn't received a copy of my contract. It was signed only two weeks ago. I need it. It appears I may need to relocate to a new publisher.'

'And did you find it?'

'No. Perhaps I'll come back in the daytime. This place is gloomy at the best of times.'

As they spoke they'd slowly moved towards the front door and the semi-gloom outside.

'Clarence was a skinflint when all was said and done.'

'So why did you stay with him?'

The older woman looked at her askance. 'Loyalty! We go back a long way.'

'So how do you feel about him being dead?'

Patricia Pontefract inhaled deeply and, in the process, seemed to grow ever taller. Was there any limit to this woman's bodily inflations?

'Everyone dies.'

Honey flinched at the sound of her voice and the darkness in her eyes. 'But everyone is not murdered.'

That superior sniff again; 'Go on. Ask me if I had a motive.'

'OK. Did you have a motive for killing him?'

'The urge to kill him has crossed my mind on many occasions over the years. And before you ask, I'll give you my reasons I would want to snuff him out. My advances could have been far better, and his calculations of royalties owed to me were often amiss. Mallory was no better. Birds of a feather flock together, and in this case they were both feathered with meanness. At least one of them had the good grace to die before his time. Old Scrimshaw outstayed his welcome.'

'So did you kill him?'

'As I said, the thought might have crossed my mind on many occasions, yeah, but as I also said, I wasn't here to do the deed. Hence my skulking around now, to get what's mine.'

'I didn't say you were skulking.'

'Only by implication.'

'Can you prove where you were on the night of his death?'

'Do I need to?' she shot back.

Getting questions in response to questions was becoming tedious. It occurred to Honey that if this woman had anything to do with the murder, she wouldn't be here now hunting for her old contract. She would have lifted it at the time, having first plied Clarence Scrimshaw with a glass of sherry laced with an arsenic chaser. That would certainly have rendered him quiet while she searched.

Following up a poisoning with a stabbing and a garrotting took some explaining. There had to be a reason. The only one Honey could think of was the possibility that, having found nothing, Ms Pontefract might have got a bit miffed. Blinded with rage, she could have taken it out on the dead man's body. It was far-fetched, but it was the best she could come up with for now.

'The police will want to know where you're staying while you're in Bath.'

Patricia Pontefract turned off her flashlight. The old Victorian gas lamp gave them enough light to see by.

'I was staying with my niece. One night was enough. She's very bad-tempered.'

Honey felt a great leap of satisfaction. She'd guessed right. 'She doesn't by any chance run that place across the road, does she?'

The light from the old gas lamp illuminated the older woman's expression. There was surprise but also suspicion.

'Ariadne. She's a very busy person. I don't want you going over there asking questions.'

The woman's attitude rankled. Honey shook her head dismissively. 'It's not your call, sister.'

The frown deepened. 'Meaning?

'The police might want to ask you questions. Your niece Ariadne might be the only one able to give you an alibi. She'll probably have to answer questions too.'

The woman's eyes narrowed. Honey shivered. Being pierced with those eyes made her feel like a butterfly pinned to a green baize background.

'I have nothing to hide.'

'Right,' said Honey, returning her phone to her pocket with great aplomb. 'So I presume you're staying with your niece over the holiday?'

'Presume all you like. I'm actually staying at the Green River Hotel.'

Honey felt her jaw slacken and head south. 'Any particular reason why you're staying there?'

'What's it to you?'

'I know the hotel.'

'So?'

'I was just wondering what attracted you to the Green River Hotel.'

Honey stood there feeling a flood of apprehension wash over her. She felt like a hungry dog waiting for a morsel of praise. All she wanted to hear was that someone had recommended her establishment. Praise made her feel warm all over.

'Nothing in particular. It's pretty ordinary but it's hosting an event, a reading of published and unpublished ghost stories. I wrote one of those being read. I believe the person holding the event is a clairvoyant. I'm interested to meet her, I'm into the supernatural. Who knows,' she added, her teeth intruding on her smile, 'old Clarence might get conjured up. Should that happen, I could ask him the whereabouts of my contract.'

CHAPTER TWENTY-FIVE

The twenty-third of December. At the Green River Hotel, doors and windows were tightly closed against the chill air of winter and all was cosy within. The smell of mulled wine, rich fruit pudding and the zingy zest of mandarin oranges scented the air.

Honey surveyed the shiny decorations, the balls on the tree, the fairy lights blinking on and off in random order. Now was the season to be jolly, keeping warm and eating and drinking too much. It made her feel like snuggling up in a chair, which she did with a glass of mulled wine, some roasted chestnuts, and a cheese and pickle sandwich. The sandwich was not exactly festive fare, but the cheese and pickle took the edge off too much sweetness.

In the hotel kitchen Smudger the chef was using both hands to push forcemeat into the orifice of a very large turkey. Following the skilful execution of that little duty, he absorbed himself in slapping half a pound of butter onto the turkey breast, rubbing it in with firm, swirling strokes.

His head still adorned with his tinsel halo, Clint was watching him.

'Some people like that done to them,' he said thoughtfully. 'Especially women.'

'What being stuffed with forcemeat?' said Smudger without missing a stroke.

'No. Being rubbed down with something oily.'

Smudger stopped and fixed Clint with a querulous lifting of one blond eyebrow. 'Are you 'aving me on?'

'Course not. Apparently it's good for the skin. Makes it supple. Makes it soft.'

Smudger went back to what he was doing. 'In the case of this turkey it makes the skin crisp and brown — and succulent.'

Clint grinned. 'Does the same to the girls I know — makes them succulent, I mean.'

Clint had only lately finished with a girl of Italian ancestry with dubious connections to the Mafia — not least her husband, who had developed murderous designs on Clint. The break had come from her side. On reaching twenty-four years of age, she had considered her opinion of Clint, and of her husband, and found both lacking, so she'd taken up with another supposed Mafioso. This might very well have had something to do with the fact that Clint had no ambition. Ambition to his ex-girlfriend meant being in full-time, well-paid employment, for a start. Clint had never been keen on that particular scenario. He regarded himself as a free spirit. 'If the Earth Mother had meant me to work in an office environment, she would have fitted me out with a pin-striped suit,' he'd said to anyone who asked why he was one of the long-term unemployed.

'I suppose one bird is as good as another,' said Smudger. 'By the way, I've already got your present sorted. That leg there,' he said, slapping one of the turkey's meaty legs. 'You can take it home with you after dinner tomorrow. OK? I take it you are staying for a bit of roast and plum pudding?'

'Of course I am. Just 'cos I'm a worshipper of the Earth Mother don't mean to say I don't have respect for the festivals of other religions.'

'Bollocks,' muttered Smudger. His grin was like a laser beam across his face.

Like everyone else, Smudger knew that Clint freeloaded whenever he could — another reason for the break-up of his relationship. Sponging off other people was a way of life with him. Winter was Clint's favourite time to work and he had a distinct preference for cash in hand jobs. He didn't do National Insurance contributions and the Inland Revenue didn't know he existed.

Questions had been asked about his love life, but if he did have a new lady in his life, he was giving nothing away. All anyone knew was that he was living alone until the spring came, when he'd be off to converse with nature — and the nudists, only returning to the Green River when he was stony broke. Washing dishes didn't amount to much in the way of readies, but the few pounds Clint earned were enough for his needs.

'What is this Earth Mother thing you keep mentioning?' asked Smudger.

Clint looked up from scrubbing the fat off a filter from the extractor fan.

'The old religion. Worship of goddesses in the form of the Earth Mother, came before the worship of a God, or the other gods. She was the protector of the earth and of horses.'

'Just horses?'

Clint frowned. 'Well, all animals really. But horses were her favourite — apparently.'

He didn't look too sure.

Not being particularly interested in any religion, Smudger took advantage of the moment. 'So how's your love life?'

Clint paused for just a nanosecond and then grinned. 'Mind yer own bleedin' business.'

Smudger laughed. 'Sod you too, mate, and Merry Christmas and all. Hey. I was thinking, wouldn't it be a cracker if Anna had her kid tomorrow on Christmas Day? That would make it almost holy — don't you think?'

'Yeah. Very holy,' said Clint, but the brightness was gone from his face.

And Smudger knew. He just knew.

CHAPTER TWENTY-SIX

In Reception Lindsey was having second thoughts about Jake Truebody. Should she tell her mother what she'd found out, or should she keep it to herself — at least for the time being? She was enjoying being an amateur detective and, so far, she didn't think she'd done a bad job, though she still hadn't managed to catch him on camera.

Truebody was not who he said he was, of that she was pretty damned sure. So far his historical knowledge hadn't been that impressive. She kept reminding herself that his particular interest was American History, but it didn't wash. She'd expected him to know more about Bath. In her estimation he should also have known a bit more about the Romans.

She mused on this as she crumpled up a brown paper bag that smelled of chocolate truffles, proof if any was needed that her mother was keeping the diet at bay until 1 January. Not until they were on the threshold of a brand-new year would the diet restart, perhaps to be focused on a special event . . . like a wedding.

* * *

Upstairs, Jake Truebody was heading for his room. A tall, angular figure was approaching from the other direction and he recognised the woman with the wild hair and red velvet reindeer antlers as a guest and a fellow American.

The look of her, the way she dressed, the behaviour he'd witnessed in the dining room, when she appeared to go into a trance before attacking her full English breakfast: all of those things made him feel embarrassed that she was American. No upstanding US citizen should be seen wearing reindeer antlers and red velvet lounging pyjamas trimmed with faux white fur. She looked quite ridiculous, vaguely resembling a gangly Santa Claus without the beard.

He kept his head down. So far he'd avoided her invitation for a congenial chat over a cup of chocolate and digestive biscuits. He wasn't here to be sociable. He had a job to do and so kept up his pace, only giving her a nod as he passed by.

After securing the door to his room, he took off his hat, coat, and scarf, throwing them into a heap on the bed.

He took out his phone and called a Bath number.

The call was swiftly answered.

'You were right. I needed to be here. We're in this together.'

The voice on the other end warned him not to get too fond of the girl.

'Of course not,' he said, and laughed. 'She's sweet, but just a means to an end. You can count on me. You should know that.'

He frowned.

'If she gets too close, she has to go. I know that. And I'm not afraid to do it. I'm a chip off the old block. Right?'

The person on the other end of the phone loved him for saying that. He could tell. However, it didn't stop more warnings and plans coming down the line.

'My cover on this job is total. I'm an old family friend, remember? I'm tolerated if not exactly accepted, but we have to be careful. Things haven't gone exactly as planned, but we'll win. I promise you that we'll win through. I'll allow nothing, absolutely nothing, to stand in my way. OK?'

Once it was done Jake severed the connection and made his way to the bathroom. He rolled his shoulders against the stiffness he was feeling. The English mists had chilled him to the bone. A hot bath was in order. After that he would make his way to the bar, have a drink, then eat in the dining room. Later on, Lindsey was going to take him to a pantomime. He wasn't really sure what to expect, though Lindsey had assured him it was wall-to-wall fun.

'It's being given by the Senior Citizens' Club. My grandmother has a starring role.'

What harm could it do? A load of oldies dressed up in fairy-tale costumes. They were hardly a threat. Too old to do anything but act like children, and certainly no threat to someone like him.

After that . . . well . . . what happened next depended on what opportunities came along. No matter what name he was going under and what job he was on, he was always open to opportunities.

CHAPTER TWENTY-SEVEN

Doherty looked surprised when Honey grabbed his arm and guided him to the lift. She'd thought about this carefully. Lindsey was being distant and she didn't like it. Appearing more caring about her sensitivities might help the situation.

'You can stay in the honeymoon suite tonight and possibly over Christmas. You can chill out in there. It's got a spa bath and a four-poster.' She sounded all bright and cheerful when she said it, but he wasn't fooled.

The lift was already there, the doors opened and in they stepped.

She avoided his eyes and he shook his head. 'Why do I get the impression that I'm getting this room all to myself?'

She shrugged. 'I just thought that you'd like to chill out and concentrate on the case . . .'

'Bollocks!'

'There's no need for that language. This is a respectable establishment.'

Doherty threw his overnight bag onto the bed while Honey pretended to check the radiator.

'Come here.'

She looked at him, chewed her bottom lip, and gave in.

He cupped her chin. 'Now. Look me in the eyes and tell me you're sharing this room with me throughout Christmas.'

She felt her resolve, and a few other things, give way when she looked up into his eyes. If temptation had legs, then Doherty was it.

'Lindsey's in a funny mood.'

'So the coach house and, in particular, your bed, are off limits.'

'Just until . . .'

'She's being childish. Is that it?'

Partly, it was. But there was also the Jake Truebody thing.

'She's being rebellious. She's never been like that before. I never expected her to react like this. And then on top of that, Professor Truebody turned up. She's acting as though she's on the rebound — as if it's me, her own mother, who's let her down.' Her eyes fluttered nervously. 'I'm worried she might do something stupid, so I'm staying close and playing safe. OK?'

Doherty began removing his clothes as they talked.

'You're telling me that you think she may have fallen for an older man just because he knew her father. Have you asked her outright about this?'

She squirmed. 'Well . . . no . . .'

'Then why don't you?' He saw her expression. 'OK. You're scared.'

She frowned. 'I can't help it. He's also a professor of history. Lindsey is turned on big time by history like some people are turned on by . . . chocolate, cream cakes . . .'

'Sod the history. I'll take the sex,' said Doherty. But she could tell he wasn't best pleased. He'd been looking forward to spending some time with her — both in and out of bed.

He discarded more clothes as he headed for the shower. By the time he'd crossed the room, he was naked. He stopped there, struck a pose, and smiled.

'Care to join me?'

'I've already showered.'

'Suit yourself.'

Lame excuse, and so obviously defensive. 'Later, perhaps. Christmas present.'

'Suits me,' he called, his voice accompanied by the sudden sound of running water. 'So what's on the agenda this evening? A swinging party? Drunken orgy with Santa Claus?'

Honey bit her lip and folded her arms. This was the difficult bit. He wasn't going to like this but perhaps if she played the family card, the same one her own mother had played earlier . . .

'It's a family gathering. We're going to a pantomime. After that we can all relax and join in the fun.'

She could have added that it was being put on by the Senior Citizens' Club and that her mother, Gloria Cross, had a leading role. But she didn't. That, she decided, would be a surprise.

Go on. He has to be told.

She blurted the truth. 'It's being performed by the Senior Citizens' Club and my mother is playing Cinderella.'

'What was that you said?' he called from beneath the tumbling warm water.

Doherty not hearing her brave declaration was a bad thing. Her courage went. She'd saved it all up and now she was going to chicken out.

Tell him. Go on. Tell him.

Gathering all her courage, she opened her mouth, the words ready to come out — though not very willing.

'We're going to a show.'

What a chicken!

'Great! That's great,' he shouted back.

Honey puffed air then addressed her cowardly image in the big mirror above the fireplace.

'Honey Driver, you are going to regret that lie.' She studied her reflection, winked, and clicked her tongue. 'But at least your hair's improved no end.'

CHAPTER TWENTY-EIGHT

Honey felt guilty about dancing around the truth but told herself she'd make up for it. Sitting through a pantomime where Cinderella was in her seventies and Prince Charming was wearing a truss beneath his tights would certainly be an experience.

Doherty and her mother didn't get on. Once he knew where they were going, he would groan, and even contemplate rushing to Manvers Street where he could lock himself in a cell.

Seeing her mother cavorting around the stage as the traditionally youthful Cinderella would probably send him into fits of laughter. He wouldn't be able to keep a straight face and her mother would be livid afterwards. Gloria Cross didn't think of herself as old. She didn't act it. She didn't really look it and if she could afford things bearing a designer label, she would go on forever.

You're overreacting. Stay calm. He'll be OK about it.

There was no guarantee that he would, but thinking the thought helped seemed to make things OK.

Wearing a black dress beneath a grey wool coat, and wine-coloured boots on her feet, Honey reckoned she looked good and could do just about anything. But convincing

Doherty that it made sense for him to sleep in the honeymoon suite fell a bit flat.

'But I'll be patient and understanding,' he'd said to her after he'd showered, and she'd helped him rub him dry, and applied his body oil, and they'd had the sort of time where one thing consequentially led to another.

Things will work out.

The night air promised a widespread frost, with ice on the pavements and white roofs by morning. Venturing out in the comfort of a low-slung sports car was preferable to walking. The pantomime was being held in a de-consecrated church across the road from Waitrose and not far from the central post office.

'You smell good,' he said as she slid into the front seat.

'French perfume. I figured you might want to smell that I was here even though you can't really see much of me bundled up against the cold.'

'So I notice. Getting through all those clothes to your bare flesh would be like going on safari. It would take some time but I'm sure I would get there in the end.'

He was keeping quiet about the honeymoon suite. She took it that he'd accepted the situation.

* * *

David Longborough opened the door of his apartment in Newbridge on the western side of the city.

'About time.'

He sloped off into the living room, leaving Sam Brown to close the door and follow him in.

When they'd first met, she'd been attracted by his offhand manner, thinking that it represented him being hard on the outside and soft on the inside. Even now she made excuses for his rudeness, telling herself that clever people were often rude because everyone else wasn't up to speed. David himself had told her that.

'Because I'm clever, I can bend the system. And I get away with it. Wear confidence like you would a coat,

Samantha, and you'll always come out on top. Everyone will believe anything you say.'

She was one of those who really had believed whatever he'd told her. Only recently had she harboured some misgivings about his nature — mostly regarding his feelings for her.

He poured himself a Jack Daniels, turned, and slugged it back in one.

'So what did they ask you?' he said.

'The police, you mean?'

'Who the bloody hell do you think I mean? Of course I mean the bloody police! What did they ask you?'

As she had been Clarence Scrimshaw's secretary, with access to his movements, contacts, and daily diary, Sam was one of the employees who'd been summoned for an interview at the station.

'Just general things, David. About Mr Scrimshaw's habits. I told them what you said for me to say. I told them he liked a bit of nookie, pinching my bum and that kind of thing, when nobody was around. Not that he did, of course,' she added quickly, suddenly worried that he might believe the lies and be jealous. Not that he should. The lies had been concocted between them, though mostly by him. But David was funny like that.

Suddenly he gripped her shoulders. 'You'd better have done it right, girl. You'd better not have opened your mouth and said the wrong thing.'

'I didn't. Ouch! Don't do that.'

His fingers were digging into her shoulders. His breath was thick with Jack Daniels.

'Just you make sure you keep to that story. He got fresh with you after you came back from an errand. That's the story you're to stick to. Right?'

'I told them that. I told them he'd always fancied his chances. That day I'd just come back from the dry cleaners . . .'

'You stupid bitch!'

The slap was hard, jolting her head. She heard her neck crack. She cupped her aching cheek, already turning red from the force of the blow that had sent her sprawling onto the sofa.

'There was no need to do that.' She turned scared eyes on him. He'd never hit her before. He'd threatened to, but never had.

His expression was as hard as stone.

'There was no need to mention where you'd been. All you had to say was that you'd been on an errand.'

'Sorry.' She hung her head, tears stinging her eyes.

'You coming to bed now?' he said brightly. David Longborough could change his mood instantly. It was as though nothing had happened, certainly not clouting her hard enough to take her head off her shoulders.

If she was sensible, she would get out now. She used to be sensible, but that was before David Longborough had come along. Doing what David wanted had become a habit, one that she was having trouble breaking. The cracks were appearing, but for now she would go along with what he wanted — at least, until she didn't love him anymore.

CHAPTER TWENTY-NINE

Doherty was looking slightly dazed having arrived late for the date — one that he hadn't particularly wanted to keep so had dawdled at the police station. 'A pantomime!' He sounded exasperated.

'Half a pantomime. We've missed at least half of it.'

'That's something at least.'

'Oh come on. They're fun. Don't deny that you enjoyed them when you were a kid.'

'That was different. Your mother wasn't playing Cinderella.'

St Michael's Church had a rounded front with handsome pillars. The walls to left and right of this ran perpendicular to Walcot Parade and Broad Street.

Crowds of people seemed to be milling around at the front of the building, the lights were still on, making the stained-glass windows shine in the darkness.

Honey glanced at her watch. 'I'm sure she said that they wouldn't be finishing until ten thirty.'

'You mean we've missed all of it?'

Honey snarled and gave him snake eyes. 'Stop sounding so pleased about it.'

He was craning his neck, seeing something over the crowd and the roofs of cars that she couldn't see. At six foot one he could do that.

'This pantomime — was it likely to cause a riot or offend public decency?' He sounded half curious, half amused.

Honey tried standing on tiptoe but couldn't see much at all. What was he talking about?

'Of course not. Cinderella only lost a glass slipper, not her underwear!'

'Well, they're not here to catch the show.'

He nodded to a police car — all warning stripes, blue light currently unlit.

Two policemen were heading for their car, carrying between them what appeared to be a yellow and purple spotted parcel.

Doherty waited until they'd stuffed the bundle into the back seat as best they could. He knew the two uniforms as Humpty and Dumpty. KFC was their lunch of choice. Both were a bit overweight and in danger of being ordered on a Police Federation fitness course.

Honey saw what had been stuffed into the back of their car. 'What's with the horse? Are the mounted police short of horses at the present time?'

'Hey, guys!'

The two uniforms acknowledged his presence.

'What's going on?' he asked them.

One of the policemen, the one Doherty called Humpty, pushed his hat onto the back of his head and wiped his brow with a man-size tissue before he answered. Meanwhile, his colleague, Dumpty, who was bent double complaining about his back, declared his intention to go back in and make an arrest.

'Not until I get some details,' said Doherty.

'Well,' said Humpty, still mopping his brow. 'It appears that this horse was stolen from the back of the Theatre Royal. The actors playing the front end and rear end of this horse were both smokers so they went outside to have a puff. No problem with that, they were merely obeying the smoking laws. They were still half-clothed — in their outfit,' he said, nodding and looking Doherty straight in the eye in an effort to make him understand. 'As a horse.'

'A pantomime horse.'

'Correct, sir. They were still wearing the lower half of their costume — the legs that is, but had taken off the upper part, the head etc., which they were carrying between them under their arms.'

'Get on with it.'

'Anyway,' he said, his red face steadily abating. 'They then decided that they wanted to use the lavatory and they couldn't go there dressed in their respective lower halves of the costume, which would of course get in the way. So, accordingly, they disrobed, leaving the two bottom halves of the horse outside, plus the upper half which forms the body, head, and tail of the horse. Unfortunately, when they got back, it was gone.'

Her ears tuned to the conversation, Honey kept her eyes fixed on what was happening outside the church. What she saw next confirmed that peace at Christmastide wasn't likely to be on the menu at the Green River.

The policeman who'd gone in with handcuffs at the ready, was now heading their way and was not alone. He had a tight hold on her mother's arm and she wasn't going quietly.

'This is police brutality!' she was shouting. 'You are contravening my human rights and I shall sue you for millions!'

Her mother had obviously been interrupted before the clock struck twelve because she was still wearing what passed for glass slippers (a cool pair of glittery Manolo Blahniks) and a sumptuous tulle dress that looked like something Norman Hartnell might have designed for the Queen back in the mid-fifties.

Honey let out a heartfelt sigh, backing it up with a good slice of indignation. 'My mother did not steal that horse!'

'She's right,' shouted her mother. 'I did not!'

The policeman was unimpressed. 'Put that in the statement.'

Some policemen had the wrong attitude, but they had a hard job to do. Honey didn't begrudge them their off days. However, although there were times when she could happily cover her mother in concrete, this wasn't one of them. Besides, she felt responsible for this happening. The horse had been requisitioned from her premises. She shoved her face up close to the red-faced copper.

'There is no way I am allowing you to arrest my mother. Your own common sense should tell you that she couldn't have stolen it. It's heavy. You know that and look at her. She's an old lady, too weak to carry two bags of Chinese takeaway, let alone a thing like that.'

'I resent that comment!'

Trust her mother not to swallow that one. Comments about her age were never well received.

Dumpty rolled his eyes. 'That's all I need. An eccentric old lady stealing pantomime pieces.'

'How dare you!' He grimaced as the toe of a top of the range designer shoe met his shin.

'That does it! I'm arresting you . . .'

Reaching too swiftly and too sharply for the pair of handcuffs fixed to his belt, proved a bad move; his back kicked in again.

'Jee-sus . . .' he groaned. He looked as though he might kick a cat if there happened to be a conveniently placed moggy handy.

'Look, lady, I'm having difficult times of late and I've no time for hard luck stories from tottery old ladies . . .'

'Tottery! Listen, sonny, I can walk in these shoes. You certainly couldn't!'

Everyone looked at the high-heeled shiny shoes. Honey shook her head. 'You've got to give my mother credit,' she said to the policeman. 'She copes with those shoes. Anyone else would be tottery wearing those shoes. I would be tottery.

But stealing a pantomime horse while wearing them? No way!'

The policeman about to put her mother in cuffs looked less sure about how to proceed.

'I don't suppose it would look good for the police, especially at this time of year.'

Honey looked to Doherty to intervene, but he was having none of it. He was leaning back, elbow resting on the car roof, probably to stop himself collapsing with laughter.

Humpty, the policeman with the tissue, brought a couple of grey cells into play. 'Well I have to agree with you there. We could barely lift it between us. Anyone old wouldn't be able to manage it.'

He yelped as her mother clocked him around the head with the fairy godmother's wand which somehow she'd ended up with.

'I'm not that decrepit!'

'Madam, I must warn you . . .'

This was getting out of hand. Honey addressed Doherty. 'Well? Are you going to say something?'

Doherty straightened and took his hand away from his mouth. Just as she'd figured, he was on the verge of laughing.

'Look, Adge,' he said, addressing the big man with the sweating forehead by his real name. 'You'll feel like a right fool when word gets round that an old dear got the better of you. You'll be the laughingstock of Manvers Street, besides which, guys, you're speaking to my future mother-in-law.'

'Is that right?' said Dumpty, the one with the bad back and a pained expression. His eyebrows were arched almost to his hairline and he was looking at Honey's mother as though he didn't envy Doherty's predicament.

Honey squeezed her eyes tightly shut. Doherty shook his head. 'I take it your mother's in the dark too?'

'Kind of. She's just ignoring the obvious.'

On reopening her eyes she saw that her mother was wearing a shocked expression and her wand no longer resembled a lethal weapon. It was bent in the middle and the star was dangling from the end.

'Abracadabra,' said Doherty, smiling as he lifted the star with the tip of his finger. 'Look guys. Can we leave this until after the holidays?'

The two constables looked at each other. Doherty knew that one of them was a stickler for never changing his mind about an arrest — even if there was a fair chance that the perpetrator turned out to be innocent. Humpty was famous for sticking to his guns.

Honey was entertaining visions of her mother locked up over the Christmas period, sleeping on a thin mattress, covered only by a plain blanket, not her usual chintzy rose-patterned bedspread trimmed with Nottingham lace. Nor would there be a hint of Chanel No.5 hanging in the air. Instead she'd have to endure the smell of boiled cabbage and sickly-sweet custard.

'We all want to get home, Adge,' Doherty said to the policeman.

'Certainly, Steve, but there was a complaint and we do have to do something.'

'Of course you do.'

'We have to ask how the object in question ended up on this stage and not the one at the Theatre Royal?'

All eyes turned to Gloria for the answer.

Honey decided that this was the right time to offer a defence. 'She saw it at my hotel, and asked if the senior citizens could borrow it . . .'

Both policemen looked at her. 'Is that so?' said Adge.

Doherty rubbed his hand over his eyes. 'Oh, Lord. Here we go.'

Honey was forthright. 'It's just a prop. Get it back to the Theatre Royal and there's no harm done.'

Humpty turned his attention to Honey. 'So *you* were the one who stole it.'

'Oh, come off it,' she yelled. 'Do I look the sort of person in need of a pantomime horse? Do I look as though I can carry it? Get real!'

'You're shouting,' Doherty said to her, placing his hand on her arm and gently pushing her to one side. He promptly placed himself between her and the uniform. 'Hey, Adge. Get into the Christmas spirit. Take the horse back and it's all over. Right?'

It was hard to judge what the policeman was thinking, but his eyes went shifty, sliding from left to right and back again like an observer at a tennis match.

'You know how it is, Steve. A crime has been committed. This woman has admitted that the stolen item was taken to her hotel. She's made a confession. She could go down for this.'

Honey saw Doherty's expression harden. It was a fair bet that he was about to lose his patience.

'This is my fiancée you're threatening.' His voice was oddly cold. 'And it's Christmas.'

Humpty shook his head. His belly shook with it.

'Sorry, sir, but the theatre weren't too pleased about losing their horse. It's a new one and the old one is full of holes caused by moths. That's because it's only used once a year, if then, so they tell me . . . Ouch!'

The policeman, who so easily fitted the role of Humpty, leapt forward. Honey glimpsed the wand heading back from whence it had been. Her mother had used the metal star to jab the copper up the rear.

'Nasty,' said Honey, though she secretly applauded.

Doherty waded in. 'Gloria, you can't go around doing things like that . . . He was only doing his duty.'

The one that had been so fired up to arrest Honey's mother was shaking his head sadly. 'And she's going to be your mother-in-law?'

Doherty took the police officer to one side so Gloria couldn't hear him.

'We all have our crosses to bear,' said Doherty, in a pretty good parody of the long-suffering son-in-law. The policeman immediately latched on to this.

'You've got my sympathy, Steve, though in all truth, she couldn't be worse than mine,' he said, his voice suddenly mournful, his expression as hangdog as a kicked-out bloodhound. 'She got widowed and then said she was lonely and my missus was concerned. So the old bat's moved in with us. That's why I'm working all over Christmas. Anything but listen to her. She nagged her old man to death. Now she's doing the same to me. I swear she is. I only wish she was young enough to get married again, but at her age?'

Gloria Cross was on the job. The fact that she'd been accused of theft was suddenly put on the back burner. She'd caught the whiff of a likely customer.

'Your mother-in-law is widowed?' she said, her eyes wide with interest. 'Well there's a thing. Now just you hang on here and take one of my cards . . .'

She took a card from a safe place next to her bosom and gave it to him. He read the card, his professional no-nonsense expression swiftly turning incredulous.

'Snow on the Roof?'

'It's a dating service for the over-sixties,' Gloria Cross explained. 'You know the old saying, don't you? Just because there's snow on the roof . . .'

He nodded. 'I know. There's still a fire in the grate.'

'Or in the old boiler,' Doherty added. He was just about managing to suppress a grin. Honey kicked him.

The policeman with the mother-in-law problem looked thoughtful. 'Do you think you could really fix the old bat up with a man?'

Gloria Cross nodded emphatically. 'Just get her to register online.'

He nodded and tucked the card into a breast pocket. His mood seemed lighter. His back seemed to straighten and his expression was less pained.

His colleague on the other hand looked resigned. 'So we're not arresting her? Never mind. Better luck tomorrow. We'll nab a few drunk and disorderlies, no doubt.'

His partner looked askance. 'Are you kidding? I need to get my life together. The sooner I go off duty and get my mother-in-law sorted, the better.'

The policeman who had looked resigned now seemed to come over all responsible. 'May I remind you that there has been a theft . . .'

Fearing her mother might still end up in a cell, Honey protested. 'Look, my mother is not a thief and neither am I.'

She threw Doherty a pleading look, but he had his back turned and appeared to be making a phone call.

'I did not steal this horse,' said Honey's mother. 'My daughter did not steal this horse. The truth is that two of her chefs got drunk and came back with it to the hotel. They couldn't remember where they got it either.'

'Is that so?' Sensing closure on this case, the two policemen moved closer. 'They were drunk?'

'Mother . . .' Honey attempted to quieten her. The last thing she wanted was for Smudger and his accomplice to be locked up over Christmas. There was a lot of cooking to be done.

Her mother pushed her away.

'Of course they were drunk. "God Rest Ye *Merry* Gentlemen". You've probably sung the carol yourself. People get merry at Christmas.'

'Not us, madam. We're policemen. We have a job to do.'

During the last events of this debacle, Doherty had been on the phone to the people at the Theatre Royal and explained the situation.

'We're all out of here,' he said. 'Just take the horse back and they won't press charges. They've got a pantomime to perform.' There was no mistaking his tone. He'd given an order. The two officers headed for their car.

'And we,' he said, turning to Honey, 'have a murder to solve.'

CHAPTER THIRTY

Honey was tossing and turning in her bed, pummeling imaginary lumps in her pillow. She twisted until she was wrapped tightly in her duvet, feet sticking out one end.

At last accepting that sleep wouldn't come, she sighed, closed her eyes, opened them again, and made an effort to disentangle herself from the chrysalis covering of feather filled down. The duvet wasn't letting go that easily. She ended up on the floor, spewed out like jam from a huge doughnut.

No matter how hard she tried, the fact that Doherty was asleep in another bed on the other side of the yard denied her the sleep she craved. And she had to have sleep! There was so much to do.

A thought came bouncing into her mind; she could sneak across the yard and into the hotel. By morning she could be back in her own bed and Lindsey would be none the wiser.

Why are you doing this?

The mature voice of reason spoke loud and clear. Up until now, Lindsey had been adult about her mother and her policeman friend. The only thing that had changed was a stranger blabbing about them marrying and the arrival of Professor Jake Truebody.

She pushed the urge to fill the empty half of Doherty's bed into the back of her mind.

Occupy yourself.

Yes. That was the thing to do. The murder of Clarence Scrimshaw was posing quite a puzzle. She stirred the facts around in her mind like the ingredients of an Irish stew.

Write it down.

Yes! That was the right thing to do. Write it down.

Stealthily opening the top drawer in her bedside cabinet revealed a notepad and pen which had ostensibly been placed there to record her dreams. The process had been recommended by Mary Jane as a way of purging the bad spirits of the past that occasionally came to haunt her.

As a matter of fact, Honey found her dreams mostly filled with general day-to-day things, such as guests who didn't pay their bills, though sometimes they were far more imaginative. A Roman legion marching through the dining room featured on one occasion. Her dead husband Carl turning up either in spirit or physical form was the stuff her nightmares were made of — hence her unease regarding Jake Truebody. Too many emotions were being stirred up by his presence.

Naked except for a dab of Chanel behind each ear, she piled three pillows behind her and sat up. Pen and notepad in hand, she was ready for action.

Now what?

Right. List everything she knew about the death of Clarence Scrimshaw. What strikes me most about this man? Honey asked herself.

That name for a start; straight out of Charles Dickens. Scrimshaw. She'd never met anyone with that name. It was archaic and far from common. With the end of the pen resting on her lips, she pondered why that was, and decided that perhaps people with that name had wanted something more jaunty and modern and changed it by deed poll.

But all that was beside the point. The blank sheet in front of her awaited words of enlightenment and words had to be written. The blank page ordered it be so.

First she noted how, when, and where he'd died. After that there came the questions and clues. Number one, why the overkill? Any one of the three methods used was enough to kill him. Someone had to want somebody dead really badly to do it three times. Perhaps it was some kind of joke designed for the police; spot the method that hadn't been used. Poison?

Scrutinising what she'd written did little to help. The methods were there in black and white, yet a 'Eureka!' moment refused to materialise.

She turned her attention to motive. Not so easy. His employees regarded him as too mean to live. Could one of them — all of them? — have decided to put him out of his misery?

It didn't gel. Surely a discontented employee would have committed a murder in anger, done it swiftly there and then, possibly grabbing something heavy to do it with. Honey recalled having seen two brass-stemmed table lamps at the scene of the crime. Anyone killing in the instant heat of anger would have grabbed one of those, given old Clarence a mighty bash over the head, then come to their senses and rode out of Dodge — or Bath in this case — as fast as their legs or a tuned-up engine could carry them.

A disgruntled author was another possibility. Patricia Pontefract was a case in point. But in Honey's opinion, Patricia seemed believable when she said she wasn't the killer. Her brusqueness could be interpreted as evidence of her honesty, but that didn't mean to say that she always told the truth.

Scrimshaw had probably made a few enemies over the years. Doherty's crew had done some swift and sure research into the old guy's life. Overall it seemed that Clarence Scrimshaw's closest acquaintances were his accountant and his lawyer. Both of them were to receive a visit from Doherty shortly after Boxing Day and possibly at their homes. Neither profession was likely to be haunting their offices until around January the fifth.

When it came to employees, there was Samantha Brown. She was pretty, a little bit empty upstairs, and, according to investigation, was a single parent. Apparently Sam's mother looked after her son for two days of the week, with the remaining three days covered by a day nursery called Total Teeny Tots. Day nurseries of any description didn't come cheap, so Sam couldn't be earning enough to pay for it. Now who, Honey wondered, was paying for that? The father? And who *was* the father? Perhaps old man Scrimshaw had had more than just a soft spot for Samantha. It was something to look into. OK, the boss of Mallory and Scrimshaw was a bit long in the tooth but, as her mother had told her, the market was out there. Snow on the roof, but a fire in the grate; wasn't that what she'd said?

She made a note that it wasn't beyond the realms of possibility. David Longborough had hinted at Sam having been close to the old man. It could have been innocent, or it could have been incredibly serious. Office flings between employee and boss could start very innocently. Sam probably used to take Scrimshaw his tea mid-morning and perhaps he'd hinted at something extra, something a bit more satisfying than a digestive biscuit. If Scrimshaw had taken a shine to her, then perhaps he may have imparted secrets to her that nobody else knew anything about.

The list only made it to halfway down the page. Honey frowned. She favoured seeing more suspects on her list. The fact was that none of them leapt from the page with a label attached saying *take a closer look at me.*

She stopped writing. There were no answers, only questions; no clues, only conjecture.

And no Doherty, she thought, studying a solitary rum truffle sitting on her bedside table. The truffle would have to do.

She awoke to the sound of something buzzing not far from her ear. At first she sat bolt upright thinking it was the fire alarm. But no, the blue light on her phone was flashing blue. Its clock face said it was three in the morning.

She spouted a few swear words in the phone's direction before picking it up.

'Who the hell is ringing my phone at this deathly hour?'

'A guy with half a bed to spare. I'm lonely.'

'Shhh. Keep your voice down!' Honey said automatically before realising it was her own voice she needed to keep quiet.

'I am keeping my voice down.'

Honey frowned, one ear trained in the direction of Lindsey's bedroom.

She threw back the duvet and reached for her dressing gown. 'I'm coming.'

She fumbled in the dark for her slippers. Unfortunately they seemed to have gone wandering by themselves. The only footwear her fingers connected with were a pair of knee-high boots that she'd worn when out shopping. She pulled them on.

Pausing outside Lindsey's room, she listened for any of movement but heard nothing. Lindsey had to be sound asleep.

Wrapping the towelling robe more tightly around herself, Honey crept to the front door, crossed the yard to the back door of the hotel, went along the corridor that led to Reception, and up the stairs to the first floor.

Every experienced hotelier was totally aware that honeymooners required a four-poster bed, a bottle of bubbly and total privacy. The last requirement was the most essential, thus the honeymoon suite at the Green River Hotel was situated on the second floor, around the corner at the far end of the landing, where on clear nights moonlight threw a pool of silver through a dramatically arched window. The window overlooked the fire escape to the rear of the hotel, the coach house roof, and the back of the buildings in the next street.

One booted foot placed neatly in front of the other, Honey hesitated. Something was wrong. The landing lights should have been on. Even at this hour their muted glow should have lit the landing in case of mishap.

But the lights weren't on. There was only moonlight streaming through that arched window. A chilling thought occurred to her. Arched windows like that figured prominently in movies. Movies about haunted houses in places like Amityville.

But this is Bath! Things like that don't happen here.

Keeping a keen look out for axe-wielding maniacs, she crept along the landing. Nothing to fear, she told herself. Of course not. She knew this old building well, and as far as she was aware it didn't harbour the ghosts of any axe murderers. There was only Sir Cedric, who might or might not be a figment of Mary Jane's imagination.

Gathering the warmth of her thick towelling dressing gown more closely around her, she prowled along like a cat burglar in search of loot.

What are you so scared of?

She was just about to obey this urge to be courageous, when a shadow cut into the pool of silver moonlight. In an instant Honey was in a half-crouch behind a carved oak linen cupboard that she'd had the foresight to install in a handy place — handy for hiding behind when shadows loomed up in front of you.

One side of her brain was suggesting Doherty was waiting for her outside his room. The other side of her brain, the more cautious side that looked left and right before crossing the road and meant that she never walked under ladders or brought hawthorn blossom into the house, told her to hang back.

The possibility that she may have disturbed Lindsey entered her head, but if Lindsey was following her, she would have declared her presence with an accusatory statement, like '*And where do you think you're going at this time of night, as if I didn't know?*'

Unless Lindsey had her own agenda for prowling around.

Her throat constricted as the worst-case scenario hit her; Lindsey and Jake Truebody . . . was it possible?

The last thing she wanted was her daughter thinking she was spying on her. On the other hand, she would really like to know if a little hanky-panky was going on here.

Now what? Should she jump out and confront whoever it was?

Ascertaining the size and shape of the shadow wasn't easy. Shadows by nature can get distorted depending on the light shining behind them.

Pulling together all the logic she could muster, she did her damnedest to work out whether the shadow had resembled anyone she knew.

Can I hear breathing, or can't I?

She couldn't. She couldn't see or hear anyone, yet she was convinced that somebody was there.

Suddenly she heard footsteps softly falling on the carpet. Someone was standing in the dark, waiting, perhaps listening because he'd heard her.

She held her breath.

If it wasn't Lindsey and it wasn't Doherty or a sleepwalking guest, then it had to be a male intruder. Her reasoning for it being a male intruder rather than female was that, on the whole, women weren't attracted to a career in burglary.

Whoever it was had decided to move. Unfortunately, they'd chosen to move in her direction.

Pressing herself tightly against the wall and behind the linen press, she crouched lower, hoping for instant invisibility and worrying her chocolate-thickened thighs might give her away. Where was a policeman when you needed one? Hanging around in his room.

So phone him!

She checked for her phone and felt for the keypad, desperately trying to recall the location of the shortcut key. She couldn't find it.

The shadow passed close by. Whoever it was would soon see her. She had no choice. Once he was at some distance, she would run to the honeymoon suite and get Doherty to deal with it.

As with the best laid plans of mice and men and people with mobile phones, things went astray. Hers began to ring.

Hearing the first notes of 'Bohemian Rhapsody', the man who had thrown the shadow spun round like a top. Never mind Queen belting it out, her screaming into the phone was much louder than that. Doherty was on the other end.

Her heart lurched painfully when big hands grabbed her arms and flung her hard against the wall. She slid down it, dazed and seeing stars of all colours, vaguely aware that someone had come to rescue her, that doors were opening, that Doherty was finally there asking her if she was all right.

'Is she OK?'

It was Jake Truebody asking the question.

'Just a bump on the head,' said Doherty.

'Is he gone,' asked Honey?

Doherty held her close as he helped her to her feet. 'Yes. What happened? Do you know who it was?'

'No. I only saw a shadow. Nothing else.'

She leaned on him heavily as he guided her to his room. Her legs were like jelly; her head felt as though a West Indian combo were playing reggae on an ancient set of oil drums.

'You've got no clothes on,' she said, doing her best to focus on the most interesting aspects of his body. They seemed a little fuzzy, but the light wasn't good and her eyesight was blurred.

'Wrong place, wrong time for us to do anything about it,' he said grimly. At the same time as holding her upright, he was giving directions into his phone.

'I presume whoever it was jumped out of the window,' he said.

Honey realised she was lolling a bit, but there was nothing much she could do about it, not until her balance came back on stream. In the meantime her robe was parting over her thighs. Doherty took a good look.

'I like the look,' he said with an approving nod. 'Bath robe and knee-high boots does it for me.'

CHAPTER THIRTY-ONE

Despite a wide search, there was no trace of the phantom intruder.

'Not even a footprint.' Doherty frowned. 'There should have been. There's a patch of frost at the bottom of the fire escape.'

Honey thought for a minute that he didn't believe her.

'I did see someone — someone pushed me up against the wall. What a way to start Christmas Eve.'

He stroked her cheek as she lay in his bed with the duvet up to her nose.

'I believe you,' he said and kissed her forehead. 'Oh, by the way, Mary Jane insists there's a bad spirit at large. A spirit from the past.'

Honey made a grunt of disbelief. 'This bump on my head says otherwise. Bad spirit or not, they don't usually clobber you with something lethal.'

'No. They don't.'

There was something in Doherty's tone that made her sit up and take notice.

'You're thinking deeply. I always know when you're thinking deeply.'

'How come?'

'I'm lying naked in bed and you're not in here yet.'

He grinned. 'You know me well.'

It was early next morning when the phone rang. Doherty told her to get dressed. They were off to visit Clarence Scrimshaw's house.

'He didn't just have the flat above the office. We had a good look round there and found nothing. He also has a house in Beaufort East.'

The journey to this other property turned out to be much shorter than she'd envisaged. Along the A36 and over Cleveland Bridge, then right onto the A4.

'How come nobody knew about this house?' she asked.

Doherty was grim faced. 'He didn't come here that often and when he did, he was always alone.'

They pulled up outside a long terrace in Beaufort East.

'This isn't what I expected,' she remarked. 'I thought he'd lived in something grand if he had a private home besides the flat.'

'He had the money to do that,' murmured Doherty. 'We've checked with his accountancy firm and his lawyers. But old Clarence wasn't materialistic as such. In fact he was quite the opposite. In a way, he was quite spiritual.'

'Religious?'

'In a way.'

'What are you not telling me? That the place is stuffed with old and very valuable Bibles?'

He placed his hand on her shoulder. 'Let's see, shall we?'

Typically for Bath, the slip road running between the building and a strip of lawn where trees and bushes attempted to thrive was chock-a-block with cars. Doherty double-parked and stuck his 'police on duty' badge on the dashboard.

The rank of houses had once been surrounded by lush greenness. Nothing much remained except for a sliver of scrubby lawn between them and the road. To the rear was the river, hidden behind a series of low-rise accommodation. Out front beyond the strip of grass the traffic lumbered along the

A4, heading out of the city. The road was still called London Road although most of the traffic was heading no further than the suburbs or villages to the east of the city.

The buildings were tall and mainly late Georgian. Originally built as town houses for the gentry, most, if not all, of them had long since been turned into flats. Clarence Scrimshaw's two-bedroom flat was situated on the second floor. Doherty informed her that the cleaner who looked after it would be there with the keys.

Mrs Florence Withers was waiting for them in the ground floor hall. She was small, of pensionable age, with darting eyes and bright orange hair. The hair colour made Honey consider taking in a second box of chocolates to the stylists at Bee in a Bonnet. She had so much to be thankful for. Mrs Withers gave Doherty a set of keys. They were a spare set and she said he could keep them in case of need.

'I've got other gentlemen to look after, so I can't be running along behind you all the time,' she said with a toss of her head.

Mrs Withers got out her key, turned it in the lock and opened the door into a carpeted hallway. As with the rest of the building, the carpet had seen better days.

Two doors went off to the left and right, another was straight ahead. Mrs Withers took them into a living room of reasonable size. Two large sash windows looked out into the bare branches of a tree. Beyond that a fire engine was charging along the road heading out of the city, siren blaring. Nobody spoke until the sound had faded.

'Probably a cat stuck up a tree,' remarked Mrs Withers dismissively and sniffed her disdain.

The living room was of reasonable size. Having been expecting good quality old furniture, perhaps even the odd antique, Honey hid her surprise at what she saw.

There were the usual things one expected to find in a living room; two armchairs, one sofa, a coffee table, small fold-down dining table, and two dining chairs. The carpet was green and the original cornice ran along three walls. A cheap paper lampshade hung from the ceiling and an ancient print hung above a well-polished though old-fashioned sideboard. The whole lot was more junk shop than *Antiques Roadshow*.

A smell of beeswax hung in the air.

'Things have been moved,' said Mrs Withers. 'I noticed it right away.'

Honey and Doherty looked around. There were few ornaments. A pair of Staffordshire dogs sat either end of the sideboard. A red and white cut-glass fruit bowl sat between them. There was no fruit in it.

Honey turned slowly around, her eyes alighting on this and that, but not really finding what she was looking for.

'Something is missing,' said Honey, her eyes scouring the room. 'Besides taste that is.'

Mrs Withers fixed her with a stern eye. 'I beg your pardon?'

Unwilling to upset the woman, Honey found an excuse for her comment. 'Men don't usually have much taste, do they?'

'What's that got to do with anything?' Mrs Withers said indignantly. 'It's clean and tidy!'

'Got it,' said Honey. 'There's no television. No DVD player. No anything.'

'Mr Scrimshaw didn't believe in television,' said Mrs Withers. 'Said it was a waste of money.'

'OK,' said Doherty. 'We've established that there was no television and no recording and viewing devices, so no one broke in to take those. So tell us what *is* missing, Mrs Withers.'

Honey heard the impatience in his voice. The room looked untouched. The lights of the city flickered beyond windows that showed no sign of having been forced. Neither was there any sign of splintering on the front door, and the lock was still in place.

Doherty asked Mrs Withers why she insisted that someone had been snooping around.

'Everything's been put back *too* tidy,' she said. 'It wasn't the way Mr Scrimshaw liked things. He liked to know he could put his hand on something if he wanted to. It was a mess but a man's got a right to live in a mess if he wants to.'

Doherty opened a drawer on an old sideboard. 'Knives and forks,' he said. There was a slight tinkling of metal against metal as he trailed his fingers across the cutlery.

Honey could see that he was thinking this through. Doherty was doubly attractive when he was in thinking mode. It was as though he'd broken out in a streetwise hardness that toughened his features and upped his masculinity.

He was wearing a dark green shirt beneath the customary leather coat — a reefer-style with a slit up the back, double-breasted. He loved that leather coat even though it was a bit scuffed in places and the collar curled up at the ends. The shabby jacket matched his jeans.

Summer and winter he wore that coat. If things had gone according to plan, he would have dressed up a bit; worn a suit or some tidy casual. A warm coat perhaps? But though the weather was cold, that wasn't Doherty's way. It didn't look as though he felt the cold. Even in this weather she suspected his body would still feel warm. The opportunity to confirm that suspicion would have to wait until later.

Mrs Withers folded her arms over her knitted jacket and beetled her brows. 'Someone's tidied everything up, and it wasn't me.'

She said it as though she were the keeper of a kingdom. Mr Clarence Scrimshaw's little kingdom.

'There's nobody else likely to tidy things up — a relative for instance?'

'Not that I know of. Certainly not locally, though if one does turn up, I'd appreciate you telling me. The old goat owes me for doing his cleaning and bits and pieces. Comes in handy at this time of year.'

'Is that so?' Doherty was all attention.

'Certainly is. We have — or rather we did have — an arrangement. I gave him a time sheet for the year and he paid me at Christmas.'

'I can see it would be useful at this time of year,' said Doherty nodding in agreement. 'I presume you have a family to buy for.'

She almost spat her contempt. 'Presume all you like. I didn't spend it on Christmas!' Mrs Withers exclaimed. 'I used it to pay for my summer holiday. I always book it the day after New Year's Day. That was why me and Mr Scrimshaw got on so well together. Neither of us liked Christmas. Neither of us liked relatives much either.'

'So who else has a key besides you?' Doherty asked her.

'Only me, as far as I know.'

There was no point in Mrs Withers staying and Doherty told her so. 'We'll take a look round, look for clues, and lock up when we go.'

Mrs Withers said that would be alright and stressed once again that if some long-lost relative turned up, to let them know she was owed a tidy sum of money.

'They had to have had a key,' mused Doherty reflecting exactly what Honey had been thinking. 'But why tidy up?'

The second bedroom was securely locked. While Doherty scrutinised the outline of each key, Honey grabbed the handle and gave the door a good shake.

'It's locked for a reason,' said Doherty, one eye on the keys and one on her.

'OK, there's something he doesn't want Mrs Withers to see. The family jewels perhaps?'

Doherty began thinking aloud. 'So what's in here and where's the key? I wonder if there's a safe somewhere . . .'

Honey pointed out that Clarence had been a skinflint. 'A safe? Just to keep a key in? Not here. In the office there's probably a very old safe stuck in a dark corner. Business dictates that. But not here.' Honey shook her head. 'Safes cost a bundle of money. He'd stick to something old-fashioned, simple, and extremely cheap.'

Doherty looked at her as he thought about it. 'I go mad for a girl with brains.'

She smiled. 'Lucky for you I've got the brains and the looks.'

He started to open drawers, looked beneath ornaments, felt behind the frames of the few pictures hanging on the wall.

'Should you be doing that?' she asked. 'What about fingerprints?'

He knew where she was coming from. 'Mrs Withers only has a suspicion that things have been moved. She can't prove anything and there are no signs of a break in. Nothing taken — as far as we know — and we don't know whether the victim entertained visitors here.'

Honey leaned against the door with her arms folded, watching him. This was one of those moments when a special person with special connections was needed. Basically, you needed to have had a slightly dotty grandparent. Honey could hold her hand up to that one; on her mother's side of course.

Aware that she wasn't moving much — well, not moving at all in fact, he looked up. 'Well? Are you going to give me a hand here or what?'

'OK.' She headed for the kitchen.

Alice Fairbairn, her mother's mother, entered the kitchen with her, though only in her head as she'd been dead for years. Her grandmother had been something of a rebel in her youth. For a start, she was possibly the first woman in the town she'd lived in to wear trousers. Trousers were for men back then and women who wore trousers were considered 'fast'. Alice had also run her own business, a greengrocery in the centre of town; that was besides bringing up a family and serving in a bar.

She'd been described as 'sharp' for most of her life which meant she'd been careful with money. Distrusting banks, Alice had secreted her money under the mattress. Jars and tins marked coffee and tea was where she had kept loose change and the money needed to pay bills. And keys. She'd also kept keys in jars and tins.

Honey's logic was simple. Clarence Scrimshaw had been well into his dotage, which meant he had been influenced by the old school of money management and basic security. One look round the kitchen told her what he'd been like. The cupboards dated from the seventies; not exactly up to date but they were clean and serviceable.

She hunted through an assortment of blue striped Cornish Ware. Had Scrimshaw been a tea-drinking man or had he preferred coffee? Somehow she figured him a tea drinker.

Her fingers skipped over the jars. She lifted the lid from the jar marked tea and dug in.

Her fingers should have touched the soft dryness of unused tea bags. Whatever she was touching was lumpy and damp. She pulled one out, holding it delicately between finger and thumb.

'Yuk!' She turned up her nose. Old Scrimshaw was frugal in the extreme and used his teabags more than once. Some were distinctly on the furry side, clustered together like baby mice.

There were limits to what her stomach could stand. Digging back in was definitely off the menu. She upturned the jar. The teabags landed in a damp heap.

The key fell out with them.

'Bingo!'

After wiping the key off in a tea towel, she headed for the locked door.

Doherty heard her cry out and came out of the living room.

'Was that a whoop of triumph I heard?'

'It sure was.'

'You're looking pleased with yourself.'

'I deserve to be.'

He shook his head as he smiled that disbelieving smile of his. He'd never exactly openly admired her logic, but that smile said it all. Her toes curled up in delight.

He stood close behind her, his front brushing her back. It was like having a shield behind her, a warm shield.

'So he's got a safe in the kitchen?' He looked hopeful.

She shook her head. 'In the tea caddy. And, seeing as I found it, I should be the one to shout open sesame. Right?'

He shrugged. 'You're the one with the key.'

Honey breathed a sigh of satisfaction. 'Now what will we find? Gold or guilty pleasures?'

The door opened on a room that was in total darkness. The light switch was on the wall. Doherty reached around her to switch it on. A single lightbulb suspended from the ceiling blinked into light. The bulb was far too small for the size of the room, but the only source of light in the place.

'It's a library,' said Honey.

'It's a gloomy library,' remarked Doherty, wrinkling his nose as he took it all in.

He was right. The single lightbulb was fighting a losing game, but she could see there were books. Lots of books.

A heavy oak table, its legs carved and bulbous in the middle, sat in the centre of the room. Two chairs, both with barley twist backrests, sat on either side of the table. There were various things piled on it, mostly lever arch files of varying styles and colour.

Books sporting the entwined M & S of the Mallory and Scrimshaw logo on their spines took up three quarters of the room. The other was filled with cloth-covered books, their gilt titles still shiny despite their age.

Recalling what John Rees had told her, Honey inspected them closely. She hadn't a clue whether they were valuable, but most were pretty old. Not all of them were Bibles, though most were about religion. All of them were too old to have been published by Mallory and Scrimshaw.

Honey walked slowly, eyeing each shelf as she went. 'They're divided into subject matter. See?'

Doherty followed where her travelling finger.

'*Celtic Faith; Celtic Rituals; Celts and the Occult.*' He slid one from the shelf and opened it. A piece of paper fell out.

Honey picked it up and began to open it.

Doherty took it from her and began to read.

Honey waited. He refolded the letter. 'Well? What does it say?'

'Did I tell you about the knife that killed him?'

'That it was sharp?'

'As I've already told you, the knife we found in him wasn't the knife that killed him. It was a paper knife. The kind you use for slitting open envelopes.'

'So not known for being particularly sharp.'

'Correct.'

'So you can't find the real weapon?'

'Not only that, but we figured that whoever did it must have valued the knife. We asked ourselves why. The only reason we could come up with was that the weapon was too easy to identify or too valuable.'

'And that piece of paper?'

'It's a receipt for a ritual knife.'

'The one used by the killer, I suppose.'

'It appears that Mr Scrimshaw didn't just collect Bibles,' said Doherty, his finger running down the spine of one old book after another. 'Look at this. *Pre-Christian Pan European Beliefs*.'

'Pagan,' said Honey.

'So. Our Mr Scrimshaw was into the occult, though perhaps only on a collector level.'

Honey had moved on, her eyes landing on one of the folders sitting on the table in the middle of the room. She opened it.

Doherty came to look over her shoulder. 'Newspaper clippings.'

She turned the pages slowly. 'They're all about bog bodies. I know about them.'

'Explain.'

Some of what Lindsey knew had rubbed off. She hadn't always turned a deaf ear when her daughter was in full flow.

'Bog bodies are usually the remains of sacrifices from Celtic times. As you may have guessed, they're found in bogs — peat bogs all over Europe.'

'Now there's a nice subject for Christmas.'

She looked up at him, fully expecting to see that his eyes had glazed over and that he was yawning. He wasn't. He had adopted his serious face, the one he reserved for serious subjects.

'Well,' she said, feeling quite pleased that she knew so much, 'I recall a bog body found in the Midlands where the details of the sacrifice were clearly visible. His smashed-in skull was due to a heavy blow on the head, but besides that he was also garrotted — the rope still around his neck, and he was also stabbed. Three methods of death; three is a sacred number in most religions you see. It certainly was for the ancient Britons.'

Still eyeing her with that serious policeman expression, he retrieved the piece of paper from his pocket and gave it to her. The paper was crisp and old. It was a bill dated 23rd February 1956. The item was listed as a ritual knife. Price paid, seventy-five guineas. 'Cheap, I reckon. A collector's piece, and if you happened to know its history, worth a lot more than that.'

'It was valuable.'

'And whoever used it wanted to keep it — but still leave some kind of knife in place.'

Doherty pursed his lips as he thought about it. 'Why bother to shove the paper knife in the old man's ear?'

'So it would still look like a pagan killing?'

'Could be. We need to make enquiries. See if he was involved with anything like that and who with.'

Honey knew just the person who might know. 'I could phone John Rees.'

Doherty looked at her searchingly. He knew John Rees was all hers if she'd just say the word.

'He's just a friend.'

He nodded. 'Sure he is.'

She called him, and he promised that he would check and phone back.

CHAPTER THIRTY-TWO

The only let-down — or rather flare-up — on Christmas Day was the excess of blue flames on the plum pudding. Rich in alcohol, the addition of and setting fire to the brandy was a huge success, except for the fact that Smudger's eyebrows got singed in the process.

'No problem,' he cried, patting his eyebrows with the palms of his hands. 'They needed a trim anyway.'

Guests and hotel staff all sat together in groups of eight. Conversation was brisk and jovial, even among the party from Mallory and Scrimshaw, though Honey did notice that the corners of Sam Brown's mouth were downturned. She also noticed that the girl's demeanour bordered on nervous each time David Longborough looked at her.

She leaned against Doherty and made it appear that she was nuzzling his ear. 'Do you think Longborough might have been jealous of the attention Mr Scrimshaw extended to Sam Brown?'

Doherty glanced at the pair. 'She did say that Scrimshaw came on to her. In which case anything's possible.'

Honey's attention shifted. Her eyes were everywhere, just as a hotelier's should be. Diners and guests were not always well behaved.

According to her calculations when setting up the tables, every seat should have been taken. Her eyes settled on an empty chair. Each placing had a name card. The empty chair she espied on one particular table should have been taken by Professor Jake Truebody.

She was about to get up from her chair when Clint arrived.

'More wine?'

Clint was doing the honours, a white cloth over his beefy arm. He was wearing a kilt and a white frilly shirt. The lights in his bow tie blinked on and off with rapid frequency. A halo finished the look, though it was a bit more bent and battered than it had been.

By the time she looked back along the table, another place was empty. Lindsey's place. She guessed that wherever the professor was, her daughter would be there too.

Honey would have gone, there and then, to Professor Truebody's room, but something happened that stopped her in her tracks.

Fingers tightly gripping the table, Anna got to her feet. 'My water has broken!'

There was an instant flurry of confusion infused with just as much activity.

Smudger the chef had been moving from guest to guest with a jug of brandy cream. He was now hovering over Anna, was the closest to her in fact. His pink face had turned white.

'Do something!'

Whoever said it was asking the wrong man.

'I don't deliver babies. Only food,' he said, nervously clutching his jug and shaking his head.

'This is most inconvenient. Will someone please phone an ambulance?' The demand was made by Patricia Pontefract.

'Done,' said Doherty.

Honey was first at Anna's side. 'Let's get you into the bar. It's cooler in there.'

Together, Honey and Mary Jane helped Anna from her chair and onto her feet. The poor girl was panting and taking deep breaths, arms cradling her belly. Doherty followed on behind at a respectable distance.

'Imagine,' said Mary Jane, her voice trembling with excitement. 'We're having a holy birth! What I mean is, Anna is giving birth on Christmas Day.'

'I was born on Christmas Day.' The speaker was none other than their favourite washer-up — Clint.

'Tell her to breathe deeply,' Doherty was saying, still keeping his distance and offering the advice to Honey.

Anna puffed out her cheeks and took deep breaths, expelling the same breath with the ferocity of a hurricane.

'That's very good,' Honey said.

Clint was kneeling, holding Anna's hand. 'Hang in there, Anna, baby. Hang in there. And don't you worry about Vicky. I'll take care of her.'

Vicky was Anna's eldest child. There was no way that Clint would not be inconvenienced by looking after her. This was because she was presently living with Anna's mother, her grandmother, in Poland. But despite his unorthodox appearance, Clint was a romantic who knew how to turn on the charm.

The sound of the front door bursting open carried into the bar. Everyone, though Doherty more so than anyone else, breathed a sigh of relief. He was telling the truth when he'd said that he'd never delivered a baby in the back of police car or anywhere else for that matter. 'Just because police doing that make the headlines, doesn't mean to say that we all do it.'

The cavalry, in the form of two paramedics and a large yellow and green ambulance parked outside, had arrived.

'Let's take a look,' one of them said. He knelt down and proceeded to prod Anna's stomach. His brow was furrowed.

'Labour pains are coming quick and the intervals between are very short. Better take you in or the baby will be born here in the bar.'

'Handy,' said the other paramedic. 'We can all stay and wet the baby's head!'

'Clint? You are coming with me?' cried Anna. Her eyes were fixed on his face.

'Just you try and stop me, Anna, baby.'

'Well wasn't that sweet of our friend Clint,' said Mary Jane once the entourage of medical personnel, Clint and Anna had left.

Honey and Doherty exchanged looks. They said nothing, but both were suddenly aware that Clint's going with Anna wasn't just about being sweet. There was something else going on.

'Right,' said Doherty rubbing his hands together. 'Let's see if there's any pudding left, shall we?'

He took Mary Jane's arm and was about to take hers when she made an excuse.

'I just have to powder my nose.'

'Take a leak,' Doherty nodded in instant understanding.

'That too.'

She did enter the ladies' cloakroom but didn't linger. A quick look into the dining room confirmed that Lindsey had not retaken her seat. Neither had Professor Truebody. Not sure what to expect, she headed for the stairs.

'Honey,' came a familiar voice from behind her. 'I've caught you.'

Doherty meant it literally, scooping her with one arm until she was flat against his chest. A sprig of mistletoe dangled from his free hand.

He kissed her.

'Merry Christmas,' he said once the kiss was broken.

'Merry Christmas,' she managed to say once she'd caught her breath. 'You took me by surprise.'

'I did consider following you into the ladies' washroom, but it wouldn't look good on my record sheet. Anything wrong?'

Her gaze kept shifting to the stairs. He asked her what was up.

'Professor Jake Truebody was not at lunch. Did you not notice?'

'And Lindsey?'

'She's disappeared too, but I know where they are. I was just about to go upstairs and confront them.'

'Do you think that's a good idea?'

Honey sighed. 'I don't know. I really don't know. I don't even know if Carl really knew him. I don't remember his name, but that doesn't mean to say he wasn't an acquaintance of Carl's. But if he wasn't, how would he have got hold of our personal details?'

'Online?'

'What do you mean?'

He looked reluctant to continue. 'I wasn't going to tell you this just yet, but John Rees phoned me. He said that there were rumours about the deceased being involved in the occult, but that they were only rumours. Nobody knew for sure. Then he went on to tell me something else.'

Doherty wasn't one for hesitating. He tended to bark it out as it was, take it or leave it. But he hesitated now.'

'There's more?'

He nodded. 'It concerns your personal details.'

For a moment Honey had the scary suspicion that her identity had been stolen and that she was currently running an overdraft at her local bank equal to the national debt.

'Go on.'

'John's been doing some online dating of late.'

'John Rees? I don't believe it!'

She was shocked. John scored high on the list of desirable men that no mature woman would kick out of bed. He'd always been decidedly single, but perhaps he was feeling lonelier than she'd thought.

'He said he found it difficult to make dates the conventional way. I can understand that . . . So he went online and purely by mistake, found a site for the over-sixties called *Snow on the Roof*.'

'My mother put my details on there.' Honey scowled. 'Without my permission.'

'Correct. That's where your details are listed, even though you're not in that age bracket, including you being listed as a widow, plus Carl's name and profession. Link into that and you get redirected to information about Carl. It was easy to find.'

'I feel dizzy.'

'Too much wine and rich food?'

'No. Too much interference from my mother, plus I didn't know John Rees was that old.'

'He's not. He just likes mature women — like you.' He grinned.

She kicked his leg.

Her attention went back to the stairs and what Jake Truebody might be doing with her daughter.

Doherty sussed it out. 'Do you want me to come upstairs with you?'

She nodded. 'That's an offer I can't possibly refuse.'

* * *

An email from Jake Truebody's sister stated that her brother's body had been found.

Taking a deep breath, Lindsey decided that the best time to do another search of Jake Truebody's room was while he was eating Christmas lunch — which unfortunately he didn't do.

Once she was in his room, Jake slammed the door behind her and lay flat against it, between her and the chance of escape.

'I came up to check the towels.'

Jake Truebody shook his head. 'I don't believe you.'

Despite the speed of her heartbeat, she put on a brave face. Folding her arms, she kept her chin up and looked him straight in the eye.

'I don't believe you either, Professor Jake Truebody — or whoever you are.'

If he was taken off guard, he didn't show it.

'What's that supposed to mean?'

'The real professor's body has been found. His sister emailed me.'

He gave a choking kind of laugh and shook his head. 'You don't say!'

He smiled like a snake as he shook his head. 'Would you believe me if I said that I worked for the FBI?'

'No.'

'Very wise. Would you believe me if I said that I was a priest?'

'Well you're certainly not an historian!'

The man who had checked into the hotel as Jake Truebody threw back his head and laughed loudly.

'You caught me out there. I didn't have much of a clue did I, even about American History, though I thought I did. What tripped me up?'

'You said that Pocahontas married John Smith. She rescued John Smith and married John Rolfe.'

He pulled a face and slapped his forehead. 'Unpardonable! My real speciality is genealogy. Tracing family trees. It went down very well in the prison where good old Jake Truebody did his duty one day a week. I was there to save their hellbent souls. Anyway, people are very interested in knowing who their ancestors are and where they came from, and I'm no exception.'

It was difficult to believe that Jake Truebody was a priest. But she had to play along. She had to play for time until someone came looking for her.

'So what's your real name?'

His whole demeanour seemed to soften.

'Father John Smith — would you believe?'

'And you were a prison padre?'

'We can all sin.'

'So why are you here?'

'I'm seeking a Bible on behalf of an old friend. Of course I didn't know that back in prison — not until later on. Old

Professor Truebody put me on to it. A very valuable Bible as it turns out, one of the first to be translated from the Latin Vulgate back into Greek. I traced it here. It was delivered to a collector who didn't care much about its origins so long as it was in his bookcase. I was going to call in on him, but then heard he'd been murdered.'

'Clarence Scrimshaw.'

'Yes.' He grinned. 'A very Dickensian name, don't you think?'

'Similar to Scrooge. And his partner was named Mallory.'

'Similar to Marley. Isn't that amazing?'

She agreed that it was. 'So why didn't you go to the police?'

Jake Truebody — or Father John Smith as he now said he was — moved away from the door.

'My client wished to keep the matter private, hence my coming up here during lunch just in case your mother's boyfriend — the policeman — made contact with me and started to ask difficult questions. After all, you suspected I wasn't who I said I was, and you're not the professional.'

'So why use Jake's name and passport?'

'There are other very dangerous people after that Bible. I knew I was being followed and knew he'd gone missing. I don't think he'd mind. Jake was a very understanding guy. And the real owner would like that Bible back.'

She hugged herself. 'So who is your client?'

He shook his head and a strange smile came to his lips. 'Someone who is very close to me.'

'A relative?'

'Something like that. You know, we're very similar, you and I. Both of us are lacking a father. Mine died when I was very young.'

'You never knew my father. The real Jake Truebody knew my father, not you. And I also don't believe you're a priest.'

His eyes turned frighteningly dark, like deep-set chips of onyx. One side of his mouth curled upwards; not a smile but hardly a sneer. It was then she remembered the shiver she'd felt on first meeting him.

'OK. OK,' he repeated, his eyes unblinking and never leaving her face. 'What the hell? You might as well know the truth.'

He told her about the night of a great storm when the real professor had taken pity on a man, lately released from the prison where he taught history and genealogy.

'He was known as Wes Patterson, otherwise known as Crispin Mallory.'

'As in Mallory and Scrimshaw?'

'Son of the deceased partner. Only found it out when I was doing this genealogy stuff. He's hiding out here somewhere close by. I'm sure of it. I think he killed Jake and killed this guy Scrimshaw.'

'You sound as though you do work for the FBI.'

He grinned. 'There. I'm not so bad.'

'Do you suppose he has a key to the flat — the apartment above their offices?'

The man now calling himself Father John Smith looked querulous. 'Well that's interesting. Why do you think that?'

'My mother had a look round there. She went there to check on the people who'd sent Mr Scrimshaw Christmas cards or presents. There were a few cards in the office, though mostly from suppliers. There were none in the flat above and it was empty.'

'And presents?'

Lindsey shrugged. 'The staff said that there had been one, but my mother couldn't find anything.'

'If there was a parcel, it must have contained the Bible. I have to get it back.' His eyes flashed open. 'How about we go take a look?'

Lindsey tried not to glance at the door. She was now in two minds about escaping. What if, after all, he *was* telling the truth.

'How do we get in?'

'Hmm,' he said, chewing his bottom lip thoughtfully. 'Let's cross that bridge when we come to it.' A smile lit up his face. 'I can pretend to be an FBI man with a bunch of skeleton keys in my pocket.'

CHAPTER THIRTY-THREE

Honey knocked on the door of room thirty-six. There was no response so she knocked again.

Doherty stood waiting patiently with his hands in his pockets.

'The birds have flown. The door's innocent. Stop beating it.'

She unclenched her fists and took a deep breath. 'I've never interfered with my daughter's love life, but this time I've got a gut feeling . . .' She brought out the master key.

'If it gives you peace of mind.'

Into the lock went the key.

In a way it was something of a relief to find the room empty, bed neatly made, and nothing out of place.

'What would you have done if you'd found them in bed together?' asked Doherty.

Honey swallowed. 'Normally when that happens, I apologise and tell them I've entered the wrong room.'

'And in this instance?'

She didn't hesitate. 'In this instance I'd tell him to leave and her to find someone of her own age to pick on.'

'Drastic.' Doherty took hold of her arm. 'Let's get a drink and think about this.'

The smell of mulled wine and rich fruit met them at the bottom of the stairs. By the time they got back to the dining room, the telling of ghost stories was in full swing.

David Longborough was reading a story he'd written himself. Honey was vaguely aware it was about a vampire and his human girlfriend. He read with confidence, speaking each character in a different voice, just as an actor would.

Doherty came and sat down beside her. 'I've brought you a drink,' he whispered.

She didn't respond. She sat frozen, her attention was firmly fixed on David Longborough. She touched his hand.

'Steve. That's him. That's the voice of Clarence Scrimshaw. The voice that made the booking.'

Doherty waited until Longborough had finished before taking him to one side.

'How about you come into the bar and we have a quiet word about Mr Scrimshaw?'

Like a lamb to the slaughter, the over-confident Longborough, thinking he was onto an amiable chat about his ex-employer, went into the bar. Doherty signalled Honey to come in too.

'A brandy would be nice,' said David Longborough. 'Quite frankly, if it wasn't for the anti-smoking laws, I'd ask for a cigar to go with it. I don't suppose there's any chance . . . ?'

Honey shook her head. 'Sorry.'

Longborough's cocky expression was barely dented. 'And the brandy? I speak better when my vocal cords are well oiled.'

'No need. I'll start the conversation off. Let's talk about the theft of Clarence Scrimshaw's debit card.'

Longborough had a wide mouth, the sort that easily slides into a smirk, a smile, or a grin. But not now. His smile dropped.

'I don't know what you mean.'

'Yes, you do. Mrs Driver recognised your voice when you made the reservation. She heard you mimic an old man's voice when you checked into the hotel.'

'And you've just read in character,' Honey added.

Steve Doherty carried on where she left off.

'Scrimshaw found out you'd paid for the shindig with his card. You argued and killed him. You knew about his connections with the occult and you were hoping the blame would fall on one of his acquaintances there.'

Doherty was firing blanks here; he didn't know for sure that Clarence Scrimshaw was involved in the occult; the man had merely collected books on various religions. He was guessing Longborough wouldn't know that. All he was aiming for was a confession.

Longborough's confidence had melted away. He looked frightened. He shook his head adamantly. 'No. It wasn't like that. It was meant to be a joke. Just a joke.'

'So how did the debit card get into his coat pocket?'

Longborough hung his head and spoke to his hands. 'I got Sam to do it. She gave him a Christmas kiss and a big hug when she did it. He always did have a soft spot for her. It was easy for her to slip it into his pocket. But I swear he was fine when we left the office, inspector. Honestly he was.'

'And the key,' said Honey. 'I'm presuming you collected the key to Mr Scrimshaw's room, then posted it in the slot the next day.'

Longborough nodded. 'The Polish girl gave me the key, but didn't ask me to sign for it. She seemed in a bit of a hurry.'

Honey needed no further explanation. She knew Anna had been in a hurry because she'd wanted to go to the loo.

It was difficult to tell but she guessed Doherty thought Longborough was telling the truth. He wouldn't get tried for murder, but he would for fraud. So would Sam Brown, though only as an accomplice.

Doherty slung his leg over a chair, turning it so he could rest his elbows on the chair back.

'So Christmas was still humbug as far as Mr Scrimshaw was concerned?'

'Too right it was. We even bought the Christmas tinsel and baubles ourselves. He wouldn't put a penny to it.'

Doherty stroked his chin. 'So you thought you'd take a Christmas bonus when he wasn't looking.'

Longborough hung his head. 'I'm in the shit, aren't I?'

Doherty nodded. 'Deep.'

He read him his rights then phoned for someone to come up with a car from Manvers Street.

Accused of aiding and abetting, Sam Brown went too. Honey found herself feeling little sympathy for the girl. It was obvious she was in thrall to Longborough; why else would a mother spend Christmas Day — even if only part of Christmas Day — away from her child?

Doherty paused outside the door to the dining room, shoulders hunched, thumbs latched into his waistband.

Honey recognised he was thinking things through.

'So David Longborough didn't kill him. It wasn't about money — well not as far as David is concerned. So what next?'

'I've got a few ghosts that need putting to rest.'

The telling of ghost stories had gone on without interruption. Doherty wanted to interview others. Honey suggested it best that she fetched them out as required.

Doherty agreed that would be OK. 'I wouldn't want to be a party pooper.'

The first was Mrs Finchley. Shocked by the death of the man she worked for and hankered after she'd looked downcast most of the day.

'You're wanted in Reception,' Honey whispered in her ear.

Mrs Finchley didn't question who wanted her. Neither did she resist. It was as though she was on autopilot; her body acting independently of her brain, moving in response to outside suggestion.

Honey led her from Reception and into the bar. Mrs Finchley raised no objection. She was a far more docile person than she had been not that Honey liked her any better for that. She was certainly no team player, aloof as she was from her colleagues, looking down her nose at them, thinking she was better than they were.

Her dress sense didn't help; she was wearing a sparkly twinset and a double string of pearls. If her hairstyle was anything to go by, she had a great fondness for the Margaret Thatcher years; the years before the ex-prime minister had taken grooming advice.

Doherty was perched on a bar stool. He signalled for Mrs Finchley to sit on the one next to his.

'I'd prefer a chair. Stools are not ladylike,' she said, regarding the bar stool as some would the south face of the Eiger.

Doherty waved instead at a club chair with deep-set buttons and bun style feet.

Honey stood at the end of the bar, one eye on the door in case of interruption.

Doherty sat casually picking at a dish of ready salted peanuts. He'd taken off his jacket. Seeing as it was Christmas Day, he'd broken his own rules and was wearing a shirt and tie. He looked cool. He looked collected.

Honey smoothed her red dress down over her hips. She'd made an effort too. The dress looked good; full marks to a new foundation garment controlling everything from just above the waist to halfway down her thighs.

Doherty began his questioning. 'Mrs Finchley. It's been reported by a reliable witness that on the night of Clarence Scrimshaw's murder, you left the hotel looking quite flustered. Can you tell me why that might be?'

Mrs Finchley shrugged her ample shoulders. 'It's simple. I forgot to bring some decent bath gel. Hotels only supply such meagre samples.' She sounded nervous and didn't meet his eyes.

Sliding from the stool, Doherty began pacing the floor.

Honey worked out what he was up to. He knew something Mrs Finchley did not know and he was about to enlighten her.

'Did you visit Mr Scrimshaw's room round about four thirty on the afternoon of the murder?'

'No. Certainly not. I'm a respectable woman. Anyway, I don't think Mr Scrimshaw had arrived by then.'

Doherty shot her an accusing glare. 'One of the chambermaids saw the door to his room closing about five minutes after you left. Would you like to change your story?'

Mrs Finchley's jaw dropped and if eyes were ever going to pop, hers were.

'Why were you there in his room, Mrs Finchley?'

For a brief moment, Freda Finchley's plump face seemed to freeze then suddenly broke. She began to bawl, her cries as loud as a braying donkey.

'Crocodile tears!'

Honey couldn't help it. Doherty looked to her for clarification.

'Her eyes are dry. It's just a noise.'

Most men are knocked off balance when women turned on the waterworks. Doherty was no exception.

Honey shouted directly into Mrs Finchley's face. 'Cut it out, lady. Your eyes are dry.'

For a moment Mrs Finchley seemed to cease breathing.

'Well go on. Tell us all what you know. We're all ears. Was old skinflint Scrimshaw making it with somebody else? Did he have a floozie in there or not? Come on, Mrs Finchley. Come clean.'

Mrs Finchley's face turned from flaccid to Florentine marble. She heaved a huge sigh.

'Mr Scrimshaw wasn't in the room.'

Honey cocked her head to one side. Mary Jane's ghost stories were entertaining enough, but this stuff was gripping.

'So if Scrimshaw wasn't in the room, who was in there?'

Mrs Finchley raised her pale round eyes. 'Mallory. Eamon Mallory. Or at least . . . it looked like him.' She frowned as she tried to recall the memory. 'It looked like Eamon alright, but as he was, not the age he would be now.'

Honey frowned. This was not the answer she'd been expecting. She suspected Doherty hadn't expected this either.

'Excuse me, but who is Eamon Mallory?' she asked.

Mrs Finchley swallowed hard before responding. 'Eamon Mallory was Clarence Scrimshaw's business partner. He died some time ago.'

'So I understand,' said Honey. Doherty shot her a look. 'Alistair told me,' she explained.

Doherty jerked his chin in understanding. He stood in front of Mrs Finchley with arms folded. 'Are you saying that you saw a *dead man* in this hotel?'

Mrs Finchley nodded. 'Though of course it couldn't be him. He's dead.'

'Where did you go to when you left the hotel in such a hurry?'

'I went to see Clarence, Mr Scrimshaw. I wanted to tell him that I'd seen Eamon Mallory — or his ghost. I haven't seen him for about thirty years. He left at Christmas time over thirty years ago. He ran away to America with a younger woman. The last I heard they'd all died in a house fire . . .' She paused. 'Well, perhaps not all of them,' she said, her brow furrowing as she fought to recall the details. 'Eamon definitely died and I think the child did too. I'm not sure about Daisy.'

'Daisy? What was her maiden name?'

'Barber, I think. I never met her. I think Mr Scrimshaw was sweet on her too. I think she was an author — an American author. I remember he locked himself away in his office when he heard the news that they'd run away together.'

'So you went along to tell Mr Scrimshaw that you'd seen Eamon Mallory — even though he's supposed to be dead. What time did you reach the office?'

She appeared confused. Honey guessed she was having difficulty getting the details in order.

Honey repeated the question Doherty had already asked. 'What time did you get to the office?'

Mrs Finchley blinked like someone emerging from a deep dark mine.

'About five fifteen, I suppose. He was alive then. I swear he was. I didn't kill him!' she cried, her eyes filled with pleading. 'There are plenty with good reason to kill him, but not me. I loved him. I really loved him.'

Doherty took Honey to one side. 'Do you think that's a woman who would kill in a fit of passion?'

'Possibly, but more likely she'd kill a chocolate gateau first. Comfort eating always comes first in healing matters of the heart.'

Mrs Finchley was allowed to go, but not before she'd intimated who might have a good reason to kill her former employer.

'Eamon would, if he were still alive. They quarrelled about books. They were keen collectors of antiquarian volumes.'

'Mrs Finchley, did you ever see any valuable Bibles in Mr Scrimshaw's possession?' asked Honey.

She shrugged. 'I saw old books. Some of them might have been Bibles.'

'Did you have sight of one very ancient one that arrived just before Christmas?'

Mrs Finchley shook her head. 'No. I didn't, but that doesn't mean that one didn't arrive. Mr Scrimshaw was very secretive about the books he collected.'

Honey turned to Doherty and voiced what she was thinking. 'Eamon Mallory's son; do you think he might have survived the fire?'

'I'll check it out.'

He phoned the details through.

'If the son is still alive, then he could have been the intruder.'

'But why break in?'

'He was looking for something?'

Doherty shook his head. 'I don't think so. I think the intruder who caught you in boots and towelling robe was a separate incident . . . Perhaps it was someone who'd forgotten their key.'

Honey wasn't too sure about that. She put herself back to that night.

It was what Doherty said next that jogged her memory.

'I liked the outfit you were wearing that night.'

Yes, her outfit had been memorable and incredibly simple; a towelling robe and a pair of knee-high boots — and something else; something very small and insignificant.

'I was also wearing perfume. Chanel No.5 Number Five. The intruder smelled of perfume — not aftershave. Perfume.'

'A woman?'

'Bingo! A female guest creeping from a male guest's room and not wanting to be discovered!' She shrugged her shoulders resignedly. 'It happens all the time, though they don't usually bash people over the head when they are discovered.'

'So who's next on the hit list?'

He stood leaning on the bar, thinking things through.

'Excuse me.'

Mallory and Scrimshaw's financial director, Paul Emmerson, had a face without softness. His nose was a straight line, his mouth was a straight line, and his cheekbones and jaw were sharp. He looked from Doherty to Honey Driver.

'I need to speak to you.'

He looked terribly pale, but then, reasoned Honey, most people who deal with money for a living, look as though they only come out at night.

'I saw your daughter go out earlier,' he said to Honey. 'I couldn't believe who she was with.'

Sensing that she wasn't going to like this, Honey asked him why, what, who the hell was he talking about?

Doherty played Mr Cool. 'Can you enlighten us, Mr Emmerson? Can you tell us who Lindsey was with?'

'Crispin Mallory. Eamon's son. It had to be him. He looks so like his father.'

Honey and Doherty both straightened.

'Tell me more,' said Doherty.

'I went up to my room to get my wife's headache pills. She takes them a lot,' he added with a somewhat pained expression. 'It's the wine,' Emmerson added with a nervous laugh.

Honey was under no illusion. This guy was attempting to distract them from knowing the passionate intimacy — or rather the *lack* of passionate intimacy — in his sex life. All the same, she felt a niggling sense of unease.

'The man you saw with my daughter. We know him as Professor Jake Truebody. Are you saying it was Eamon Mallory's son?'

He nodded. 'Yes. He looks just like his father, though twenty-odd years younger of course. I worked with the two of them back in the old days at Mallory and Scrimshaw. I'm hoping to retire shortly, and I know I'm getting on, but my memory is still good and I've seen the old photographs Clarence kept. There's no doubt in my mind. That person you call Jake Truebody is Crispin Mallory.'

Doherty ordered the accountant to sit down. 'This son. Where has he been living up until now?'

'In the United States. I think his mother was an author based in Idaho. I understood that he died with his father in a house fire, but it's obviously not true. He looks just like Eamon. There's no doubt about it.'

Honey sucked in her breath.

Doherty thanked him. The moment the door closed, he was punching in numbers on his phone.

'Get me what you can from the FBI on a Crispin Mallory.'

The information would be a while coming through. Although Honey was desperate to find her daughter, she didn't know where to look. However, things had been clarified. Just as Anna had pointed out, Jake Truebody had avoided being seen. They had presumed he was avoiding her or the police. Now it seemed that he had, in fact, been avoiding the older employees of Mallory and Scrimshaw simply because he looked like his father.

Honey spotted her mother, her outfit shining like a sardine in the moonlight.

Patricia Pontefract was reading her story, her voice rolling over the words as though she'd bled every one of them onto the page. She looked full of herself, puffed up to twice her size.

A lectern was provided that put the readers' two steps up from the audience. Patricia Pontefract stood tall and erect.

Honey sat down next to her mother and whispered in her ear. 'Exactly how much detail about me did you put on that website?'

Her mother shushed her, frowning. 'I'm listening.'

There was no way of moving her when she'd made up her mind and she never took the blame for anything.

'You could have put your granddaughter's life in danger,' Honey hissed.

Still frowning, her mother looked at her. 'I can't see how. It was only family things.'

Honey shook her head in exasperation. This conversation was going nowhere. She got up.

'Where are you going?' whispered her mother.

'To find my daughter.'

'I'll come with you.'

'No. Stay there. It might be dangerous.'

'You've just told me that my granddaughter is in danger. Of course I've got to come.'

'No. This is police business. Stay here and enjoy the readings. Mary Jane will want you to.'

Gloria sat back down. 'OK. But as soon as it's over, I'll follow on. Mary Jane will drive me. She's only had a sherry or two, so she'll be OK.'

Having experienced Mary Jane's driving when she was sober, the idea of her driving under the influence — even of a small sherry — was too terrible to contemplate. She advised her mother to stay put and wait for them to call.

The sound of applause came from the dining room preceding the emergence of Patricia Pontefract, her face pink with satisfaction.

'That showed them!' Her statement was delivered with confidence and pride. 'I need to speak to you.'

Her demand was aimed at Doherty who wasn't entirely sure who she was.

Honey filled in the details.

'Patricia Pontefract. She's an author. Mallory and Scrimshaw were her publishers.'

'Ah!' Doherty indicated that she take a seat.

Patricia Pontefract didn't move. She stood there taking up a large amount of room. It wasn't hard for her to do. She was a big woman and presently wearing a voluminous dress capable of housing the crowd scene from *A Midsummer Night's Dream*. A gang of chains rattled around her neck, her bosoms heaving up and down like a pair of giant bellows.

Her eyeshadow was luminous and deep purple. Her deep-set eyes looked as though they were set in amethyst. She narrowed them further when she turned her gaze on Honey.

'We can do without you. This is a private conversation.'

Just as Honey expected, Doherty didn't respond well to Patricia Pontefract's sharp attitude. His mouth straightened. His shoulders stiffened.

'A private conversation concerning what?'

'A crime, of course! I need to speak to a policeman. You are a policeman, are you not?'

'I am and if this is about a crime, then yes, you can talk to me.'

'Fine.' She turned to Honey. 'Please leave.'

Doherty refused to be intimidated.

'This is Mrs Driver's hotel. She is also the official Crime Liaison Officer for Bath Hotels Association and is working on this case with me. I insist that she stays.'

'No. Absolutely not.'

'Yes. Absolutely yes,' he shot back.

They were like two bulls about to lock horns — except that Patricia Pontefract was female and would thus be a cow. Honey thought the description was a good fit.

Doherty stood his ground. If he *had* been a bull and a matador had been present, Honey's money would have been on the bull. Doherty didn't give in easily.

The voluminous tent seemed to expand to greater proportions, then contract when Patricia Pontefract heaved a huge and defeated sigh.

'You know that Clarence was a pagan, do you?'

'Do you mean he dressed up in white robes and danced around at Stonehenge twice a year?'

Patricia Pontefract pursed her lips. 'Pagans take their religion very seriously, Mr Policeman. The old religion is embedded in this island, even in the Christian calendar. Even Christmas was established at a time of year when the pagans celebrated the Winter Solstice. They feasted and gave thanks around this time of year, just as we do.'

Doherty wasn't too hot on the religious front. Honey could see he was trying to surmise where this was going. 'So you're saying that Mr Scrimshaw viewed Christmas as humbug for a very good reason; he wasn't a Christian. He was a pagan,' said Doherty.

'That's what I'm saying. I think you should bear that in mind in your investigations. You may find it useful.'

She spun on her heel and marched out, her gown billowing like a giant windsock behind her.

'Well,' said Honey. 'So Scrimshaw wasn't Scrooge, he was a pagan.'

Doherty looked sceptical. 'I don't believe it.'

'I quite fancied investigating the world of nature worship and dancing around a fire at midnight,' Honey mused.

'Keep your clothes on. Wait till summer and we'll fly out to Corfu.'

The overbearing author had disappeared into the ladies' cloakroom.

Honey looked at the closed door. 'That's a woman who believes in herself.'

Doherty made no comment. He was examining a text message he'd just received.

Honey craned her neck, but at that angle, the screen was too small to read.

He raised his eyes without raising his head; such a simple action making him look both threatening and alluring. Honey felt her toes curling up, and her stomach trying to get friendly with her spine — it was that taut.

'Where would you suppose the professor's gone?'

Honey felt herself turning cold, any pleasant feelings towards Doherty instantly forgotten. 'He could be anywhere.'

His eyes locked with hers, and then he was moving.

'Crispin Mallory and Professor Jake Truebody are one and the same. He was serving sentence under the name Wes Patterson. Our friend is known to the FBI as a murderer and a liar. To put it in their words, he's like a chameleon and can change his spots to suit. He's had dozens of identities over the years, but the name he was born with was Mallory — Crispin Mallory. Jake Truebody was murdered by Crispin and an accomplice. The accomplice too has disappeared. Probably buried in cement somewhere.'

Honey could tell just by the tone of his voice that there were more details that would fill her with less than glad tidings.

'What else?'

'Let's get to the car and I'll tell you. Right now, we have to find Lindsey.'

'Let's go.' Grabbing her old, padded jacket from behind the bar, she pushed past Doherty and headed for the outside world.

'Honey,' Doherty put a hand on her arm, 'we don't know where they've gone.'

'He's got no reason to kill Lindsey.' She sounded confident. Inside she felt like ice. 'Why would he?'

Doherty hadn't brought his car and response at the skeleton-staffed police station was understandably slow.

They hailed a taxi. Doherty told the driver to drop them off at Manvers Street. His aim was to initiate a search, though where they would start searching was sheer guesswork.

Honey sat on the edge of her seat. Doherty was silent. Only the driver, a guy with a skinny beard, attempted to strike up a conversation. Honey recognised him as having called in at the Green River Hotel to pick up a fare.

'Hey. How is that hotel? OK, is it?'

'Fine.'

Usually when asked about the Green River Hotel, Honey responded giving the full marketing spiel. But not today.

Undeterred by her silence, the taxi driver continued.

'Pretty zany in there. I mean, I pick up some pretty cool characters; pretty off the wall ones too, but the passenger I picked up in there a few days back took the biscuit. A horse! Would you believe I picked up a horse as a passenger? Not a real horse, of course. A purple pantomime horse with yellow spots, the sort two guys get inside to make it happen. Know what I mean? Well, this cute honey behind the reception counter got a barman to help me out with it. Can't understand what a cute girl is doing working in a hotel; should have been a model. Though perhaps she's decided to split; know what I mean? Perhaps she's escaping. She got in my cab earlier with this cheesy older guy. No horse though.'

Honey suddenly tuned in with what he'd just said.

'My daughter! You're talking about my daughter! Where did you take her?'

'Hey, I can't divulge where passengers want to go. It's private.'

Doherty brought out his ID.

'Police. Now tell me. Where did you take them?'

CHAPTER THIRTY-FOUR

Snow resumed falling at around four in the afternoon. Evening closed in with it. The flakes were big and came in flurries, just like those depicted on Victorian-style Christmas cards, the mail coach outside a snow-covered inn.

Those who had ventured out to walk off their festive food were fast disappearing back inside. Warm houses, more food, and glasses of mulled wine were beckoning, that and repeats of favourite television programmes.

Cobblers Court was deserted.

Lindsey Driver was stripped to her underwear and already shivering.

'Take a good look,' he'd said to her. 'See how cold it is? A few hours and you won't even notice how cold it is. You'll be dead. I'll come back and retie you to suit the scenario; the evidence will point that you had had kinky sex with your lover — Jake Truebody. But it got out of hand and you ended up dead like deep-frozen belly pork.'

Lindsey stared wide-eyed out of the upstairs window which was ill-fitting and let in the draught. He'd placed her in the coldest part of the room.

Unlit windows stared back at her from buildings turned into grey phantoms by the mist. Snow was falling with it. How was that for a Victorian atmosphere?

It was easy to imagine a time when gas lights flickered in dark streets and horses' hooves and wagon wheels clattered over the cobbles and Jack the Ripper had roamed Whitechapel in London.

The snow was forecast to stop soon, the sky would clear and the temperature would drop to minus five.

Regard for the weather was a very British thing. Lindsey tried to steer her mind away from the forecast and her probable fate. She had to keep positive.

'Priests don't call themselves John Smith,' she murmured, angry that the lowdown swine she'd come here with had trussed her up like a Christmas turkey.

Whatever this guy was, and who he was, she didn't believe he was a priest. Neither did she believe he was Professor Jake Truebody, but then he'd already admitted he wasn't, so no need to go there.

So he wasn't Father John Smith and he wasn't Professor Jake Truebody; so who was he?

She looked appealingly at him.

Jake, John, whoever, was sensitive enough to work out what her eyes were asking him.

And he was totally dismissive, shaking his head in mild rebuke.

'It's your own fault. You snooped. If you hadn't started asking so many questions, we wouldn't have had to do this.'

We? Who was we?

He smiled. 'Sorry, honey, but no time for hugs and kisses. Don't want you getting warmed up by a hug and lasting longer than I'd planned. Anyway, I have to be going. Nice knowing you. Shame, I might have taken pleasure in knowing you more.' His fingers left an icy trail across her shoulders. 'Shame, but no way. You know too much. Still, under the circumstances, I've got a few minutes so might as well tell you the rest of my story, right?'

No! She shook her head and squeezed her eyes tightly shut. She'd be a witness — if she lived.

'Here goes. The truth, the whole truth and nothing but the truth; so help me God.'

He laughed at his own words. 'I was abandoned as a kid, believing both of my parents to be dead. Fact is, only one of them was dead, but I didn't know that. It was down to Scrimshaw. News got to him that I was still alive, but he hid the truth from my mother for years, which is possibly the reason for me growing into such a wayward boy. But I had my wits. I lived on my them and yeah, OK, I ended up in prison. While I was there, I got interested in genealogy. I traced my parents, did the research, and plotted revenge, because, you see, the fire that killed my father had been started deliberately. Scrimshaw never forgave my father for stealing the woman he loved away. He hired somebody to kill him. Our house was burnt to the ground. I was always a bit of a wanderer and had wandered miles that day. Nobody knew who I was. Nobody knew where I came from and I was only about five years old. I ended up in an orphanage; prison followed later on. As I said, I lived on my wits. I found out all kinds of things. Great thing, the internet, don't you think? You can find out anything if you look hard enough and me, I'm a whizz at it. That's how I located my mother. I told her what I knew, and she told me the rest. To say she was furious is an understatement.'

This man, whom she now realised was Crispin Mallory, threw his head back and laughed.

'And my father? Carl? Did you really know him?'

'I used to clean his boat for him,' he said as he began to wind a gag around her mouth. 'Your father was responsible for getting me my first jail sentence. He got me arrested for stealing a few dollars. I won't lie about it, I wanted revenge, though not as much as I did on Scrimshaw. But that was back then. It was sheer chance that I punched in his name and your mother came up on some zany dating website. It did cross my mind to seduce your mother, but when I saw her reaction to me saying I was a friend of your father — well, she wasn't pleased to see me. Guess they didn't get on too well, huh?'

He smiled into the flashlight, scraping back his hair with the blade of the knife he was holding.

Lindsey closed her eyes for a moment, reminding herself that he wouldn't use the knife to kill her. He'd trust the cold to do that.

He turned round at the sound of a footstep on the stairs outside.

Lindsey tried to turn her head to see who it was. She couldn't move, though she knew she needed to. She was freezing to death.

'Well. I can't sit around here chatting,' he said. 'I have to go.'

'Come on,' somebody hissed out of the darkness.

Lindsey shivered and took a deep breath. She could smell perfume. Expensive perfume.

What she wouldn't give for a blanket. This place was as cold as a tomb. Clarence Scrimshaw had kept this place in the dark ages, only improving those facilities he had to by order of the local authority. Central heating and double glazing obviously hadn't rated high on his list of priorities.

'Crispin!' There was warning in the hissing voice.

'OK, I'm coming.' He leaned over her and kissed the top of her head. 'Sorry to cut short our time together, but I've got work to do. We're looking for a very valuable Bible that old Clarence had just bought. Don't suppose you know anything about it, do you?' He shook his head. 'No. Of course you don't. So you just sit tight there and I'll have a look-see around. Enjoy the view — while you can.'

Two sets of feet clumped their way down the stairs. The sound of the main door hushing shut drifted up the stairs. A blast of cold air came with it.

Her shivering intensified.

She panned the window in front of her. If she could break a pane of glass, someone below might see the falling debris and raise the alarm — if there was anyone around — which didn't seem likely.

She tried rocking the chair on its legs, anything to keep moving, but the chair was heavy. It wouldn't budge.

Cold sweat broke out on her forehead. If she couldn't move, she wouldn't survive. All she could do was wait and shiver, getting colder by the minute, more light headed as her systems began shutting down as hypothermia set in. The night was getting colder, the snow heavier. She needed a miracle, an angel in disguise.

CHAPTER THIRTY-FIVE

Honey was as tense as a squashed bed spring.

Doherty filled her in on the information from the FBI.

'Crispin Mallory is like Doctor Fu Manchu, a man of many faces. Killed Truebody, killed his prison buddy, and killed Scrimshaw.'

'They had no idea who they were dealing with,' he said. His tone was grim. 'He's a conman. The best there is. He's also totally without scruples. They didn't stand a chance.'

'Your tone of voice tells me there's more to this.'

'I don't want to worry you.'

'I'm worried already.'

'Shame the immigration authorities didn't question the passport.'

Honey tossed her head. 'A friend of my mother's boarded a plane on her dog's passport.'

'Nobody noticed?'

'Nobody notices old ladies, and those guys at the airport deal with thousands of passports per day.'

'So what's your point?'

'A little tweaking of the features, a little dyeing of the hair, and you could be anyone. Passport photos are uncomplimentary. They're not even accurate. And remember what you said about this guy who calls himself Truebody resembling a TV professor — it's a cliché.'

Ahead of them was a diversion sign.

The taxi driver shouted over his shoulder. 'I'll have to take a detour. It could take a little longer.'

'No way!' Honey poked the taxi driver in the shoulder with her finger. 'Just get me there. Fast!'

'Are you going to shoot me?' He was wide-eyed, but his voice was cool.

'It's my index finger and it's not loaded,' she snapped, no time for humour. 'Just go warp speed.'

'Hey, missus! This is a taxi, not the Starship Enterprise.'

Doherty grabbed her shoulder and pulled her back into her seat.

'Honey. It's best we wait until the units are on their way.'

'No way.'

There was determination and then there was determination; a mother out to protect her cub had ten times the determination of any normal human being. If she could beam down there in the middle of Cobblers Court, she most definitely would.

'Have you found out who's been gluing red noses onto reindeers?' the cab driver asked Doherty.

''Fraid not.'

'That's good. I'm not into this artistic stuff, and my kid — he's five — just loves the red noses. It's like being invaded by a whole herd of red-nosed Rudolphs. More than enough to pull Santa's sleigh.' He stopped the taxi. 'That'll be twelve quid.'

Doherty told the cab driver to put the bill on police account.

'Hey!'

It was a disbelieving pronouncement of the word 'hey'. Pound to a penny, the cab driver didn't believe them.

They ran into Cobblers Court was deserted. There was no one around; no lights in the buildings. The gas light hanging from the wall flickered through the falling mist and did precious little to lift the gloom.

Doherty was ready to heave into the door with his shoulder, but when he touched the handle, it creaked open.

Inside was how Honey remembered it from her first visit; the emergency lighting signal was flashing on the wall. The cold was intense. She guessed there was no provision in place to turn on the heating in freezing weather.

Doherty retrieved an LED torch from his pocket. Guided by its chill blue light they headed for the stairs.

He stretched out his arm, preventing her from following him.

'Stay here,' he whispered.

'Okay,' she whispered back.

He set off up the stairs. Honey was right behind him. Doherty sighed and muttered something under his breath.

'The stairs can be a bit . . .'

A stair squeaked beneath Doherty's foot.

'Squeaky,' she whispered.

He carried on, more slowly now, placing his foot gingerly on each stair tread.

Only one more stair squeaked, and that one was only three treads down from the landing.

They paused; listened; took a breath. Nothing.

It struck Honey that they would know if someone was there. On her last visit, she'd heard Patricia Pontefract quite clearly. Her heart sank. There was nobody here.

Doherty spoke to her over his shoulder. 'You check the office and I'll check the apartment.'

'Right.'

She followed him up the next flight of stairs to the apartment.

He stopped on the top landing, turned and said, 'am I speaking in a foreign language? Is there an impediment in your ear that's restructuring my instructions? Or do you have a good reason for ignoring me?'

'Lindsey,' she said.

He sighed. 'Fine.'

The door to the apartment was slightly ajar. Doherty pushed it open, keeping his hand on it so it didn't happen too quickly.

Once it was fully open, he flattened himself against the wall. Honey did the same. Her heart was in her mouth. She wanted to look into the first room of the apartment but was afraid to.

Doherty entered, flashing his torch over the prim, plain furniture, the bookshelves, the worn Turkish rug that lay between the sofa and the fireplace.

The bookshelves were almost empty, most of the contents scattered in heaps over the floor. Drawers and closet doors had been wrenched open.

Doherty switched on the light. 'Someone's given this a right going over.'

While Honey stood there, trying to keep calm, Doherty searched the rooms.

'There's nobody here.'

For a moment they stood there, drinking in the silence, their breath steaming on the cold air.

Then a sudden thud made them start.

The office.

Doherty took the stairs two at a time and got there before Honey did.

'The door's locked. Someone's been here. It wasn't locked before.'

Yet again Doherty laid his shoulder into a door. Honey was thinking it must hurt but comforted herself that he had the muscles for it. He had the attitude too. When something needed doing, he barged straight in.

The door burst open and the torch picked up the underside of a chair that had fallen onto its side. A pair of feet was visible tied to the legs, plus a hand tied to the chair arm. Honey turned on the main light. To say she almost had a heart attack was putting it mildly.

Honey ran over to her daughter and bundled her close. Lindsey's teeth were clicking together like a pair of castanets.

'He told me his real name was Crispin Mallory,' she managed to say.

'We know,' said Doherty. 'Somebody saw you together and recognised him as being a dead ringer for his father.'

Honey and Doherty both pulled off their jackets and draped them around Lindsey's shivering body. As Honey rubbed her daughter's extremities to get the blood flowing, Doherty asked the questions.

'Where is he?'

'Gone. There was someone else with him. I couldn't see who. How did you find me?'

'The cab driver saw you with Crispin. He remembered you from when he picked up the pantomime horse the other day.'

Lindsey managed a shivery chuckle. 'Great stuff. I was wishing for an angel. A cab driver is as good as it gets.'

'You didn't hear them discuss where they were going?'

'He was looking for a Bible. He'd given up on it being here, I think.'

Doherty looked around him. The place was a shambles. Desk drawers pulled open, boxes of stationery upturned.

'So he didn't find it here. Where would you hide a valuable book of any description?'

'Along with other religious books?'

There was a clumping of heavy feet running up the stairs. Lindsey started but Doherty said, 'It's just my units, don't worry.'

But he was wrong. The door swung open.

'Hey,' said the cab driver. 'Are you straight about where to send the bill?'

Doherty stared at him incredulously for a moment. 'Of course I am. Now take her back to the hotel,' he barked. He turned to Honey. 'We'll get a squad car to take us along the London Road.'

Lindsey intervened. 'No. I want you both to arrest Crispin. You can't afford to wait.'

There would have been an argument.

The four of them made their way downstairs, Lindsey safely held between her mother and Doherty.

On reaching street level, Honey cried, 'I see a pink Caddy!' The cavalry, in the form of her mother and Mary Jane, ploughed through the packed snow and slewed to a halt.

'Get him,' shouted Lindsey to Doherty as Mary Jane floored the old car.

Doherty opened the door of the cab wide for Honey then hesitated. 'You don't have to go there. You've got Lindsey back and it's Christmas.'

Honey stuck out her chin. 'I want to face that son of a bitch! I want to tell him exactly what I think of him.'

CHAPTER THIRTY-SIX

Crispin Mallory and his partner-in-crime had not expected any problems at Clarence's place on Beaufort East but had met it head on.

The Crommer family had been playing charades and generally enjoying their after-dinner entertainment when Crispin had arrived.

The most unfortunate thing was that he didn't have a key for any of the doors. First he'd smashed open the outer door, then the inner one, behind which sat a stack of old Bibles.

The noise had reverberated around the whole house, and Mr Crommer was not amused. On top of disturbing his family's fun, the noise had awoken the youngest Crommer, who was nine months old and teething.

Mr Crommer was a big man and had friends staying. The three of them, all men with arms the size of Crispin's thighs, came out with fists clenched and shoulders squared.

Crispin Mallory was taken by surprise.

The sound of a screaming baby sounded from inside the house. Heads popped out from upstairs windows, demanding to know what all the fuss was about.

Honey and Doherty arrived just as the furore was spilling out onto the pavement.

Fists were flying and Crispin Mallory had been caught off his guard.

'Spoil our Christmas, would you!' shouted Neville Crommer.

If Crispin Mallory had been a Bathonian, he would have known he was messing with a prop forward from their top-notch rugby team. He would have recognised the other two men as Crommer's teammates and made a decision to come back another day. But he didn't know that and had instead charged forward and felt like he'd collided with a barn door.

'Look, I'm sorry, folks . . .' His voice was as slick as an oil spill as he changed tack. But it was just as unwelcome. The blows kept coming from Crommer and his two teammates, all big men with fists the size of shovels.

A police car pulled up behind Doherty and Honey, having been redirected from the publishing office by Doherty en route.

Mallory had no chance to make a dash for it.

A man dressed in crisp white shirt, blue cravat, and neatly pressed chinos, noticed the police car. He automatically took it that Doherty and Honey were part of the cavalry come to assist them.

Mr Crommer looked very pleased. 'Full marks for coming so quickly, chaps. We've only just phoned.'

'We happened to be in the area,' said Doherty, after which he ordered the uniformed bods to take Mallory downtown. 'Pleased to be of service,' he added.

'One down and two more to go,' said the man who introduced himself as Frederick Selkirk-Jones. 'The two women are still up there, fighting like cats and dogs.'

Honey and Doherty exchanged a swift look and dashed for the stairs.

The door to Scrimshaw's home was wide open. The place was a mess and Mrs Withers was in the thick of it, the terms of abuse coming thick and fast. She was holding a sweeping brush aloft.

She turned round as they came in. 'So you two are here again, are you?'

'What are you doing here, Mrs Withers?' asked Honey.

'Mr Crommer phoned me and told me somebody was smashing the doors down, but that he would hold the fort until I got here. I came right away. I only live on the end of the row and good job too! Look at the mess they've bloody made. Old Scrimshaw will be turning in his grave. Uppity sorts coming in here and getting it upside down . . .'

It was noticeable that Mrs Withers didn't blame the members of Bath's rugby team. She was probably a staunch supporter.

'The other one's still inside,' explained Mrs Withers. 'She ran in before I could stop her.'

Honey and Doherty headed for the library.

Mrs Withers, who was clinging to a sweeping brush, followed on.

'She won't come out.'

She?

Mrs Withers waggled the sweeping brush. 'She tried to hit me with her handbag. Well I wasn't having none of that, thank you very much!'

Honey made an instant judgement. Handbag against sweeping brush. No contest.

'Do you know the woman?' Honey asked Mrs Withers.

'I know 'er,' said Mrs Withers, nodding, sucking in her lips in disapproval. 'She was always harassing the old chap, especially of late. Used to come 'ere when she was younger, too, with 'er old man.'

'Her husband?'

Honey smelled the beginnings of story here — almost a ghost story.

'Used to be in partnership with Mr Scrimshaw. They fell out for some reason. But 'er, she kept coming back.'

'Crispin Mallory's mother?! She's not dead!'

Doherty banged on the door. 'Come on out, Mrs Mallory. This is the police.'

Slowly, the door opened.

Honey's jaw dropped. Patricia Pontefract.

'I'm in shock,' said Honey.

Patricia Pontefract sniffed imperiously. 'Must have been that bump on the head I gave you.'

Honey sniffed. The perfume worn by Crispin Mallory's mother was unmistakable. The huge necklace she wore would have done a smaller woman as a breastplate. As she stood there, the light caught it, heightening its brightness. Nobody could fail to notice it — even on a foggy night.

Tallulah!

The woman was smiling as though she were thinking of something very special.

'I could write a book about all this, you know. It'll probably be a bestseller. That bastard Scrimshaw told me my son was dead. That he'd died in the fire with his father. That was just to keep me close at hand. Not that there was anything physical in the later years. But he should have told me. My son found me. He's good at finding things out.'

Honey felt some sympathy for the woman. For someone to part a mother from her child was unforgiveable.

'You sound proud of him.'

'Of course I am. Wouldn't you be?'

Honey grimaced. 'To a point. Your son killed Clarence Scrimshaw, among others.'

Patricia puffed out her substantial breasts. 'No, he did not. I did. I did it for my boy. All these years of being apart. It wasn't fair, but then, Clarence was never fair. I thought the police would have gone after the stone-huggers and moon-worshippers,' she added bitterly.

'Because of the way he was killed?'

'That's right. The number three was sacred to the pagans. I didn't go into overkill leaving lots of leads for you to follow. Just enough to confuse.' She turned to Doherty. 'If you're wondering where the knife is, I sold it. It raised enough for a good lawyer.'

CHAPTER THIRTY-SEVEN

Patricia Pontefract and her son, Crispin Mallory aka Professor Jake Truebody and sometimes Wes Patterson, both spent Christmas Day and into the New Year banged up at Her Majesty's pleasure.

Patricia Pontefract would be charged with murder, her son as an accessory, before being extradited to the USA.

Honey was determined that New Year's Eve was going to make up in every way for the chaotic Christmas they'd endured. Though there had been definite advantages to dashing around after villains; for a start Honey had not had chance to overindulge. A box of chocolate-covered marzipan was still sitting in the top drawer of the reception desk. That white silk kimono Doherty had bought her would still fit. And she could help him into the boxer shorts she'd bought him — or help him out of them if he preferred.

Yes, she thought, New Year is going to be wonderful. The whole family was here, the staff had opted to stay over and enjoy the party. In order that work was kept to a minimum, Smudger the chef had laid out a cold buffet.

Lindsey had learned that the internet could not be relied on to tell the truth about anyone. Her mother had learned not to give too much information away.

'I've got it. Less is more with the internet,' she said. 'Just like underwear.'

The comparison was lost on Honey.

Crispin Mallory had set up a phony site to field sightings of his alter ego, Jake Truebody. There never was a sister; only him. On the one hand it was quite a sensible approach; he'd kept track of presumed sightings at the same time as erecting a smokescreen to cover his exit from the USA and the murder of the real Jake Truebody and his own inmate. On the other hand, it was also something of an ego trip; Crispin thought he was too clever for anyone to catch. The fake message had been something of a challenge. Unfortunately, it had been Lindsey who answered it.

* * *

Honey's happy New Year bubble was unfortunately burst by her head chef.

He looked worried. His mouth was moving from side to side as though he couldn't find the words he was searching for. 'We have a problem.'

'What is it? Are you ill?' Honey asked. Panic loomed like a black cloud on her sunny horizon. The last thing she wanted over the rest of the holiday and New Year was for her head chef to be ill. Maybe he was just drunk, if not, he no doubt would be soon — she'd seen him whirling around in a tartan kilt on past New Year's Eves. This year would be no exception.

'Spill it,' she said, half inclined to shove her fingers in her ears, convinced that this was something that she didn't want to hear.

'Clint is stuck to his chair.'

Their washer-up had taken a break from helping with the preparations for the buffet. He'd decided to wait for Smudger to change and sat himself down on a chair. Unfortunately, he'd secreted a tube of super glue into the back pocket of his stonewashed jeans. Even more unfortunately, the tube hadn't been sealed properly. Clint, or at least his jeans, was stuck to the chair. Worse still, a stash of red plastic noses — left over from the BBC's Comic Relief event, had been found in the cold store. They didn't belong to the Green River Hotel. Clint admitted to them having been purloined from the Zodiac Club.

'It keeps them stiff,' he explained when asked why they were in the cold store.

'I'd prefer not to know that,' said Honey. Folding her arms, she pinned Clint with an accusing glare. 'The noses and the glue say it all. Worse still, you've implicated the Green River Hotel in your prank. I am not happy.'

Clint hung his head and groaned.

She showed no mercy. 'I don't think we want Doherty to know about this, otherwise you could be spending some time in a police cell. It won't reflect well on the rest of us. Whatever possessed you to do it?'

When Clint wrinkled his face, the spider tattoo on his forehead fell forward over his eyes as though his skin had worked loose over his skull.

'It was just a joke. I reckoned they looked all the better for it. More festive. Don't you think?'

She sighed. 'Get out of those trousers. I've got a spare pair that will fit you.'

While he slid away from his jeans and the chair to which they were attached, Honey fetched the pair of clown's trousers from the laundry room. An entertainer they'd hired for a children's party had left them behind. Honey had contacted him, but he'd declined to collect them. He'd decided instead to accept a job on the deli counter at one of the big supermarkets.

There were other trousers she could have given him, but Clint deserved to be taught a lesson.

The trousers were made from alternate diamonds of green and red material that shimmered in the light. A pair of overlarge black shoes made of stiff felt was attached to the legs of the trousers. The shoes were large — very large. 'Put these on.'

Clint stared at them as though she were offering to clothe him in an iron maiden — complete with nails and cast-iron belt.

'I'm not wearing them!' he spluttered. 'Not unless you cut the feet off.'

Honey shook her head. 'We can't do that. The feet are joined onto the trousers and I don't want to ruin them in case the clown comes back for them. You wear these or your boxers. Go on. You're the clown. You make the choice.'

'Them jeans are brand new.'

His voice was full of protest, but she saw the look in his eyes. He had no choice. Tonight he'd planned to visit Anna and the new baby. He had to wear something, at least until he could get home and change.

* * *

Honey couldn't help giving her daughter a big hug each time they came into contact. Lindsey was OK with that for a while, but eventually the incessant squeezing got to her.

'Look, I've been thinking, marry him if you like.'

Honey shrugged. 'We're having second thoughts. After all, what's the point? We don't intend starting a family. Not at our age.'

Lindsey smiled in a girlish manner. 'What's age got to do with it? Anyway, having a baby brother or sister might be quite fun.'

Honey shook her head. 'Not for the parents it isn't.'

'I approve of whatever you two want to do. It's OK by me. Honest.'

The fact that Lindsey was being so reassuring made Honey feel warm inside, though her attitude to having a half-brother or sister was a little disconcerting. Plus there was Rachel of course, Doherty's daughter by his first marriage.

She toasted her daughter. 'Never a dull moment in this game — even at Christmas, though I must admit I'm glad things have calmed down. Everything is going to be smooth as custard for the rest of the holiday.'

Lindsey raised her glass. 'Amen to that.'

THE END

ALSO BY JEAN G. GOODHIND

HONEY DRIVER MYSTERY SERIES

Book 1: MURDER, BED & BREAKFAST
Book 2: MENU FOR MURDER
Book 3: WALKING WITH MURDER
Book 4: THE JANE AUSTEN MURDERS
Book 5: MURDER BY LAMPSHADE
Book 6: MURDER BY MUDPACK
Book 7: MURDER AT THE ROMAN BATHS
Book 8: MURDER FOR CHRISTMAS

Thank you for reading this book.

If you enjoyed it please leave feedback on Amazon or Goodreads, and if there is anything we missed or you have a question about, then please get in touch. We appreciate you choosing our book.

Founded in 2014 in Shoreditch, London, we at Joffe Books pride ourselves on our history of innovative publishing. We were thrilled to be shortlisted for Independent Publisher of the Year at the British Book Awards.

www.joffebooks.com

We're very grateful to eagle-eyed readers who take the time to contact us. Please send any errors you find to corrections@joffebooks.com. We'll get them fixed ASAP.

Printed in Great Britain
by Amazon

14541394R00154